SCARLET
CARNATION

ALSO BY LAILA IBRAHIM

SCARLET CARNATION

A NOVEL

LAILA IBRAHIM

LAKE UNION
PUBLISHING

Published by Lake Union Publishing, Seattle

www.apub.com

Amazon, the Amazon logo, and Lake Union Publishing are trademarks of Amazon.com, Inc., or its affiliates.

ISBN-13: 9781542020756
ISBN-10: 1542020751

Cover design by Shasti O'Leary Soudant

Printed in the United States of America

To the wide, loving, and generous circle that surrounded us in the midst of a global pandemic.

Arise, then, Christian women of this day! Arise all women who have hearts, whether our baptism be that of water or of tears! Say firmly: We will not have great questions decided by irrelevant agencies. Our husbands shall not come to us, reeking with carnage, for caresses and applause. Our sons shall not be taken from us to unlearn all that we have been able to teach them of charity, mercy and patience. We women of one country will be too tender of those of another country to allow our sons to be trained to injure theirs. From the bosom of the devastated earth a voice goes up with our own. It says "Disarm, Disarm! The sword of murder is not the balance of justice."

Julia Ward Howe,
Mother's Day proclamation of peace, 1870

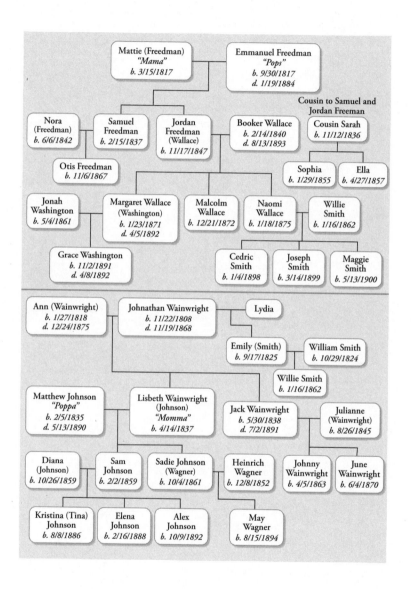

PROLOGUE

NAOMI

We make joy in spite of the indignity—or perhaps because of it. Delight in my well-lived life is a most satisfying weapon against the hate and trampling. God calls me to build the common good and make my own days glad. I do both with every breath I'm given.

Naomi Wallace

CHAPTER 1

MAY

May 1915

"I don't believe it would be wise," May whispered in John's ear. She resisted the warm tug of his body pressed against hers. His fingers released their tight grip on her skirt.

He pushed against the mattress, cool air rushing into the gap between them, and looked into her eyes while he stroked the hair at the nape of her neck—a lovely shiver ran down her spine.

"We are almost engaged," he assured May.

Her breath caught. He was finally expressing the sentiment she felt in her heart. "Are you certain?"

He nodded slowly; desire filled his brown eyes.

She took his face between her hands. Her thumbs caressed his cheeks as she gazed up at him. May combed her fingers through his sandy brown hair. He smiled down at her, his eyes sparkling with love. She brought her lips to his, ready to signal her consent with a passionate kiss, when the clock chimed the half hour.

She dropped her head back on the mattress in his studio apartment. Not like this—when they were expected at Professor Kroeber's for dinner.

May exhaled hard and cleared her throat to push down her own desire. "Soon, I promise. I'll be ready soon, but not tonight when we have to rush off."

He nodded and smiled, but the slight droop of his head told her he was disappointed.

"I'm getting Margaret Sanger's pamphlet on family limitation from my cousin on Sunday," she reminded him, hoping her assurance would prevent hurt feelings.

"You are practical, as always," he said, and sighed.

She shrugged. He gave her a peck on the lips and rose from his bed. May couldn't read John's emotions. Was he angry? She shouldn't have let it go so far, but it was so pleasurable. She considered apologizing.

John gazed at her like he knew her mind. "Don't imagine my state to be anything other than pure devotion to you." He exhaled. "I don't want to rush into anything until you are as certain as I am."

A thrilling flood washed over her, causing her heart to race and her breath to shorten. This was love. May smiled, reached for his arm, and squeezed. This man who was both kind and intelligent was her treasure. She took a deep breath and forced herself to turn away from him—for the moment.

May and John walked from his tiny Northside apartment near the University of California in Berkeley to Professor Kroeber's house in the Berkeley Hills. In fifteen minutes it felt as if they'd been transported to the Napa countryside. John held her hand as they climbed steps through tall redwood trees and bright-green bunches of grasses.

The staircase ended at a narrow street. May paused and turned around to catch her breath and take in the view. Spread out below, the bay sparkled in the sunlight. Tall, modern buildings in San Francisco rose on the other shore. Constructed since the 1906 earthquake and fire, they were a testament to the resiliency of the city and its people. To the north the warm, brown hills of Marin County were marked by circles of oak trees and squares of bright-green farms. The Pacific Ocean sparkled beyond the gap of the Golden Gate until it ended under a thick blanket of gray fog.

John took her hand. May's heart sped up in anticipation. This was the moment she'd been expecting for weeks. They'd been dating for nearly a year and he was graduating in a few days. John gazed at her and swallowed. She smiled at him, her eyes shining in joy; she nodded in encouragement for his formal proposal. He bit his top lip, and inhaled, readying himself to ask. Then he turned back to the vista.

Her stomach dropped.

"Nearly as splendid as the view from Indian Rock," he declared. "I don't believe there's such a lovely view in all of San Francisco. Don't tell my parents, but this is the more favorable side of the bay."

She took a deep breath to slow her hurt heart.

Hiding her disappointment and misunderstanding, she bantered, "I won't tell your family, nor anyone else from that city. More than enough of them inundated Oakland after the earthquake. I don't need to encourage more to make the East Bay their home."

"Am I such a burden to your fair city?" he asked.

She paused, tapped her lip with her finger, and stared upward as if in deep thought. "I suppose there is room for you, but only you." She laughed and kissed his warm lips. She intended a peck, but his hand cupped her cheek and she found herself lost in the moment.

When they broke away his shiny eyes expressed the longing in her heart, confirming her understanding that he shared her deepest desire. May had to trust he was waiting to secure work.

On Wednesday, John would be conferred a Doctorate of Philosophy in Anthropology. Ideally, he would get a professorship in Northern California at Stanford University or Mills College to be close to their families—his in San Francisco, hers in Oakland. If not, he would seek a position at one of the many institutions of higher education in Southern California. A degree from the University of California was so well regarded that she was confident they wouldn't need to leave the state.

After graduating from Oakland High School two years ago, May applied for jobs only at the University of California. As the secretary at the Department of Anthropology she met many wonderful college men. A few months of flirtation with John turned into the respectful romance she desired and would soon become a lifelong marriage.

She shook her head to clear it and reminded him with a smile, "We don't want to be late."

He turned left, walking a few yards down the street to the brown shingled home where Professor Kroeber, his advisor and her boss, lived.

They were gathering in celebration and farewell. As a secretary in the department, she'd never received a coveted invitation to a dinner party at Professor Kroeber's home, but she was confident she would be warmly welcomed as John's date. Professor Kroeber was forward thinking about social equality and never showed any class prejudice toward May. She was proud to have supported his research and would miss working with him.

Mrs. Kroeber, a plain but confident wife, ushered them into a stunning redwood-paneled living room.

"A genuine Maybeck!" John whispered into her ear, reminding her that the renowned architect he so admired designed this home.

"Almost the equal of a Julia Morgan design," May retorted.

He laughed, as she intended. She was forever championing the up-and-coming female architect. They were unlikely to ever afford a custom home, but they enjoyed conversations about designs. They were both favorably inclined toward the modern simplicity of the arts and crafts movement rather than the ornate Victorians they each lived in as children.

Thomas King, another graduate student, and his date, Judith Hunt, were seated on a couch across from Professor Kroeber. Ishi was seated by the professor in a high-backed upholstered chair. His dark hair and skin stood out from the cream fabric. She glanced down. His bare feet spread on the red Oriental rug, an amusing juxtaposition with his Western suit. A small, sweet smile spread across his face though he didn't look at May. In the custom of his people he didn't make eye contact or speak directly to her, a woman not in his family; nevertheless, he conveyed warmth and calm.

Ishi's life was as heartbreaking as it was inspiring. For several weeks in 1911 he made the headlines in the newspaper. The whole state, perhaps the entire nation, followed his story with great interest. Nana Lisbeth had been so moved that tears ran down her cheeks as she read the account in the *Oakland Tribune*.

Ishi walked into Oroville, California, barefoot and emaciated— wrapped in mystery because he spoke no English. Before she worked there, the professors in May's department read about his plight in the newspaper and arranged for his release from jail to the university.

In time Ishi explained he was the last of the Yahi, a tribe of Native Californians. Soon after the Civil War, his community was nearly annihilated in the Three Knolls Massacre. A small band hid in the hills for five decades, dying one by one until Ishi was alone. Close to starving, he exposed himself to an uncertain fate in a society that destroyed his people.

In the four years since he emerged from hiding he lived and worked in the University of California Anthropology Museum at the Golden Gate Park in San Francisco.

Nana Lisbeth and Momma were very impressed May met him more than once, when he came to the department office to meet with

Professor Kroeber and his students or to make a record of the Yahi language and mythology.

On Sundays Ishi displayed his skills in bow making, arrowhead carving, and fire starting at the museum to the public. May had yet to see his survival talents, but planned to when she attended the Panama-Pacific Exhibition, the months-long, world-famous exhibition in San Francisco celebrating the opening of the Panama Canal.

Mrs. Kroeber stood in the doorway and pronounced, "We are all here and dinner is ready, so please come to the table."

May flushed at the memory of why they were late. She raised her hand to her face, as if she could feel that her cheeks were red. She didn't dare look at John for fear of blushing further.

Over a simple dinner of roasted chicken and potatoes they discussed the news of the department.

"Tell them our news," Judith prodded Thomas.

"I've accepted a position at Whittier College in Los Angeles County," he declared.

"Congratulations!" Mrs. Kroeber said.

"Wonderful," John replied, but May heard the jealousy in his voice.

"Well deserved," Professor Kroeber chimed in.

"Judith and I will be married next week and then head south at the end of June," Thomas continued.

Envy shot through her. She wanted her future settled too. May took a deep breath to calm her heart, forced a smile, and added her congratulations. John squeezed her hand.

Judith looked at May. "You'll be my maid of honor, won't you?"

"Of course," May replied, but her voice sounded hollow to her own ear. She enjoyed Judith's company well enough, but the woman she went on double dates with wouldn't stand by May when she got married. That honor would go to her cousins: Elena and Tina. Judith didn't have any family near, so it made sense that she asked May.

"Saturday, two o'clock at the campus chapel. We hope you all will be there," Thomas said to the whole table. To May and John he said, "Our joint excursion to the Pan-Pacific Exhibition shall be our last double date, I'm afraid." The couples had plans to ferry across the bay to visit the world famous fair.

John said, "May is looking forward to seeing your skills on display, Ishi. I have told her that you seem to make fire out of air."

Ishi gave a single nod.

Professor Kroeber spoke up in his authoritative voice: "I was most grateful to have Ishi's skills as a counterbalance to the eugenicists. Their excessively large booth was very well funded by Kellogg. They advocate for limiting reproduction to the original stock of this nation and forbidding immigration except from Northern Europe. Their dangerous Darwinian argument will lead to forced sterilization."

Disgust in her voice, Mrs. Kroeber explained, "They actually advocate for a eugenics registry to create a pedigree of breeding pairs—for humans. It seems they would make it illegal for a Norwegian to marry a Greek if they were able."

May gasped. She'd known there was a huge rift in the anthropology field, but she didn't realize the eugenicists were so well organized and extreme.

John replied, "Wouldn't they be horrified by our student body—women, Negroes, Chinese?"

The table murmured their agreement. The University of California was extremely proud that the student body was not limited to white men like so many institutions of higher education. It had been forward thinking from its very foundation.

The conversation continued and the evening flowed by quickly. May studied Mrs. Kroeber, watching how she kept everyone engaged with ease. She asked questions, made comments, and changed topics as needed. She balanced being the cook, the maid, and the hostess with grace. May took this opportunity to learn, since she would be in this role soon.

"Not one mention of the *Lusitania*," May said as they rode the trolley to her home a mile below campus in the Santa Fe neighborhood. The development of small craftsman homes, far from the Oakland city center, was one of the many springing up along the train route between Oakland and Berkeley in the past ten years.

Days after May graduated from high school, in 1913, Nana Lisbeth sold their boardinghouse close to downtown to purchase this home in the suburbs with modern amenities such as electricity and a gas stove. The two-bedroom bungalow was a bit tight for the three of them but would be the right size for Nana Lisbeth and Momma once May was married and had formed a separate household.

"Honestly, I avoided the topic because it would have taken up the entire evening's conversation," John replied. "We only have a few more days to think about our research together. The speculation about joining in the European War is growing tiresome. We will or we won't. I am not sure how it will affect my life."

"I agree. There are good arguments on both sides, and my opinion won't sway our leaders one way or the other." May switched topics. "Professor Kroeber's description of the eugenics booth was disturbing. I can hardly imagine something that offensive in San Francisco in 1915."

"We'll see for ourselves soon enough," John said. "So many of our colleagues do not respect other races at all. I want to see their evidence for myself—though I know most of it is derogatory and inaccurate."

May was heartened that they agreed on such a controversial topic. They stopped walking where the stairs to her house met the sidewalk. It was late, too late, for May to invite John in. However, only the front porch light was on; Momma and Nana Lisbeth were most likely asleep, so May leaned in to kiss her beloved. When she pulled away, her heart pounded and her lungs were tight in the best way.

She whispered in his ear, "I cannot wait for the day when we won't have to part at night."

He squeezed tight, then released her with a heavy sigh. She shared his frustration . . . and longing. This was a major step, but she was ready to take it with him. As long as he was devoted to a future together and she used the means of preventing a pregnancy, she saw no reason to delay the pleasures of the body. Fortunately her cousin Elena's copy of Margaret Sanger's pamphlet, the very one on family planning that caused the activist for women's empowerment to be imprisoned, would be in her hands soon. Mrs. Sanger, the most celebrated advocate for birth control in the nation, was a hero to May and most Unitarian women. May considered Mrs. Sanger's powerful words, with which she wholeheartedly agreed: *Enforced motherhood is the most complete denial of a woman's right to life and liberty.*

At the front door May looked back for a final wave. John's lusty smile confirmed parting was hard for him too, and made her heart dance. *Such sweet sorrow,* she thought with a smile.

May forced her body to turn away from him and go into the dark, quiet house. She rested against the closed door and stopped for a deep breath. *Only a few more days of this,* she reassured herself.

She took off her shoes and got ready for bed in her stocking feet. As she climbed into bed her mother turned over and whispered, "Good night, May."

May exhaled. "Good night, Momma. Sleep well."

May lay in bed, her back to Momma, longing for the day she would be climbing into bed next to her husband, Dr. John Barrow.

The next morning Nana Lisbeth carried clippers and straight pins when they walked out the door for church. They stopped in their front garden and she went to work harvesting the blooms she'd nurtured for this day—Mother's Day. The white-haired woman clipped one carnation followed by another until all the white blooms, representations of love and protest, were in her hands. She clipped two scarlet ones but left the rest.

At May's church, congregants wore white carnations to honor deceased mothers and scarlet ones to honor living ones. The tradition began after the Civil and Prussian Wars when Julia Ward Howe encouraged mothers to wear white carnations to protest sons being sent to be killed in battle. Decades later, Anna Jarvis popularized the symbol as an honor to motherhood, going so far as to successfully advocate for a federal law making the second Sunday in May a time to honor mothers.

With the war raging in Europe, many congregants would wear white carnations for two reasons: a protest against the United States joining the fight and to honor their deceased mothers. The symbols were getting muddled.

Nana Lisbeth handed Momma a pin and a white carnation. She touched her hand to her chest and said, "For Ann Wainwright."

Momma attached the white flower to Nana in honor of her mother. Ann Wainwright was only a name to May. Nana's mother, father, and brother, Jack, died on the other side of the nation in Virginia long before May was born. They were characters in Nana Lisbeth's stories but didn't feel like family.

Nana Lisbeth held out another white flower for Momma to pin on her. "For Mattie Freedman."

May smiled. This flower honored Nana's enslaved caregiver from the family plantation—Fair Oaks. Nana Lisbeth called Mattie her "real mother," the person who shaped her the most.

May hadn't met Mattie's son Samuel or his descendants that lived in Chicago, Detroit, and Memphis, but the branches of their two families that lived in Oakland remained close. They saw each other a few times a year. Auntie Jordan, Cousin Naomi, and Cousin Willie were extended family—a treasured part of the fabric of love woven into their life, less close than Uncle Sam and Auntie Diana or her cousins, but definitely beloved family.

"And for peace." Nana Lisbeth held up another white flower for Momma to pin onto her chest.

Each flower placed on Nana's chest seemed a prayer.

Nana Lisbeth turned to face May and pinned a scarlet carnation on her granddaughter's chest. "To honor your mother."

May heard the command in her grandmother's mature voice. She'd not been gracious to Momma lately. She believed she was responding to her mother's attitude, but Nana Lisbeth wanted them both to be kinder to one another. May was ready for more distance, to share a bed with her husband rather than her mother. She longed for her own home and family separate from her elders. Momma hadn't done anything wrong; May simply wanted a different life than Momma had settled for. After her husband died Momma never remarried, never traveled, and served people: first in the boardinghouse and now as a grocery store clerk.

May was going to be a professor's wife, surrounded by interesting conversation and intellectual rigor, nothing like Momma—a store clerk living with her elderly mother. May *was* grateful for the life her mother and grandmother gave her after her father died. She knew they worked hard, but she wouldn't be held back by her mother's ennui.

Nana Lisbeth held out a white carnation and raised her right eyebrow in question. Did May want to wear one for peace? May sighed. Of course she wanted peace, but was she against this war? There were sound arguments for staying out of it and equally strong ones for joining in the fight. She'd yet to decide where she stood and didn't want to wear one simply to go along with a common sentiment. She shook her head.

"I will have one of each," Momma declared.

Nana Lisbeth handed over two carnations, which Momma pinned herself.

"Did he propose last night as you'd hoped?" Nana Lisbeth asked May as they rode the train down Telegraph Avenue.

They were going for worship at the Unitarian church in Oakland. The Berkeley church was closer to their new home, but her mother and grandmother were loyal to the congregation where they'd been active since they'd become involved in the suffrage movement in the 1890s.

May found their attitudes when it came to women's freedoms to be both amusing and annoying. They assumed she would get married and live independent from them after high school, but seemed to think she was being too independent in accepting John. She suspected it was because he refused most of their supper invitations. He was too busy with his studies, and he didn't find her family interesting enough to have dinner with them every week. He'd come often enough for May—even to a Sunday supper where he met Auntie Diana, Uncle Sam, and her cousins.

May shared their fears that her marriage to John might take her far away, but they needed to accept that she was an adult and would be living her own life separate from them.

Neither Nana Lisbeth nor Momma were married. When she was an infant, May's father traveled for work to Hawaii and died there. They didn't even have a grave to visit. Momma was so disturbed by his absence that she never spoke of him, not on the anniversary of their wedding or his death or on his birthday.

May only knew two facts about her father: he immigrated alone as a young man from Germany and he died alone in Hawaii. He was a gaping hole in her heart and in her mind. As much as she wished Momma was strong enough to speak of him, she wasn't.

In contrast, May's childhood was filled with stories about Grampa Matthew and the produce business he and Nana Lisbeth started after they moved to Oakland in 1873. She heard so many stories about him at family gatherings that she felt as if she'd met him. Every week Nana Lisbeth visited Grampa Matthew's grave in Mountain View Cemetery. May accompanied her when she was young, but the habit fell away as May matured.

May simply shook her head in answer to her grandmother's question. She didn't elaborate because she wasn't interested in either defending John's actions or hearing their opinions about her life.

May's aunt, uncle, and cousin were already seated in their usual row in the sanctuary. She took the chair next to her cousin, and leaned over Elena's belly and said, "Hello in there!"

Elena laughed and rubbed the small protrusion.

"How are you feeling?"

"The nausea has dissipated at last—and I have energy again. Hallelujah!" Elena declared.

"Wonderful."

May beamed. She and Elena were as close as sisters—especially since Elena's older sister, Tina, moved to Martinez four years ago. May confided in Elena more than anyone else in her life. They saw each other at least once a week—at church followed by Sunday supper at Aunt Diana and Uncle Sam's. Hopefully Elena becoming a mother would bring them even closer. May intended to be as helpful as possible.

"How was the dinner?" Elena asked.

"Lovely," May declared and then added, "And a touch disappointing."

"No question?"

May shook her head. "He paused our journey at the top of a staircase. We took in a gorgeous view of the bay. He agreed that the East Bay is preferable to San Francisco. When he cleared his throat in a way that caused me to believe this might be it, my heart raced in my throat. But we only kissed again and moved on."

May let out a sigh.

"What is he waiting for?"

"He wants a settled position before he makes such a request; I'm sure of it. His future is still uncertain."

"Well, that is practical," Elena said, her voice cheery, but her eyes held a different sentiment.

"What?"

"We always spoke of our children being as close as sisters, like us. I am happy for you. John is a successful and kind man. But selfishly, I don't want you to move away."

May teared up. "I agree. It is at once thrilling and horrifying to imagine moving. I still hope a local college will extend an offer."

Reverend Simmonds walked down the aisle and worship began with one of May's favorite hymns: "My Life Flows on in Endless Song." She always took the choice in music as a sign of how enjoyable a worship service would be. She looked at the beautiful stained glass window of the sower and the huge redwood beams above her head. Sorrow bubbled up. May would miss worshipping with her family each week. John showed no inclination to attend regularly, though he did express enthusiasm for Unitarian values. *Mills College*, she hoped or prayed—sometimes it was hard to tell the difference. She would hold out hope that John would be offered a position at Mills so they could stay in Oakland. May hooked her arm through Elena's and gave her a squeeze.

After the closing hymn and benediction the family walked to Uncle Sam and Aunt Diana's home for Sunday supper. Wanting privacy, May and Elena trailed behind the group. May whispered in her cousin's ear, "Do you have the pamphlet?"

"As promised."

"It worked for you, right?" May confirmed.

Elena nodded. "For two years, until . . ."—Elena rubbed her belly—"it didn't." She laughed. "Peter and I are mostly ready. In an ideal world this would have happened after our house was more finished, but we will make do. Even though she's a surprise, she's a welcome surprise."

"You sound so certain you are having a daughter."

"If I say it enough God will grant my prayer."

May laughed. "You know that's not how it works."

"So the scientists say. But my Bubbi is certain God is still deciding if there's a boy or girl coming."

May laughed again.

"I'm happy to use science when it suits me and folklore as I see fit," Elena declared.

May said, "Remember when you used to insist you were going to marry another girl?"

Elena looked wistful. "Oh, to be young and naïve."

"I'd insist, 'Two girls can't get married!'"

"And I'd argue back, 'Why not?'"

"And I'd say, 'I don't know any girls that are married.' And you would declare, 'You will when I am.'"

They both laughed.

Elena returned to the topic of family planning. "The pamphlet isn't very long. It's written in the plainest language and easy to read. I used the sponge soaked in carbolic acid and glycerin. I've never found a place to purchase a pessary—though they sound more pleasant. I always douched with Lysol after the act. I didn't always take the laxative as Mrs. Sanger recommends." Elena made a face as she rubbed her belly. She continued, "And I think that's what got us this little treasure."

"It sure is a lot of work!" May observed.

"Less work than having a baby, and if you have a good man, more fun." Elena laughed, her mouth wide and her head thrown back. She looked like Aunt Diana—full of life and joy.

And the holder of a secret that May was ready to be in on.

CHAPTER 2

NAOMI

May 1915

"My next-door neighbor is moving to Stockton. Might you be interested in purchasing his home?" Mrs. de Hart leaned in to ask Naomi Smith. They were in Mrs. de Hart's elegant living room for the executive meeting of the Northern California branch of the National Association for the Advancement of Colored People.

The mere thought of buying a house sent Naomi's heart racing. She'd met all her dearest goals in life excepting that one. She was certain it would ensure them, and their three children, Cedric, Joseph, and Maggie, economic security. If she and Willie owned a house they could maintain it, make improvements, and never be forced out of their home. And if it were large enough, Gramma Jordan could live with them too, though these compact bungalows were built for modern, smaller families and typically only had two bedrooms.

Naomi's husband didn't share her dream—or rather, he believed it was unattainable, so he dismissed it. When she raised the longing to own a home, Willie declared he had simple needs and was very satisfied with their life. Naomi feared he took her desire as a criticism of his ambition, but she never meant it as an insult.

Naomi smiled at her friend. "I should enjoy living near you in this lovely suburb. However, we do not have those kinds of funds stashed under our mattress."

"Perhaps he can arrange for payments over time? I've heard that is becoming more common," Mrs. de Hart replied. "After the meeting we can knock on his door."

Naomi nodded consent while reminding herself to balance out her desire and reality.

She told her companion, "I will love the house, if it is anything like yours."

"It is nearly identical, only reversed. They were built at the same time in 1908. You might be pleasantly surprised at the price. These houses are much more affordable than custom."

They'd formed this branch in 1913, soon after the esteemed W. E. B. DuBois, a founder of the national NAACP, visited their beloved city to raise passions. It was one of the stronger branches in the country, with 150 members. Naomi had signed up immediately and became a founding member of this executive team.

Colored people were losing their limited political rights and economic opportunities in too many states. Mr. DuBois firmly believed the freedoms enjoyed by their race in California would set an example of the possibilities in other places. Instead of allowing the forces of oppression and hatred into Oakland, a city known for its progressive views, they would be a shining example of harmony and equal freedoms to the rest of the nation. Naomi refused to sit idly while colored people were trampled by unjust laws and images in the press.

Their first campaign for the dignity and rights of colored people in Oakland was to end the showing of the picture *The Birth of a Nation*, which portrayed Negroes as barbarians and only served to raise animosity. President Wilson revealed his prejudice by showing that vile movie as the first moving picture ever to be screened at the White House.

They'd lost the injunction against the film, but continued gathering with signs in front of the theater to protest it. As a small minority in the East Bay, colored people were no threat to the white majority; however, a few cruel men were determined to oppress her family. Naomi could ensure her children's future by advocating for equal rights and opportunity.

Mr. Butler of San Francisco, the president of this branch of the NAACP, called the meeting to order. Today they were planning their part of the program for Alameda County Day at the Panama-Pacific Exhibition. Naomi's mind kept wandering from the conversation and she gazed around the living room and imagined it as her own home. Her red-and-gold rug would contrast beautifully with the shiny finish on the hardwood floor. She pictured her favorite vase with dried flowers on the mantel. The caramel tile surrounding the fireplace was obviously crafted by artisans, lending a simple elegance to the space. The apartment she'd lived in for more than twenty years was built in the last century. With no modern amenities and a great need to be painted, it felt run down and dirty no matter how much they cleaned.

Naomi shook her head and told herself to stop daydreaming. She turned her attention back to the group and their plans to show the accomplishments of their race.

"Our children are our greatest pride and asset. I believe we should feature them on our float—decorated in flowers from our gardens," Mrs. de Hart declared.

"Few people outside of our community know that Virginia Stephens is colored," Naomi added. "They know her name as the child who won the contest to name the exhibition—The Jewel City—but not her race. We should ask her family if she can be at the center of the design with her name in large letters. That will put aside any doubts about the capabilities of our kind."

"That is an excellent idea," Mr. Butler agreed.

Mrs. Simmons looked at Naomi and said, "Mrs. Smith, I understand your daughter has been working at the fair."

Naomi nodded. "Yes. Maggie is working for Sperry Flour Company booth selling pancakes."

"Has she been treated fairly?"

Naomi remembered the moment she first saw her beloved Maggie degraded by the vile costume required by her work. The long gray gown covered with an apron and her hair wrapped up in a white kerchief was an instant signal: "Aunt Jemima."

Fifty years after the Emancipation Proclamation, three thousand miles from the town where Naomi's mother and grandmother were enslaved at their birth, white men still profited from restricting her daughter's place in society.

Naomi felt her bile rise. She shook her head. "They must dress up as mammies while they distribute pancakes."

She looked around at faces shaped by disgust. Shame passed through her. *Maggie plans to be a nurse, she's a smart girl.*

"She wasn't told about the costume when she was hired," Naomi explained, ". . . and then she knew she could easily be replaced were she to object. It is only for the summer. She'll return to high school when it resumes."

Mrs. de Hart took her hand and reassured her, "Our young'uns need jobs."

Naomi smiled at Mrs. de Hart. She didn't need to defend her daughter to these fine people. The meeting continued with a discussion about their ongoing campaign against *The Birth of a Nation*. They decided to write a letter to the *Oakland Tribune* twice a week for the next two months. In addition, Miss Delilah Beasley, a valued NAACP member and special contributor to the *Tribune*, would submit editorials condemning the race-hating film.

They were fortunate that the largest and most respected newspaper in Oakland was willing to have a Negro, and a woman at that, contribute, but sometimes Naomi felt as if they were Sisyphus. It was good there were many of them rolling that stone uphill. Together they might not get crushed by the weight, but would they ever succeed?

After the meeting concluded, Mrs. de Hart reminded Naomi of their plan to see the house next door. As they walked to the west, Naomi admired the well-kept lawns and bright flowers growing in the surrounding yards. The neighborhood exuded a simple and clean spaciousness. Each detached house was painted a unique color and had a long driveway—some even had private automobiles parked in them. It was lovely.

A young white man, not more than thirty years old, opened the door painted in Willie's favorite color—deep green.

Mrs. de Hart introduced Naomi to him: "Mr. Thomas, this is my good friend Mrs. Smith. She might be interested in buying your home if the terms are right. Are you willing to show it to her?"

"Come in!" he declared, looking pleased.

The living room was an exact reversal of Mrs. de Hart's, but felt entirely different. Though these homes weren't custom built they could be personalized through their decor. He walked through an archway into a dining room with dark redwood paneling. She could see the kitchen through an opening in the built-in cabinet. It was one of those modern pass-throughs that made serving so simple.

Past the swinging door, the kitchen was filled with light from two sides. A small table in the nook had a lovely view of the backyard. Naomi imagined serving breakfast to her three children in such a bright space.

"Gas stove and water heater are included," he explained. "My wife says they are a dream come true."

Mrs. de Hart asked, "And the icebox?"

"Certainly, if you wish," he replied, smiling at Naomi.

He moved to the modern bathroom. Bright-pink tile rose most of the way up the walls around the bathtub. A single thick stripe of shiny black tiles ran around at eye level. Willie would laugh at such dramatic colors, and Naomi would love the ease of cleaning.

"The bedrooms are one to each side. They have built-in closets so you don't need wardrobes," Mr. Thomas explained, but didn't move toward them. It would be strange to see such a personal space.

He led them back through the kitchen, down a few stairs, and into the backyard.

It was small, but private. Her current yard had four separate gardens, one for each unit in the building. Naomi found it insufficient for their needs. But this yard would be all hers.

"Our lemon tree has been so prolific this year," he explained as he crossed to it. He pulled two off and asked, "Would you like these?"

"Thank you," Naomi replied.

"As you can see"—he pointed to the low fence—"Mrs. de Hart keeps a lovely yard."

Mrs. de Hart smiled and said, "We are going to miss you and your family, Mr. Thomas. You have been wonderful neighbors."

"Likewise," he said. "We will be fortunate if our new neighbors in Stockton are half as gracious as you are."

Naomi smiled at Mrs. de Hart. It would be most amazing to live next to her. She allowed herself to imagine sharing lemons, recipes, and kindness.

Naomi asked, "Do you know how much you are selling it for?"

"If we can avoid using an agent and their high fee," he replied, "we believe a fair price is $3,800."

Naomi's heart dropped like a stone down a well. Their savings account was just over $1,200—nothing close to that number.

"Can you take payments over time?" Mrs. de Hart asked.

He scrunched up his face and shook his head. "Unfortunately, we cannot as we need to invest in a new home in Stockton." He looked at Naomi. "I understand some banks are extending home loans with five- or even ten-year terms."

Willie would be reluctant to go into debt. Still, she did a quick calculation. Even without interest that amount of money divided by 120 payments was more than she was comfortable taking on. And with only two bedrooms there really wasn't adequate space for the five of them. Even though Cedric was away most of the time, and Joseph would probably be doing the same soon, she wanted them to have a bed in her home, whenever they were in town, for as long as they wished.

Naomi forced a smile and told a half truth. "I will bring this to my husband's attention when he is home and get word back to you if he agrees. I fear he will not be willing to live this far from downtown."

"Please let me know should you decide you would like to make the purchase. I'm sure the de Harts would love you as their new neighbors."

"That would be wonderful," Naomi agreed.

Naomi was near to tears as they walked back through the house. It was a lovely dream.

She rubbed the green door before she stepped onto the front porch. She sighed. This house was beyond their means, but it didn't mean they would never own their own home.

Naomi prayed, Lord, send me the residence you want me to have.

CHAPTER 3

MAY

June 1915

It was a glorious day to be on a ferry headed to San Francisco. They traveled to the Panama-Pacific Exhibition with the newlyweds, Dr. and Mrs. Thomas King. There was so much to celebrate—the two men graduating, Thomas and Judith's wedding, and a fabulous job for John. He'd been offered and accepted a position at Dominican in Marin County—only a ferry ride away from San Francisco. Now that everything was falling into place, May was confident that the formal proposal would come.

Mrs. John Barrow. May wished he would use Jonathon. It sounded more mature to her ear, but he insisted it made him feel like a child to be called Jonathon, as his parents used for him.

May stood at the boat railing, her arm hooked around John's, watching the tower of the ferry building grow closer. She leaned her cheek against him. He kissed the top of her head.

A line from the hymnal came to mind.

All things are mine, since I am His—how can I keep from singing?

His in the hymn referred to God, but for May, it was John. She looked up at him and smiled. Humming the tune, sheer joy filling her heart and mind. She was so very fortunate. In a matter of weeks she would be starting her true life—moving out of her mother's house and establishing a home of her own.

The exhibition was as grand as the accounts in the newspaper reported. Blocks and blocks of the city of San Francisco were transformed into a walled fortress along the waterfront. Dome-topped buildings in art deco designs anchored the four corners. The city was declaring to the entire world: we are recovered from the 1906 earthquake, ready to be an important city of the future.

The two couples strolled through the Joy Zone, a midway lined with games, rides, and attractions. It spread blocks and blocks from Fillmore Street to Van Ness Avenue, making what had been a familiar neighborhood entirely unrecognizable. Each booth's distinct and dramatic façade broadcast the attraction in order to draw customers.

"Oh dear!" May exclaimed as she tapped John's arm and pointed.

Ahead was a grotesque caricature of an African man. His chin rested on his hands and a large ring passed through his nose. The words *African Dip* filled in the space between his arms. It was one of those horrid dunk tanks that were supposedly an improvement over the African Dodger game. But May disapproved of anything that encouraged white men to hurl abuse at colored men. Dropping a man in a tank of water was scarcely better than throwing baseballs at his head.

She teared up. "I believed San Francisco was better than stooping to such degradation for profit."

John patted her hand. "We certainly have our work cut out for us, showing there is value in primitive cultures."

John sounded as if he were agreeing with her, but May somehow felt insulted. She didn't know why, so she didn't respond. Instead she pushed away her feelings, not wanting to let her sour mood taint the day.

They continued strolling, past the Ostrich Farm and candy stand, until they came to the Chinese Village. They'd been told to have lunch there if possible. The cuisine wasn't different from what they could eat in a Chinese restaurant, but the setting was a charming replica of an authentic rural Cantonese village. The four of them shared several plates of food. The garlic shrimp was the best May had ever eaten and the mushroom mushu was a new, and delicious, taste.

After lunch they parted ways with Judith and Thomas, who had already seen Ishi's skills and were not interested in using their time here visiting his booth at the hall of science and culture. May suspected the newlyweds actually wanted privacy. As she hugged Judith goodbye May was surprised to feel a lump in her own throat. They would likely never see one another since Thomas's family was in Monterey and Judith's family had moved to the Central Valley. May hadn't realized she'd grown so fond of Judith.

"I'm truly going to miss them," May told John as they walked arm in arm to find Ishi.

"You are a sentimental one, aren't you?" he replied.

"Am I?" she asked. "More than most?"

"I can't say if you are more than most, but more than my mother at least. I'm not too familiar with women."

She smiled at him. "I say I am just the right amount of sentimental. Agreed?"

He laughed. "Agreed."

A small crowd gathered at the railing of the display. Ishi, dressed only in a loincloth, looked vulnerable and exposed. May felt protective toward him, but he seemed comfortable revealing most of his body in his traditional clothing.

Ishi said "hello" to John directly, speaking one of the few words of English he'd mastered in the four years he'd lived in San Francisco. The fifty-six-year-old man gave a small, silent bow in May's direction. She smiled, hoping he caught a glimpse of her face, but she didn't speak to Ishi out of respect for his cultural taboo against unrelated men and women talking to one another.

He crouched over a piece of shiny obsidian. With a large hammerstone in one hand and a buckskin in the other for protection, he struck the obsidian on alternating sides, over and over until it was the right size. Then he switched to the flint flaker, a deer antler attached to wood with skin, and alternately struck the left and right sides with a quick, quiet force that seemed to do nothing until suddenly a small flake dropped off. He repeated the motion over and over, panting with the exertion, until he was satisfied with the sharpness.

He held it up and the crowd clapped. The arrowhead was passed from hand to hand through the audience.

"Careful!" parents cautioned their children, for good reason. It was as sharp as any knife that May had ever held.

He then moved to the stone where he would kindle a fire. He placed a stick in the well-worn hole and put moss around the base. He crouched down and spun the stick back and forth between his palms, sweat beading up on his forehead from the exertion. After a few minutes smoke spiraled up from the moss. Ishi continued at a constant pace, the sound of his hands making a fast and steady beat. The moss turned into tiny pieces that looked like black ash. Suddenly a bright spark glowed and Ishi placed dried grass over it. He leaned over and blew a whisper of encouragement. The grass burst into flame. The crowd gasped and he was rewarded with clapping once again.

He looked tired, but pleased.

May declared, loud enough for Ishi to hear, "That was very impressive!"

Most likely he didn't understand her words, but she hoped her tone conveyed her respect and enthusiasm to the gentle man who survived the massacre of his people.

John nodded and replied, "I'm grateful so many visitors from around the world can see him demonstrate his humanity. All of us were like that once. There is no reason to disregard our primitive origins—even though we have moved past them."

John pointed to the Race Betterment booth. "I want to pop into here to see the public arguments from the eugenicists for myself."

May nodded with a lopsided smile that probably looked like a grimace.

They turned into the large corner exhibit that took up at least four spaces. There were chairs stationed around a table with pamphlets and brochures. Frescos of classical Greek statues were painted high up on the walls.

May picked a brochure up and read about the dangers of race mixing. Another brochure advocated for forced sterilization for "lunatics, idiots, paupers, epileptics and criminals." It said these "unfit persons" have reached a vast multitude—"500,000 lunatics, 80,000 criminals, 100,000 paupers, 90,000 idiots, and 90,000 epileptics"— that were a drain on the "sounder population." They argued that in one generation there would be no need for hospitals or prisons if people with "superior genetics" were the only people allowed to have children.

She felt her bile rise.

"I don't understand why people are so cruel. It is just vile nonsense," May declared.

"They do have some valid points—though there is much I disagree with or find detestable."

Her heart filled with an inexplicable rage. Her emotion must have shown on her face because he responded as if she'd expressed her feelings.

"You agree that we want healthy babies," he said, pointing to a passage in a pamphlet about nutrition. "Their arguments are very much in line with Margaret Sanger's. Women not having more babies than they can afford to rear . . . and all that."

"How can you equate their goals with Mrs. Sanger's?" she challenged.

John replied, "The betterment of all of humankind is a noble goal—that is all that I am saying."

"Mrs. Sanger wants women to have the freedom that comes from choosing motherhood," May argued. "These people want to create a master race."

John shrugged. "They do take it too far, I agree. They are well funded, but I don't see them as dangerous."

Again, John sounded as if he agreed with her, but she felt as if he hadn't. May stewed as they walked away from the booth. John seemed to be making light of her heartfelt views. It was hard to explain to him why it mattered so. She supposed having relatives of another race made her more aware of the offensive nature of this line of thinking.

"Do you remember my story about the colored nurse who attended my birth on the train? I was so premature that we are certain I would have died without her skills."

John nodded.

"I don't believe I told you she married Willie Smith, my mother's cousin," May said, her heart pounding hard though she didn't fully understand why. John should be forward thinking.

John's brow furrowed. Then his eyes opened wide in understanding.

"They are extended family. We visit only a few times a year, but Naomi is a genuine heroine to me."

"I understand." John nodded. "For you this is personal, not an academic debate."

Relief rushed through May. She smiled at him. "Yes."

They walked in silence. May wondered what John was thinking. Eventually he asked, "Your family is from Oberlin?"

"Momma lived there until she was ten or so. Nana Lisbeth grew up . . ." May hesitated, then continued, "Nana Lisbeth was raised on a plantation, the daughter of the owners."

John stopped and stared at May, his eyes wide in surprise. "Your family were . . . slaveholding?!"

"Not *my* family. It was long before I was born."

"Not that long," he replied.

May's head spun.

"And then your mother's first cousin married a colored woman?"

Was he judging her family negatively?

"Yes," May said.

"Your family is very progressive!" he responded, admiration in his voice.

"We are?"

May thought about Nana Lisbeth, who always said what was best in her—courage, faith, compassion—came from Mattie. Their family was tied to Auntie Jordan and to Cousin Naomi by blood and by marriage—but also by Mattie and Nana's love for each other. May hadn't sorted through the web that connected their families. Mattie had taught Nana Lisbeth who taught May. Like Grampa Matthew, May felt Mattie's presence in her life though she'd never met her. *Progressive.* She'd only ever thought of her family as adequate. She liked to think of them in a more interesting light.

Then she agreed out loud: "We are progressive!"

John kissed the top of May's head. "I think it is dear that you care about all kinds of people. You know that, right?" He squeezed her hand. She smiled at him, relieved to have his understanding and support.

"Would you like to stop by my home before we cross the bay? My parents are likely to be there, so I can tell them the news about Dominican."

May's heart leapt at the idea. It would be her first visit to John's childhood home, having only met Mr. and Mrs. Barrow twice at large, more formal gatherings such as John's graduation last week. May nodded.

"I should like that very much," she agreed.

They got off the cable car at Mason and headed up Russian Hill. Arm in arm they walked up the steep incline, past the mansions of Nob Hill, one of the most expensive neighborhoods in the city. Just a block or two to the east was a world apart: San Francisco's Chinatown, a favorite tourist destination and lively commercial district. The decor, the street signs, and the smells made it seem as if you'd actually traveled to China, especially on the main thoroughfare, Grant Avenue. In contrast, Oakland's Chinatown was lively, with great markets and delicious restaurants, but not an attraction like the one in San Francisco.

At the top of the peak a glorious view of the bay and Oakland delighted May.

"It is beautiful," she whispered.

"As a professor, I will never be paid well enough to afford this view. Hopefully I can find one close to it."

"I'm sure we will," she replied.

John squeezed her hand in assurance.

They turned left on Vallejo and John stopped in front of a lovely, three-story Victorian. It was packed in tight, with no space between it and the next building.

John knocked on the door, a level of formality they didn't practice in her family. She walked right into her aunt and uncle's and her cousin's homes—as they did with hers.

"Jonathon," his mother declared. "What a surprise. Come in."

May watched John kiss his mother's cheek. She waited for her elder to signal how they would greet one another. Mrs. Barrow put out a hand, so May did the same. In the middle of their handshake his mother smiled and opened her arms. May gladly accepted the unspoken offer of a quick hug and took the liberty of kissing the woman's cool skin. She wanted to impress Mrs. Barrow, to show her respect and that she was ready to be a good wife for her son.

Mrs. Barrow's deep-blue dress was simple, but elegant, and she wore pearls around her neck and on her ears. They were unexpected company, so this was her everyday wear.

"We cannot stay long, not even for tea, but I want to share my news with you," John explained. "Is father home?"

Mrs. Barrow nodded. She pointed to the parlor and walked up the stairs. May studied John. He looked nervous, and younger than usual. Like most men, he probably longed to earn his father's respect. Mr. Barrow hadn't expected his son to become an academic. While he hadn't expressed strong disapproval, he told John that a professor's salary would not afford him the finest lifestyle. May admired John for being willing to follow his mind rather than his pocketbook when it came to choosing a career.

John explained the layout of the house to May. "Father's study is on the third floor. Bedrooms are on the second. This floor has the kitchen, dining, living room, parlor, and a laundry area—though mother sends it out."

"It's lovely," May said.

"A typical railroad Victorian." He shrugged. "With an amazing view in a wonderful location."

They sat down and waited for his parents. May was delighted to be here when he shared the good news, appreciated being brought into this circle of family life. She looked around the formal room. Above the fireplace was a portrait of a girl who looked to be seven or eight.

"Who is she?" May asked.

John pulled his lips into a sad, tight smile. "That is Anne. She died when I was ten and she was eight. Scarlet fever."

"I'm so sorry," May said.

"It was a long time ago. I was too young to be affected, but please do not speak of her with my mother as it upsets her." He shook his head. "I don't understand why she keeps that portrait so prominent."

An older, equally handsome version of John walked in, asking, "What's your news, son?"

"Dominican in Marin has made me an offer which I have accepted."

"Wonderful!" Mrs. Barrow replied.

"Congratulations, son. I know your mother will be relieved to have you close by. When do you start?"

Mr. Barrow kept his tone measured. He would not be considered a warm or kind man, but neither was he harsh or angry. She wondered if she could ever win his heart over. In contrast, she was confident she and Mrs. Barrow would have a warm and mutually supportive relationship much like Auntie Diana and Nana.

"Faculty meetings start on August fifteenth," John replied.

May hadn't even thought to ask. Two months away. That would be plenty of time to make arrangements. This was extremely exciting and becoming a reality. Her life was about to change entirely, for the better. She was about to have her own home in Marin County.

They chatted for a few minutes about the exhibition, which John's parents visited several times already. They'd enjoyed it, but wished the event to be over. For months the traffic had been bothersome and on far too many nights the sounds and the lights from the fair were disruptive.

Mrs. Barrow hugged May farewell, ending with a squeeze that confirmed May's belief they would be close. Mr. Barrow bid them goodbye with a nod of the head.

May buzzed as they traveled back to the East Bay. It was such a nearly perfect day together. Despite her being upset, John was able to forgive her poor temper and then bring her to his home to have time with his parents.

She stood at the railing of the ferry, wrapped from behind in John's arms. He leaned in ever so slightly against her back as his thumb stroked her hand. A pleasant shiver traveled down her spine.

"It's like we are leaving the Emerald City," she said as they sped away from the tall buildings.

"Back home to Kansas?" he replied.

She smiled. Dorothy only wanted to return to Auntie Em, but she was a child. May yearned for the comfort of home and the excitement of the Emerald City. She looked across the water at the hills in Marin. Somehow her wish was being granted, not by a Good Witch, but with this wonderful man.

John whispered into her ear, "Do you want to come to my studio?" He cleared his throat. "For a private supper?"

Her heart surged with joy. She'd been to his studio many times, but never with the thought of becoming intimate. Now they would be since everything was in place—he'd graduated, gotten his position, and she'd made a thorough study of Mrs. Sanger's pamphlet. She was a modern woman, prepared for this moment with a sponge and solutions in her bag. Thanks to scientific research she was able to follow her heart while keeping her head.

She nodded and murmured, "Mhhm."

He kissed her neck. A delightful tingle traveled down her spine and out to every edge of her body.

"Are you certain?" he asked.

Yearning filled her every pore. She turned around to look him in the face. "I am if you are," she replied.

He smiled and nodded, showing equal desire in his beautiful eyes. She grinned back; they were ready to make this official.

"I don't have a rubber," he said in a low voice.

"Mrs. Sanger has other methods," she told him. "I'm prepared."

They gazed at each other and finally consented to give in to the desire of their flesh.

CHAPTER 4

NAOMI

June 1915

Naomi burst with anticipation as she left her job at the Booth Home for Unwed Mothers. She was proud to work at the Salvation Army clinic that gave young women a safe place to deliver and good choices when it was over. Far fewer babies were abandoned to the elements in communities with clinics like this.

Nearly half of her patients left without their babies. The clinic found responsible infertile parents eager to welcome a newborn. Those who left with their babies would as often as not become the baby's older sister in the eyes of the world—their mothers claiming a late-life pregnancy to protect their daughters. Most of the young women who came to the home to deliver their babies were hiding their condition from someone.

It was a light day of work—no births on her shift—but even if she'd spent hours in a grueling delivery she would be excited to get home because tonight her family would be together. By the grace of God, Cedric's first return since becoming a coal man coincided with Willie's two days off. She stopped at a market in Chinatown on the way home to buy each of their favorites: catfish for Cedric and sweet potatoes for Willie.

Walking to the front door she measured her home against the house she'd toured in the Santa Fe Tract with Mrs. de Hart, and found it severely wanting once again. Everything lacking in her house seemed magnified since envisioning them in something better. The two slats on the porch that were bare of paint and so cracked that she avoided stepping on them for fear of making a large hole taunted her. Spots of bare redwood showed through where chips of color popped off the door and the wooden siding.

Inside was no better. They had no electricity, so the slight smell of kerosene permeated the air. It was so familiar she hardly noticed it, but it was unpleasant. With only two bedrooms in the house, Maggie slept in the laundry room, which felt oppressive now that she was a young woman of fifteen years.

Naomi didn't consider her kitchen to be an undue burden until she pictured using the gas stove to cook and hot water from a tap for cleanup. *Someday.*

Naomi sighed as she started a wood fire in her oven. *Be grateful for what you do have,* she reminded herself, and then added, *but you do not have to give up your dream of a better life for all of you.*

While the fire got started, Naomi pulled six plates from the cherrywood breakfront that matched their rectangular table. These red-rose-trimmed dishes were only for special occasions. As she set, each flowery plate brought to mind its future user. Willie at the head, with Gramma Jordan next to him; then Cedric. She would sit at the foot with Joseph to her left and Maggie to his side. She paused to take in the moment of anticipation. All six of them would be together.

Her firstborn walked into their dining room just as she set a knife by Willie's plate. Her breath caught and love swelled in her heart. No matter his age, he was still her baby.

"Cedric!" she squealed and rushed to him.

They embraced, Naomi savoring the connection—and noticing he was thinner and more muscular.

"It's good to be home," he said, his eyes welling up.

Naomi's throat filled. She cleared it, cupped his cheeks with her hands, and replied, "It's so good to have you home."

Cedric was subtly transformed in the two weeks since he'd left Oakland to be a coal man. He wore a maturity that came from measuring yourself in a new way. He'd lost some of his innocence. Maternal protection rose in her, but there was nothing for her to say or do.

She wanted her children to be confident, hard workers who knew their own worth in a society that didn't measure them by their skills or diligence. They'd never been far from Oakland and only read about the worst degradations of colored people. Even Willie spared them stories about the many abuses he faced, to keep his own dignity. They were surrounded by a stable community of church and family that cherished them since the day they were born. She feared she and Willie made a mistake in not preparing them to take their place as adults in society.

Naomi fought Cedric—arguing that seventeen was too young to work on the rails. She suggested he find a job in Oakland or San Francisco while being careful not to insult her husband for his labor. Railroad work paid well and was honorable, but the cost of being in a hostile world, and away from family, was a price she didn't want for Cedric. However, her son disagreed. As soon as he finished at Oakland High School he took a train job. Gramma Jordan reminded Naomi to be grateful he'd waited until then, because so many young men didn't understand the value in the diploma and did see the benefit of earning money.

"Cedric!" Maggie, Naomi's beloved daughter, exclaimed from the doorway, "You look like a real man now."

"And you still look like my scrawny little sister," he teased.

Naomi watched them embrace, her heart filled with joy as they clung to one another for an extra breath, demonstrating their love with a pat and a squeeze.

After they broke apart he challenged, "What are you wearing?!"

Maggie twirled around in her Aunt Jemima wardrobe: a long gray dress with a white apron and matching kerchief.

"This is what I have to wear to work!" Maggie shrugged. "It pays well."

Cedric said, "You smell sweet . . . like syrup."

"I will NEVER want to eat another pancake after this job." Maggie laughed and then she yelled "Cedric's HOME!" into the air, letting Joseph and Willie know the exciting news.

Joseph arrived in a flash. Her boys pounded and hugged greetings in the way of young men.

"I'm taller!" Joseph declared. "Right, Ma?"

"I haven't been gone that long," Cedric bickered. "There's NO way you are taller than me after two weeks."

Naomi laughed and replied, "Don't bring me into this."

To her eye they were still the same height, but it was only a matter of time. With fifteen months between them, Joseph would most likely grow taller than his older brother. Maggie passed Naomi last year, leaving her the shortest in the family.

She was also the darkest, though Maggie was closest to her complexion while Joseph and Cedric were the exact combination of her dark and Willie's light skin tones.

Willie, out of his blue Pullman porter's uniform and in his green lounge clothes, walked in saying, "What's all the fuss about?"

"Hey, Pops." Cedric smiled. They embraced, so long and sweet it raised emotion in Naomi again. She blinked the moisture in her eyes. It was plain to see that these two now shared something she didn't understand or have a part of.

"Cedric, take your things to your room, and wash up. Dinner will be ready when you are."

She returned to the kitchen to see to the food. Maggie followed.

"It's good to have Cedric home, isn't it, Mama?" Maggie asked.

Naomi nodded. "It hasn't been the same without him."

Maggie gave her a hug. "It's okay. He's still our Cedric."

"Always," Naomi agreed, "no matter where he is. Can you run down to tell Gramma Jordan that Cedric is home?"

Jordan Wallace, Naomi's mother, lived with her friend Mrs. King, less than two blocks away. The widowers, neighbors since the 1890s, decided to share a flat after Mr. King died.

Maggie, lanky and energetic, rushed out the back door without a thought to change. Naomi wondered what the neighbors might make of her outfit, though in truth they'd seen her coming and going in it for many weeks.

Maggie wasn't nearly as bothered by the outfit as Naomi and Gramma Jordan. They thought it demeaning. Maggie seemed to think it was humorous, and thought her elders were taking her job too seriously. She was thrilled to be making good money over the summer. Naomi feared it would hamper her ambitions, but Maggie said nothing would stop her from becoming a teacher like her Gramma Jordan.

Naomi finished cooking, plated the food, and carried it out.

"Oh, Ma. You made my favorite!" Cedric beamed in delight at the catfish when he saw it.

A wave of satisfaction traveled down Naomi's spine. Cedric had a measure of distance from her since leaving childhood. He loved her, she knew that, but he didn't have much use for Naomi. His companions, young women, even his father—they all held more interest to him than she did. Maybe the time away would help him to have more appreciation for family.

Maggie returned with Gramma Jordan. The silver-haired woman hugged her grandson long and hard. She cupped his cheek just like Naomi. Then they all sat down around the table.

They'd lived in this home in West Oakland for Cedric's entire life—with Willie's parents until they passed, and then the five of them. Naomi appreciated this simple Victorian, but it was small, outdated, and a rental. Several dear friends had been forced to move when their landlords sold their homes out from under them. Large profits from the rising price of real estate were hard to resist even for the kindest landlords.

Not wanting to give any additional cause for an eviction, Willie and Naomi didn't request repairs, let alone improvements. Over the years this fine apartment became increasingly dilapidated. If they lived in a home that they owned they would never be forced to move and they could make repairs and improvements as they chose.

"Tell me about it, son," Willie proclaimed, his hazel eyes wide with interest.

Cedric responded, his voice weary, "As the low man I have the overnights along with the other new guy. It's hard. I'm off from ten until four."

"That's eighteen hours of working!" Naomi exclaimed. "You are supposed to have eight hours off each day."

Cedric shrugged. "They don't care about 'supposed to.'"

Fierce protection welled up in Naomi. Her son could not possibly get enough sleep if he was worked that hard. She stole a glance at Joseph, hoping he was listening and learning—the railroads were no friend to their people.

Willie patted her hand. "Leave it be, Naomi. It's just the way it is on the rails. Cedric can handle it as well as any of us do."

Naomi felt tears push against her eyes. She didn't want her son to have to bear the same lifestyle as Willie. He worked four hundred hours a month—and was away from home far more nights than he slept there. It was a good income that provided well for them, but Naomi wished her husband was able to share the day to day running of their lives. She was accustomed to making do without Willie, but she missed his insight, humor, and warmth when he was gone.

She declared, "This is precisely why we need our own union."

Willie replied, "Well, we don't have one—and the AFL isn't concerned with colored workers."

"Someday soon," Gramma Jordan declared, "the time is coming."

When Naomi married Willie in 1895 he was a conductor for the Pullman Company. He'd been passing for white to have that more prestigious, higher paid, and less strenuous job. When Cedric was still an infant a white coworker realized the truth of her husband's blood and warned him to "voluntarily return to his rightful place." Willie understood what was on the other side of that threat, and he put in to become a Pullman porter instead of a conductor. Losing the pay was rough, but the relief from fear was a weight from Naomi's shoulders.

And now Cedric was a coal man—an even more strenuous, and lower paid, position.

Years ago she mistakenly believed that in Oakland their race would not be a barrier to their success, but she'd learned otherwise. She didn't have the same work options as white nurses, and her children were not being offered positions in offices like their white classmates.

Naomi returned her attention to her family, looking around the table at her three children, her mother, and her husband—together for just this night. None of them knew when they would be together again. She would not allow her frustrations from the past nor her fears for the future to interfere with this time with them.

Naomi reached her arms out. Cedric placed his left hand in hers. She rubbed it with her thumb. Joseph took her right hand. She gazed at the circle of hands. The Holy Spirit filled her heart. She nodded to Willie, signaling him to lead grace.

His deep, faithful voice spoke out clear and strong: "Lord, we thank you for this most beautiful day. We are grateful to be gathering in health with your blessings spread out before us. We remember that all our good and all our glory come from you. Amen."

All of their voices echoed his affirmation of the sentiment in her heart.

CHAPTER 5

MAY

July 1915

"Did your monthly come yet?" Elena asked.

Fighting back the wall of tears that threatened to cross the spill-way of her eyes, May turned her head side to side. It had been three weeks since that night. Three weeks of seeing John, feigning non-chalance as she waited for a proposal . . . and for her monthlies. She followed all of Mrs. Sanger's suggestions. She took Beecham's Pills morning and night for each of the four days before she expected her period. She'd continued the vile practice when it didn't come, but it wasn't working. Her breasts grew tenderer, she felt faintly nauseated, and, the strangest of all, everything smelled more strongly. But no bleeding.

"When do I tell him?"

"Soon," Elena advised. "You want to be married quickly. There's no need to have whispering seven months after your wedding. Especially for a new professor!"

May blushed and her stomach dropped. She'd been so certain she wasn't risking anyone's reputation. That their choice would be personal and private, never to be revealed to the world, but Elena was right. They must fix this soon.

"I'll go see him when we finish supper. Thank you for your wise counsel. I'm so emotional these days I can't seem to think well."

She squeezed Elena's hand.

Elena asked, "I suspect you have not told Nana Lisbeth and Auntie Sadie."

May bit her lip and shook her head.

"They will understand," Elena declared.

May shook her head again. She blinked back her tears. "I don't want their pity. Momma never said so directly, but it was obvious she didn't trust John's intentions toward me. If she learns we are marrying only now that I am pregnant she will forever believe she was in the right."

"You want to be engaged before you tell them?" Elena asked.

May shook her head for a third time. "I want to be *married* before they know."

"I understand," Elena said. She twisted an imaginary key on her lips. "Your secret is safe with me."

"I'm sorry to bother you with my dramatics," May said. "Your baby should be the most important topic of conversation."

Elena waved her hand, dismissing May's concern. "We're fine. We have months until the baby comes. Plenty of time to get our things set up. You know my mother . . . Mitta is ready to spring into action to take care of everything."

May nodded. She envied Elena's settled life with a lovely home, a kind husband, and a cheerful mother nearby to welcome her baby. May didn't have any of that and somehow found herself in this precarious situation.

"Our babies will be less than a year apart!" Elena declared. "I know you expected to have more time before welcoming children, but I'm delighted the second cousins will be close in age."

May took in a breath. It was so like Elena to see the best in a hard situation. She was correct, though: it would be lovely to have them grow up together.

"You are right, Elena. I look forward to watching them play together," May said.

Momma looked surprised when May said she was going directly to John's after Sunday supper, but she didn't ask and May didn't tell why she was visiting her beau after dark.

May's heart pounded as she rang the bell. It felt an eternity waiting for John to come to the front of the building. Through the glass in the door she saw him walking toward her. He looked confused and then suddenly his face lit up when he realized who was calling on him. Her angst melted a bit.

"What a delightful surprise!" he declared.

"I just couldn't stay away from you," she teased.

He took her hand and led her down the wide carpeted hallway and up the stairs to his floor. As soon as the door to his studio closed behind them he held her in his arms, kissing her passionately. Her body leapt in response and before she knew it they were entangled on his bed.

She broke away from their embrace, and said, "I have something I must tell you."

She swallowed hard, her throat nearly swollen shut with nerves.

"You sound so serious," he teased. Then he studied her. His eyebrows shot up in question, and then pulled downward as he read her emotions. "What is the matter?"

"I fear that I am pregnant," she rushed out.

John bolted upright; he sat on the edge of the bed, his feet on the ground, and faced away from May. Her heart pounded so hard in her chest that she heard the rush of blood in her ears. She couldn't see his face.

"You assured me," he stammered, "that you were taking the right precautions."

"I did everything that the pamphlet recommended." May sat up slowly, looked at his panicked face, and touched his back to comfort him.

"I can't . . . I'm sorry, but no," he said, shaking his head.

May exhaled and her throat closed up tight. She'd been upset too as she slowly accepted that her monthlies were not coming. It *was* too soon—for both of them. And yet, here they were.

May soothed, "I don't feel ready either. I was very upset at first too. I wanted to be a newlywed couple for a few years before adding children. There's still a chance it won't last. However, I wanted you to know so we can be married as soon as possible. Neither of us wants a fancy wedding. We can do it this week."

John stood up. He shook as he looked down at her. Was that pity in his eyes? May swallowed hard.

"May, I'm sorry." He seemed close to tears. "I let things go too far. I'm afraid you have misunderstood my intentions."

"What?!" Her throat closed up tight.

"I think you'd best leave," John declared.

"What?" she stammered; fear and shame made her heart race.

He took her hand and pulled her to the door. He kissed her cheek and said, "You are a lovely girl. You will make someone a great wife. Just not me. Take care of this . . . situation."

Her knees went weak. She could hardly hear him through the pounding in her head. John turned the knob, and led her by the hand into the hallway, then spun her around like he was twirling her in a dance rather than exiling her.

"Goodbye," he said solemnly. "And good luck." He closed the door in her face.

The shiny white wood mocked her as tears rolled down her cheeks. She'd run through this scene many ways in her mind. She'd imagined him joyful, confused, upset, or practical, but never pictured *this* would be the outcome of her revelation. John showed such devotion.

She braced herself on the wooden frame and took a few breaths. She put an ear to the door, pressing so hard it hurt, but she couldn't hear anything. May made a fist, ready to pound, and then fought the impulse. He needed time to adjust. Surely he would change his mind once he'd grown used to the idea of becoming a father.

She let herself cry as she walked through campus, but once she got to Bancroft she wiped her tears. She didn't want Nana Lisbeth and Momma to see her distress, and ask questions. She found her book and sat on the old davenport looking as if she were reading, but mostly gazed through a small opening in the curtain waiting for John. Certainly he would come to his senses and come over.

Late, long after Nana Lisbeth and Momma were in bed, May sat watch. When her legs cramped up from sitting, she stood by the window, gazing through the glass and rocking from side to side; rage and sorrow alternated through her. Adrenaline kept her awake until well after midnight, when she finally faced the truth: John wasn't coming tonight. She left her sentry and went to her bed.

Momma's heavy breathing filled the air as she slept without a care in the world. May climbed under the covers. She recalled the conversation with John, tried to remember his exact words, and wondered how she should have approached the topic. Eventually sleep overtook her, but dreams troubled her rest.

In the morning May hid her dilemma at home and at work. Distracted and morose, she blamed a headache. She hardly slept the next night and could hardly function at work on Tuesday. She feared she would burst into tears or scream at the smallest frustration.

May gave John two days to acclimate to the idea, but couldn't give him more time to come around on his own. They had to marry soon. At the end of her workday she walked across campus and up the steep incline to his apartment.

The hill and her nerves combined to cause her heart to beat hard. She rang the bell, breathing deeply to steady herself. It always seemed a long wait for him to come to the door, but today it was interminable. She studied the leaves of a bright-green maple tree. The light shining through them made the veins stand out.

He didn't come. *He's avoiding you!* flashed through her mind. That was a foolish thought because there was no way for him to see it was her. John must be out. Still, she pushed the button again, two long, firm, satisfying presses. Next to her, a hummingbird darted in and out of a flower. It was beautiful. And working so hard.

May sat on the steps. He had to return eventually and she would not allow him to put this off any longer. Every time a bubble of fury rose in her, she reminded herself that she too didn't feel ready for a child. She'd done what she could to prevent a pregnancy—and prayed each day for it to end. It was hypocritical of her to think that his immediate response would be more mature than hers had been.

She wished she had a book, or a newspaper, or something to distract her. She hummed "Amazing Grace" and hoped he would show grace in this situation. The apartment wasn't at the top of the hill, but she could see a nice view of the campus below and a bit of the bay to the west. She sat there long enough to watch the setting sun change the color of the sky. Bright blue transformed to orange and red mottled with pink clouds. She felt the beauty as a blessing, even in her agitated state.

The door behind her opened. She turned around, expecting a stranger, but it was Mr. Lee, the building manager. He didn't know her well but was always friendly and kind.

"Good evening, Miss Wagner," he said.

"Hello, Mr. Lee," she said. "I'm waiting for Mr. Barrow."

Mr. Lee's eyebrows drew in, then empathy filled his eyes. May's stomach dropped. Was that pity?

"Mr. Barrow moved out last Monday," he explained too kindly.

Stunned, she asked, "Where?"

"I'm afraid I don't know."

"Was it sudden?"

"He gave notice more than a month ago," Mr. Lee replied with a verbal punch to May's stomach.

Weeks ago? And he hid it from me! A heat wave of anger dried any tears that threatened to well up.

"Thank you for clarifying the situation for me," May said. "Good night, Mr. Lee."

"Good evening to you, Miss Wagner," he said. Then his voice dropped in sympathy. "And best wishes."

Mr. Lee's kindness broke through her rage. She spun around, toward home, and let her tears flow. John lied to and then abandoned her. He gave notice before she told him she was pregnant. Was he only waiting for graduation? For relations?!

Did he ever have genuine feelings or intentions toward her or was it only a dalliance? She replayed the last year. How could she have been so stupid, naïve, and foolish? She was in an untenable situation and had to find a way forward that didn't include him—or becoming an unwed mother, responsible for a child without a husband.

May took the train past her stop and rode through downtown Oakland until she got to Fourth Street and Broadway. She would talk this through with Elena, because time was of the essence.

May walked into her cousin's living room and yelled, "Hello."

"In here!" Elena's voice came from the kitchen.

"Good evening, May," Peter said as he stood up from their kitchen table. The tall, black-haired man enveloped her in a bear hug and then said, in a knowing voice, "I'll give you two some privacy . . . ," and left.

"He knows?" May asked.

"You know I can't keep things from him," Elena reminded May. Her dark hair was braided back from her face. "Mitta, yes, because she will tell everyone. It is not easy either—being with her at the produce market all day. But with Peter, your news may as well be in a vault."

May nodded, then teared up.

Elena read her and asked, "It hasn't gone well?"

May frowned and shook her head. Elena opened her arms and May gladly accepted a calm, comforting hug.

Elena put on the kettle and gestured to the table. With a nod, she invited May to tell her story.

May sighed and started, "After I left Auntie Diana and Uncle Sam's on Sunday night I told John." Choked up with emotion, May took a breath so she could continue. She forced words out from her tight throat. "He said I misunderstood his intentions. That I'd find the right man someday . . . and then—somehow I was in the hallway."

"He pushed you out the door?!" Anger filled Elena's voice.

May nodded.

"Oh, honey!" Elena said.

May teared up at her cousin's sympathy. She was such a fool! A nauseating wave of shame flowed through her.

She continued, though she sounded pitiful. "I gave him two days—two long, terrible days to change his mind. After work today I went to his apartment. I rang and rang. No answer. I sat on the steps determined to wait for him. Eventually his building manager, Mr.

Lee, came out. He told me John moved out last Monday—as arranged more than a month ago."

Elena's eyes grew wide in outrage, but her lips drew in and she didn't speak.

May said in a high voice, "He planned to drop me for weeks. Maybe months." Heat rose in her chest, evaporating her tears. "I cannot believe I was ready to marry someone so devious!"

Elena sighed. "This may not be a comfort, but I feel it is better that you discovered his true nature now rather than when it's too late. However . . ." She eyed May's belly.

May stared into her cousin's brown eyes. "You know who can end this condition for me."

Elena nodded. "It's expensive," she replied and stated the price.

May sucked in her breath. That was much of the savings she'd expected to use to set up a household with John.

"Not more dear than having a child I'm not ready for," May countered.

"Are you certain this is the right choice for you?"

"Motherhood by choice, not by chance," May said, modifying Mrs. Sanger's quote just a bit. Her entire life would be changed, and not for the better, if she became a mother now before she was married. Though she fervently believed no one should be shamed for having a baby out of wedlock, she did not want to bear that mark for life. Society had moved beyond making women wear scarlet letters, but the stigma was still ever present.

Elena patted her arm, left, and returned with a card.

"Miss Turner's pills worked for me and for Tina, but they will make you feel horrible. For many days," Elena warned. "Ask her for the French Tonic to *immediately* bring on your menses. The *immediately* tells her your cycle is past due."

"I don't know what I'd do without you," May said. "I'm so grateful you and Peter haven't moved far away to Martinez like your sister."

"Me too. I don't wish for land or a big house. I like walking places and having all of you nearby. Do Auntie Sadie or Nana Lisbeth know yet?"

"No!" May exclaimed. "And I don't plan to tell them, ever."

"They would understand . . . and be supportive," Elena said.

May shook her head. She teared up. "You don't know what it's like—to still live with your mother when you are nearly twenty-one. I already feel as if I have failed. This situation is humiliating. I will not, cannot, admit it to them. Please don't tell Auntie Diana. I know she will mean well, but I fear she would . . ."

Cousin Elena interrupted: "Your secret is safe with me and Peter. He finds no satisfaction in repeating news about other people."

Elena opened her arms. May accepted the comfort of another hug. She rested her head on Elena's shoulder, letting her tears flow. This was too much to bear. Her beautiful future was torn away from her and she must get through a most terrible ordeal.

First she'd end the pregnancy, and then she would plan for what came next.

The next morning May tucked a large fold of cash into her underclothes before she left for work. She was glad John was no longer a student so she didn't face the possibility of seeing his face. Each thought of him brought a swirl of unpleasant emotions. Anger made her heart pound and sorrow burned her eyes. She pushed aside any rising of either rather than risk an embarrassing breakdown.

Fortunately in early summer the department was quiet, with little to be done immediately. She finished everything that would be best done if she were to be away for a few days and feigned a stomach upset, giving her cover for departing and staying out for several days. If all went according to plan she'd actually be sick soon.

The trolley took her from campus to downtown Oakland. She expected to find a dim shop hidden away up a staircase, but the doorway was right on Broadway, just above Grand Avenue. Gold letters on the window proclaimed:

WOMEN'S WEAR

DIRECTLY FROM

FRANCE

A pleasant bell sounded as May opened the door.

A smartly dressed woman called out a greeting as she entered: "Good morning. How can I help you?"

"My cousin recommended your French Tonic to me." She flushed and her voice sounded high even to her own ear.

"Immediate or monthly?"

"Immediate, please." Her heart pounded.

The woman disappeared behind a curtain. She returned with a dark-brown bottle and stood at the cash register.

Without apology she declared the high price. May reached into her neckline and took out the money. She thought her hand might shake as she passed it over, but it looked steady.

The large woman placed it in the till then leaned in close though the store was empty.

Miss Turner instructed, "Take three pills each night and each morning spaced twelve hours apart until they are gone. It is unlikely you will be capable of being out of bed for at least a week. Drink a good amount of lemon water with honey and garlic or ginger. Good luck."

Those words hung like a warning as May left the shop.

———— ❧ ————

Anxious to get the process over, May unscrewed the bottle as she sat on the trolley. She kept it low on her lap, hidden in the fold of fabric between her legs. She tapped three pills into her left hand. May sent a silent prayer: *Please release me from this condition.* One by one she swallowed them without water, leaving a painful lump in her throat. She swallowed repeatedly but the uncomfortable sensation stayed with her as she traveled home.

The pills were in her belly, hopefully taking effect, as she walked through the front garden. The white carnations, representing motherhood, taunted her. She wanted a child eventually, four actually, but not one who'd been abandoned by his father. She marched by the flowers and through the door.

Nana Lisbeth quizzed her by raising her eyebrows.

"I fear I caught a stomach virus or perhaps a food illness," May lied directly to her grandmother. Up until now her deception was only of omission. She didn't like being a person who hid the truth but preferred it to being pitied.

"Up to bed," Nana Lisbeth said. "I'll bring you some tea. Ginger and lemon sound good?"

"Yes, please," May replied, grateful for her grandmother's kindness. "With honey too."

May was in the bathroom vomiting when Nana Lisbeth brought the cup. After settling May back into bed she returned with a large ceramic bowl and a damp washcloth. Nana Lisbeth gently wiped May's brow and arms.

"Better?" she asked.

May nodded. She mouthed, *thank you.*

"Of course," Nana Lisbeth patted May's arm. "You rest. I'll be back up in a bit. Do you feel ready for plain rice?"

Her stomach lurched at the thought of food. She shook her head. Nana Lisbeth left and May lay there; sitting up, she dozed with a white porcelain bowl on her lap. The dry retches were horrid, but she could rest between bouts of heaving.

May heard the front door open and close. Momma was home from her job at the market. Soon she came upstairs with another cup of tea, though May had hardly drunk any of the first. Momma looked down at May, concern in her eyes.

"Has anyone been ill at work?"

"No, I suspect it's from my lunch yesterday. I'm sure I will be fine soon."

"Shall I send word to John?" Momma asked.

His name sent her stomach low; May shook her head. Momma's features pulled inward, showing confusion, then understanding opened them wide.

"Your relationship has . . . ended?" Momma asked.

May blinked and nodded.

"Oh, I'm sorry," Momma said, patting May's arm.

Momma looked sad too, like her own heart was breaking. May bristled at the pity, but the kindness caused her to tear up. She wanted to hide.

A bout of intestinal cramps came upon May, causing her to rush to the bathroom to empty her bowels. It was disgusting, but she examined the bowl to see if the tonic was achieving her desired results. There was nothing red in there that indicated it was working as she hoped. She returned to bed, sweaty and spent. *God, please let this be over soon.*

Back in bed, she let Momma wipe her brow with a cool, wet cloth. It was so kind, so soothing. May considered telling her mother the truth of her state, but couldn't imagine adding to her concern nor engaging in any conversation. She only wanted to curl up and close her eyes.

Momma raised *Anne of the Island*. "Want me to read out loud?"

She picked the perfect story. May had plowed through the first two in the series so many times the pages were falling from the novels; she'd longed to be like the spunky heroine in *Anne of Green Gables*.

"Thank you." May nodded.

Momma started at the beginning as May rested with her eyes closed, interrupted by trips to the bathroom. May was as sick as she'd ever been in her life. Many fluids left her body, but none of them red.

Five days later May left her bed, recovered from the treatment, but not cured of her dilemma. If her calculations were correct she would be delivering a baby in March 1916, but she didn't have to raise it. She wasn't surrendering her future to a mistake.

CHAPTER 6

May

July 1915

During worship Elena leaned forward past her mother to peer at May. Her raised eyebrows asked a question. May pursed her lips and shook her head slightly. Then May shrugged, took in a deep breath, and sighed. Nana Lisbeth patted her leg. In the days since she recovered, Momma and Nana Lisbeth showed kindness while allowing her much-desired distance. They read her preference for privacy accurately, but didn't know the true reason. She allowed them to assume her pain was solely from John breaking off with her.

Elena was at her side as soon as worship ended.

"We'll see you at home," Elena told her mother. She grabbed May's hand and they strolled to her aunt and uncle's.

"Well?" Elena inquired.

Glad to finally speak of it, May said in a rush, "It was awful. As ill as I have ever been. But I never saw anything red come out of me."

May swallowed hard. Elena squeezed her hand. They walked for a block in silence. Overwhelmed and embarrassed, May felt her head pound in uncertainty.

Elena asked, "Are you still hiding it from Aunt Sadie and Nana?"

May nodded. "I won't keep this baby! I can't bear the shame of being a mother before I'm a wife." Her voice broke. "I'd be dependent on Nana Lisbeth and Momma forever."

"I think you are being harsh on yourself, and all the other women who find themselves in your position."

May took a breath and exhaled hard. "Before I was in this position I would have said the same. But now? I want this behind me, I want this baby to have a good home and I do not want Nana Lisbeth nor Momma to ever learn of it."

"How can you conceal it from them?" Elena asked. "While you are living with them."

"It will be winter when I am as large as you are. Heavy coats and sweaters along with a girdle will hide my condition."

Elena made a distressed face. "Ouch!"

"It won't be simple or comfortable . . . but I can't bear the shame of facing Momma's quiet disappointment. She never cared for John. Though she attempted to keep her feelings hidden, I could tell she didn't trust him. I thought *she* was wrong, but it turns out I was the fool."

"May, don't be so hard on yourself," Elena chided. "You took every wise precaution. He led you to believe he was honorable, that there was good reason to put your trust in him."

"Did he, really?" May said. "Or did I only want to see him as trustworthy?"

"May! Kind and respectable men do not date someone for more than a year, meet her family, and introduce them to his own if they are not intending an engagement. *He* is the one who let things go too far. He should have broken it off before you crossed that line. It's why he has behaved so horridly. He knows he should be ashamed of his reprehensible behavior."

"You really believe so?" May asked, sounding like a pathetic schoolgirl.

"Absolutely."

"Thank you," May replied. "It shouldn't, but it means very much to me to know you don't think me a fool."

"In matters of the heart we all become foolish," Elena said. "Nature, God, needed it to be so."

May's resolve hardened. "I am not going to let one imprudent mistake ruin my life."

"What's your plan?" Elena asked. "How can I help?"

"As you know, Cousin Naomi is a nurse at the Booth Home for Unwed Mothers. She's mentioned they arrange adoptions," May explained. "I can deliver there, and they will find a good family for the baby."

"You are certain?"

"Absolutely," May declared, sounding more confident than she felt. This next year was going to be an ordeal, but she was determined to get through it. "Can I stay with you after the New Year?" she requested. "It will be extremely difficult to hide my belly in the last weeks. I'll help with your baby."

"Of course," her cousin agreed readily.

"Peter will approve?"

"He's very fond of you—always has been," Elena replied. "I think secretly he still holds a hope Leonardo can win your heart."

Three years ago, Elena and Peter encouraged May to allow his younger cousin to court her. At the time they were classmates at Oakland High. Leonardo was kind enough, but so shy that she hardly knew him though they'd been in school together for many years. May wasn't interested in settling for an Oakland boy. She'd set her sights on marrying a sophisticated San Francisco man. May had firmly rejected the suggestion then and she felt the same now.

May shook her head and laughed. "Would Leonardo want my heart now that I'm tarnished?"

"May! You are being ridiculous."

"If I do not make fun of myself, I fear I will feel sorry for myself," May said.

"You will be more than welcome to stay with us, whenever you need a place to live," Elena said, returning to the subject at hand.

"Thank you," May replied, so very grateful. "I can come sooner if you want my help with your baby before then."

Elena nodded.

May continued with her plan: "I will keep working for the anthropology department for now, but I do not intend to stay at the University of California after the New Year. It is a painful reminder of . . ."

May stopped talking. Fury and sorrow twisted her heart into a knot. Sitting at her desk, she remembered the excitement and joy when John came to see her. She'd spent much time daydreaming about a home with him . . . and now that future was lost forever.

May said, "In seven months this will be behind me and I will get on with my life. John Barrow will become a distant memory."

"That's the spirit," Elena said.

May looped her arm through Elena's. The foggy morning was now a sunny afternoon. A seagull flew overhead in the bright-blue sky. May was satisfied with her plan for her future.

Many weeks later May delighted in the delicious scent of garlic and onions as she walked in their front door after work. Finally past the nauseated phase of her pregnancy, she looked forward to eating dinner. She enjoyed the taste once again, and food stayed inside her. She'd miss Nana's cooking when she moved out and was grateful for it while she lived here. Nana Lisbeth was in the kitchen stirring their largest pot.

"Elena is in labor," Nana Lisbeth exclaimed, excitement filling her voice.

May wished she shared her grandmother's unequivocal enthusiasm. Of course, she was delighted for her cousin, but it was complicated to be welcoming this baby as she was hiding the presence of another. She wished she could just be happy for Elena, but a jealous knife cut into her heart—and then she was mad at herself for being unkind to her dearest and most supportive companion.

"Diana said that Naomi is attending the birth!" Nana Lisbeth declared.

May smiled.

"It will be a most amazing welcome to the newest member of our family. I have not seen Naomi since . . ."—Nana Lisbeth considered, her white eyebrows pulled together in thought—"too long! Perhaps Jordan's birthday the year before last."

Nana Lisbeth shook her head, and continued, "Can you believe Naomi saved you twenty years ago . . . and today she will be welcoming my next great-grandchild. What a blessing!"

May felt the heavy weight of her secret. She wanted Naomi to midwife her delivery, but wished for Nana Lisbeth to never know about it. Would she really keep this secret from her grandmother forever? Telling her seemed more distasteful than keeping it private.

Oblivious to May's torn state Nana Lisbeth said, "I told Diana we would bring soup and bread—and stay as long as we are helpful. It's all ready. I've only been waiting for you."

"What about Momma?" May asked.

"Leave her a note. She works until closing tonight and may be too tired to join us."

"Let me change clothes and then I'll be ready," May replied.

"Wear something comfortable because you may be sleeping in it," Nana Lisbeth declared, sounding like they were going to a party.

Comfortable, May thought to herself as she walked to her room. She'd been terribly conscious of her clothing for weeks. Her womb was barely starting to bulge out, but so far she could hide her condition without a corset. Soon enough she'd be adding that to her morning routine. May put on her loosest dress, which made her look like she was going out in a nightgown. Nana Lisbeth approved of her outfit with a nod and they set out into the dark and foggy night to welcome a new member of the family.

Uncle Sam and Peter were chatting when May and Nana walked into the living room. The father-to-be looked scared and a little lost. Nana Lisbeth patted his cheek after they exchanged a hug.

"Your life is about to change . . . forever," she declared. It was almost a taunt, but also an invitation. She leaned in close to his chest.

In a loud whisper she spoke to his heart: "You are about to feel more love than you have ever imagined. It can be a little painful to make room for so much devotion."

"Ma!" Uncle Sam chastised. "Don't scare the boy. He will be a fine father and make his way like most of us do!"

May's heart sank. She put her hand on her own belly and then quickly raised it so as not to reveal her secret. *Little one, you will have a father who loves you . . . just not John Barrow.*

"They are in the bedroom," Uncle Sam directed. "We aren't allowed, but I'm sure you are."

Peter hugged May, clinging on a little longer than typical.

"She's strong. They'll be fine," May reassured him.

He scrunched his whole face tight and nodded repeatedly for a few seconds.

"I didn't know I'd be so scared," he said. His voice broke. Peter loved Elena so much.

She patted his arm, smiled her reassurance, and said, "It will be over soon, and you can meet your baby."

"Not soon enough, unless I hear a cry before you open that door." He laughed. "Tell Elena I love her." Peter's eyes shone with tears. May's matched his—for many reasons. Not all of them generous.

Elena lay on her side under the covers, thin strands of her brown hair stuck to her sweaty face. Her eyes were closed and she bleated like a sheep. May looked from face to face, but no one seemed alarmed by her state. Auntie Diana sat on the edge of the mattress, close to her daughter, breathing so obviously that May could hear the long exhale.

Peter's sister, Alexandra, sat wide-eyed in a chair nearby. She looked like May felt, scared and excited. This was the first birth for both of them.

Naomi sat at the foot, patting Elena's leg over the blanket. May instantly felt reassured to see their cousin. Naomi turned and welcomed May with a nod.

The animal sound stopped and Elena opened her eyes. She blinked a few times.

Aunt Diana looked up and smiled a welcome at Nana Lisbeth and May. "Come say hello."

Nana Lisbeth walked to Elena, gave her a kiss on her cheek and said, "You are about to be a mama. I can't wait to hold that precious one."

Elena smiled, but didn't move. She looked like she was in a different world, asleep with her eyes open.

May leaned over and whispered, "Peter says he loves you. And so do I." Her voice broke and tears burned behind May's eyeballs. Elena opened her mouth to reply. Suddenly she gasped, and a loud bleat came out of her throat.

Auntie Diana rubbed the back of Elena's pelvis and inhaled loudly and slowly once again. When the surge stopped Naomi said quietly,

"They are coming very fast now. Do you feel as if you have to go to the bathroom with the labor pains?"

Slowly, Elena nodded once.

"That sensation means your baby is ready to come out. You can help as much as you wish. Soon it will become so strong that you cannot resist. Then you will bear down with each pain. Do you understand?"

Elena gave another small nod.

"I will lift the blanket and perhaps your leg. Your family will help too, yes?"

Elena's eyes scrunched as she worked to understand or reply.

"Your body knows what to do, you don't have to think about it," Naomi reassured. "And I am here to do what needs to be done."

"*We* are here too," Aunt Diana said.

Elena visibly relaxed.

Naomi gestured for May to come to her. May leaned over and her cousin whispered, "Stay there in case I need you to hold her leg up, yes?"

"Yes," May agreed, hoping she would be adequate to the task. Nana Lisbeth came behind her and said, "You get the best seat in the house." She patted May's arm and went to the chair near Peter's sister.

The next wave came and the midwife raised the blanket. Elena's legs were curled together.

"I'm going to lift your right leg so I can see what is going on with your body," Naomi said. "May will hold it up to help you."

Naomi gestured for May to sit to her side. She showed May how to rest her elbow on the mattress with her hand open. The confident woman rested Elena's leg in May's palm. The calf was warm and sticky, and notably heavy.

"Hello, baby!"

Between Elena's legs was the top of a head with dark, wet hair. The infant was right there! May could not keep her eyes off it as it bulged out the slightest bit. Naomi's brown finger ran around the edge where Elena's body ended and the baby's head rested. The opening grew ever so slightly.

Elena grunted, yelled, and then was panting. The head retreated until May could not make it out in the dark recess.

"Rest now. You did wonderfully. It won't be long now."

The calm woman nodded at Alexandra and said, "We are ready for your job. The basin of warm water, and the rags that you prepared earlier."

"Would you like your leg up or down, between labor pains?" Naomi asked so gently.

May listened for her cousin's reply, ready to follow directions. Instead Auntie Diana spoke. "She pointed up."

"Will you be okay?" Naomi asked May.

She nodded, determined to be supportive no matter how heavy the leg grew.

Naomi nodded back in approval. "You are doing great," she whispered to May.

May smiled, so grateful to know that she was being of assistance. And in admiration of Naomi's kindness and skill.

Elena gasped. "Another one," she said in a hoarse voice.

The laboring woman grunted and strained. May was entranced as the head emerged ever so slowly until a purplish, reddish circle of skin the size of a daisy was showing.

"I can rub your baby's hair. I think it will be golden-brown when washed up," Naomi chatted.

Elena grabbed her thigh, and pulled her leg to her own chest; May followed, rising to reach the calf and foot dangling in the air. She stood right by Auntie Diana, who was alternating her gaze between Elena's face and the crown of the baby's head.

"Keep going," Auntie Diana encouraged her daughter.

And then it ended with a panting Elena. She didn't lower her leg; the baby stayed where it was.

The sound of fast, heavy breathing filled the room. They waited in anticipation. Everyone was calm, reassuring May all was fine, but it was like nothing she'd ever witnessed before. She looked at Nana. Her grandmother was beaming. She nodded encouragement but to whom was unclear—to May, Elena, or Auntie Diana? Probably all of them.

"Argggg," Elena growled. She curled up, her face powerful and intent.

May looked at the spot where the baby was emerging. Naomi stretched, while more and more of the head bulged out until the very tips of ears smashed against the scalp were visible. This baby was nearly here. It was a strange color, a mixture of white and bluish-purple.

"Keep going if you can, Elena. This could be the end . . ."

Suddenly the whole head was out. In a swift motion Naomi tugged in a few directions and then a whole body was in capable hands, leaving only a white-and-blue cord dangling out of Elena.

"He's out! Welcome, little one," Naomi declared.

She placed him on Elena, now on her back, her leg somehow out of May's hands. May felt tears streaming down her cheeks.

"I can't believe you are here . . . ," Elena declared, quickly returning to this world.

Auntie Diana gazed in adoration, looking as if the infant were Jesus Himself. The circle stood in awe, watching the pair panting together.

Dazed, May looked around. How much time had passed since she'd entered the room? The baby didn't cry, but he looked calm and content, his color changing from bluish purple to reddish pink. She saw his little back moving up and down with each breath. A new member of her family that she already loved. Her . . . her? He would likely call her Auntie May. She would call him nephew—though he was a cousin.

May exhaled and looked at Elena. "That was remarkable. You are so strong."

Elena smiled. "I'm glad you are here. You held my leg up?"

May nodded.

"It was like a dream. I hardly remember it though it was just a few moments ago," Elena remarked.

May felt a movement in her own belly. Most likely a bubble, but it could be the baby. Soon she'd be in Elena's position but she'd be alone, without the love of her family to cheer her on and give her strength. May swallowed her own fear and sorrow, pushing it down to focus on the joy of this moment.

Three months later, Elena and May walked to Sunday supper after worship at the Unitarian church. Baby Matthias was wrapped in a blanket knit by Nana. The warm wool kept out the chill of the fall air. He was a perfect bundle of joy.

"Can I raise a difficult topic?" Elena wondered.

Curious, tinged with concern, May replied, "Of course." Perhaps there were challenges between Elena and Peter or Auntie Diana.

"Have I done something to disappoint or anger you?" Elena asked.

May's stomach dropped. She thought she'd been better at hiding her jealous feelings. She shook her head, not able to share her true, but uncharitable, thoughts. Elena nodded, looking resigned, but not satisfied.

Shame welled in May. Her cousin was only generous and kind. She and Peter were keeping her secret, and allowing her to move in with them after the New Year.

May's unpleasant emotions shouldn't have been apparent to Elena during this time when baby Matthias was the priority. Elena and Peter deserved to be surrounded by joyous and comforting people, not the sullen and depressed.

"I am sorry, Elena," May said, hoping her tone conveyed the depth of her feelings. "I want to be happy for you, and I keep telling myself I should be, but each time I look at you my shame overwhelms me. I am angry . . . at John, at myself. I don't know how I have managed to be in this position. Pregnant, hiding my condition, a servant to my body, lying to my mother and Nana. To Aunt Diana. Am I never going to tell anyone?

"I'm scared and alone—except for you. But I am so jealous I could burst. And then I am ashamed because you have been nothing but helpful to me. And then I'm afraid that you will hate me back for being so cold."

Elena nodded. Her lips drew in and she gazed off into the distance. May's heart beat fiercely. She'd said too much. Now Elena would abandon her, and for good cause.

"Oh, May, that is ever so much to manage. I have never been in your position, so I can't say I understand how you feel. However, I am relieved to know that you don't think me cruel or insensitive." Elena teared up. "I'm aware that this cannot be easy for you. I'm sorry that my great joy is coming this close to your profound sorrow."

May wiped away the stream on her face. Tears, like so many fluids, flowed more freely than ever before. Tears of anger. Tears of frustration. Tears of fear. In this case they were tears of relief that Elena seemed to hold no resentment for her neediness and sour attitude.

Elena slid her arm through May's.

"I will never hate you. Somehow we must hold my joy and your sorrow at the same time," Elena said, so sweetly and wisely that May cried even more. "Neither of us wished for these to occur right now.

As Nana Lisbeth says, 'It's a mystery how God decides what we must bear and when. Our only decision is to choose how we will face it.'"

May nodded though she was still a jumble of emotion.

Elena continued, "Our 'how we will face this' is together, right?"

"Thank you," May said.

Elena squeezed her arm; they strolled past some particularly gorgeous maple trees. Their bright red and yellow leaves would fall to the earth soon, but in this moment they were painfully beautiful—a reminder of the glory, mystery, and brevity of life.

The day after Christmas, Boxing Day in England, May followed her mother and grandmother into their church's sanctuary. Sunlight shone through the large stained glass window over the chancel, making the bright colors and images particularly salient. She took a seat on the aisle and studied the vibrant Sower window.

In the foreground a farmer casts seeds onto a plowed field bordered by a hard path on one side and thorny ground on the other. In the background his wife guides a plow pulled by two oxen. As a child May decided they were married, which made her love the scene all the more. Small black birds peck at the seeds that landed on the hard path.

The Parable of the Sower was Nana Lisbeth's favorite Bible passage, perhaps because this window was in their church. Nana reminded congregants, especially her grandchildren, that this particular image was placed at the front of the church to remind them to be fertile soil for spiritual truths. As Jesus instructed in his brief, profound parable, distractions, skepticism, and disappointments test your deepest convictions, but if you tend to your spirit in good times you will grow deep spiritual roots to keep your faith strong in challenging times.

May appreciated her Nana's interpretation of the message in that sacred text—and had added her own when she stared at that image during uninteresting sermons: you reap what you sow and tend, a sentiment she was too well aware of nearly all of the time.

The baby stirred inside her. It was all she could do not to touch her belly. This had been going on for weeks. And would go on for many more. She had close to three months before this baby would be born. This was *the* most challenging of times for her.

Hiding her condition from Momma and Nana Lisbeth, and at work, was a constant weight pressing down on her. She was grateful that the end of her pregnancy was coinciding with the arrival of cold weather and the need for bulkier winter clothes. She only had one more week at home to get through. On the first day of 1916 she would move to Elena and Peter's home. She'd told Momma and Nana Lisbeth it was to be a help to them, but that was not the true reason.

Momma and Nana believed the true reason was she had growing pains and needed to be away from them. May didn't tell them her growing pains were of a physical nature more than a social one.

This Christmas service began with the children's choir singing "Mary's Cradle Song." May choked up over the line "Wonder baby mine."

She telegraphed a message to her belly: *Little one, some woman will joyfully call you "mine," just not me.* May found enormous comfort in that sentiment. After she'd felt those movements May became protective of the being growing inside her. She understood why quickening was considered the beginning of life in some religious traditions.

May sighed and tried to keep her mind on the service, though during the sermon her attention return to her belly when Reverend Simmonds asked them to imagine how afraid Mary must have been, delivering a baby in a manger, surrounded by strangers far from home. He preached that Mary, a mere human, had done that ordinary and extraordinary task: birthed a child who was the greatest of blessings to the world. He reminded them that they were capable of doing the same, in their own fashion.

May imagined she related to the story of Mary, a woman surprised to be carrying a child, more than most of her fellow congregants. May didn't subscribe to the virgin birth, but she believed that Jesus's message of love and compassion for all beings changed the world for the better. May felt a sudden certainty that *every* baby was a blessing from the Great Creator, so the one growing in her was no exception.

A flash of grace struck, followed by an instant of pure peace. It was a strange, fleeting sensation that left a beautiful echo in her heart. She took a deep breath and blinked back tears.

The shadow of that feeling was still with her as she sang the closing hymn, "It Came upon a Midnight Clear." The third stanza spoke directly to her, offering sympathy for her current plight as well as hope for a better future.

> And ye, beneath life's crushing load,
> whose forms are bending low,
> who toil along the climbing way
> with painful steps and slow,
> look now! for glad and golden hours
> come swiftly on the wing.
> O rest beside the weary road,
> and hear the angels sing!

Golden hours would come after she walked this long, weary road. This was her dreary winter with a crushing load, but in the spring things would swiftly change. This baby would be born and received as a gift to an infertile woman who longed for a child. May left church with a poignant sorrow, and yet she was uplifted too.

CHAPTER 7

NAOMI

March 1916

Naomi rose before the sun and kindled a fire in the oven for their breakfast: oatmeal and dried fruit that she would leave on the stove for Joseph and Maggie to eat before school. In the bathroom, she tested the water from the tap; it was cold, but not so cold she would heat up water on the stove to mix with it. She washed her face, smoothed on face cream, and braided back her hair.

While the oatmeal cooked she read her Bible. It gave her something important to think about, and an opportunity to remember that all people, always, have challenges to overcome.

In her room she sighed at a wrinkle in her uniform. Naomi stepped back to see how obvious it was. She shook her head and carried the dress into the kitchen. She didn't care for ironing but she could not be seen in such a state. She placed the iron on the stove to heat up and pulled down the ironing board. She dampened a cloth and used the iron to quickly smooth out the wrinkle.

After putting on her white dress she placed the starched white nurse's cap on her head. Twenty years ago she got her first one—and Naomi was still proud to wear it.

Her children continued to sleep when she left. She sent a silent blessing to them, as well as Cedric, Willie, and Gramma Jordan, before she stepped into the foggy spring morning and walked to the Booth Home for Unwed Mothers. She didn't know exactly what her day would hold, but it was always an honor to be God's hands on earth.

"May?!" Naomi exclaimed from the doorway when she saw her young cousin sitting upright in the hospital bed.

May's already pale face drained of all color. Naomi immediately regretted her unprofessional manner. The right side of May's mouth raised up and she shrugged. Compassion rose in Naomi. She walked to May and patted her arm.

"Lisbeth and Sadie are unaware of your condition?" Naomi asked to confirm her suspicion.

May nodded.

"Your privacy is assured here."

This wasn't the first time Naomi was acquainted with one of her patients. More than once a young woman from her church, Fifteenth Street AME, had delivered here. Some even stayed in the dormitories for several years, caring for their babies in the only home available to them as unwed mothers. Discretion was an important skill in this position.

"Thank you."

"Would you prefer another nurse?" Naomi inquired even though she wanted to support May in the delivery. "I can exchange patients with Nurse Hand if you like."

May shook her head. "I was hoping you would be my midwife. It's nice to see a familiar, and kind, face," she replied, her voice high and tight. She looked on the verge of tears.

Relieved to hear that answer, Naomi sat on the edge of the bed. A clipboard in her hand waited for answers to medical questions.

"The last time we saw one another was at Matthias's birth," Naomi said.

May nodded.

"Did you know . . . ?"

May nodded again.

More questions swirled in Naomi's head, but she would not ask them. May would share the intimate details of her situation, or not, as she saw fit.

"Shall we start with my questions?" Naomi asked.

May nodded.

Naomi began with the date of menstruation and ended with the most important query.

"Will you be taking the baby with you when you leave?" Naomi asked, though she believed she already knew the answer.

May shook her head. "You can arrange for an adoption," she stated, but it sounded like a question. "Not you, Naomi, but you the Booth Home."

"Yes. All arrangements can be left to us," Naomi replied, compassion in her voice. She was sad May found herself in this situation. She continued with an often painful, but important question. "Do you want to hold the baby or see the baby after delivery?"

May nodded. "Will you be there when he is born?"

Naomi heard the longing in the young woman's voice. She nodded assurance. "Most likely. Occasionally something unusual causes me to miss the birth, but I usually stay until the end—and will make a special effort to do so with you."

Naomi remembered May's birth, long ago on a train somewhere between Chicago and Oakland. She'd been born many, many weeks premature. Naomi had been just out of nursing school and saw to the precarious delivery in a smoking car on a moving train. She'd managed it without fear only because she was so inexperienced. She'd yet to see all that could go wrong in labor and delivery. Faced with the same situation today, she'd be terrified. It was remarkable that the fragile and tiny newborn grew into this lovely young lady.

"Will you say a blessing over him . . . or her"—May's voice cracked—"while I hold the baby. Can you pray for a good, kind family?"

Naomi teared up as well. She nodded. She'd seen this too many times: young women, good people, facing a hard decision. Most were abandoned by charming men. She wished, not for the first time, for a pill that would protect women from this terrible choice. Too many women used unproved concoctions from dubious sources.

"How soon will it be?" May asked.

"That is impossible to tell with certainty," Naomi replied. "Mother Nature has her own pace. She does not deliver by clocks like the milkman. You started cramping last night?"

May responded, "I've cramped for three nights in a row. However, the first two stopped by dawn. Today, they kept on." She stopped talking. Closed her eyes and took a deep breath. Naomi put her hand on May's belly. She felt the tightening of the uterus—rock hard from top to bottom. May's body was working hard to get this baby out. Naomi waited while the labor pain passed. May exhaled heavily and opened her hazel eyes.

"I'm sorry. It just overcomes me."

"You are doing just what you are supposed to do to get through this. First babies don't come easily. Have you seen any bloody show?"

May blushed. "Yes. I have rags in my drawers."

"That is a good sign that you are moving along as we would like. I'll be back with some water and fresh rags. I expect we'll see this baby by the next dawn, but no guarantees."

"Thank you. For your kindness and for being here with me." She took Naomi's hand. "I'm so comforted by your presence."

Naomi smiled. "You've overcome a lot since I first saw you on that train. You'll overcome this too," Naomi assured her.

"One or two more days and then I can resume my life," May said.

"It's not easy to hide this condition," Naomi said.

May nodded. "I moved in with Cousin Elena after the New Year. It has been terribly difficult keeping this secret from Momma and Nana," May said, shame covering her face. "But I just couldn't . . ."

"It will be over soon," Naomi soothed. "You'll want to bind your breasts to stop the milk. They will most likely hurt for many days, but in a week or two you will be able to leave this in the past and move on with your life."

May forced a smile, but it was obvious she was not happy. Who could be, in these circumstances?

May was in the midst of a strong pain when Naomi returned with water, rags, two novels, and an unfinished baby blanket that a recent patient left behind. She waited for the contraction to pass.

"It's going to be like this for most of the day. Let's see if we can keep you distracted between labor pains. Do you crochet?" Naomi asked.

"I cannot say that I'm skilled, but I do know how."

"Would you like to work on this?"

Naomi held out a blanket with pale green and yellow squares. Two skeins of cotton yarn were still attached. It was left behind by a woman who delivered a stillborn baby last week. Had they seen the blanket they would have wrapped the infant in it before sending her for burial, but it was too late now. The beautiful cotton was too valuable to simply throw out.

May reached her hands out for the incomplete blanket. "Thank you. I shall give it a go."

"And two books in case you didn't bring any: a new one, *The Bent Twig*, and a classic, *The Wonderful Wizard of Oz*."

"You are very kind," May said.

"Of course," Naomi replied. "I will be in and out until you are in constant need of me. Ring this bell if you require anything."

"Must I stay . . . oh, here comes another one."

May closed her eyes and groaned. Naomi placed a hand of support onto her shoulder. The moaning got louder. She was moving right along. Then it subsided. May exhaled loudly.

"That was very uncomfortable," May said.

"It hurts, but it is not hurting you," Naomi explained. "Each one brings the baby closer."

"Must I stay in this bed?" May asked.

"Not at all. Most women find it more comfortable to be on their feet. You are welcome to be out of the bed so long as you stay in this room," Naomi said.

May nodded, then her eyes widened. "It's going to hurt more, isn't it?"

"I won't deceive you. It will become more intense. And somehow we women bear it, as women have since the beginning."

"I'm afraid I cannot do it." May teared up.

Naomi took a deep breath. How many times had she heard those words? Every woman seemed to share that sentiment.

"You'll have no option but to bear what comes—that is the nature of birth and life," Naomi replied, hoping she sounded kind while being honest, though not so frank as to mention death.

In truth the only choice a woman has in childbirth is how she bears what she's given. Resisting the pain seemed to worsen it. Some women fought their bodies and others surrendered to the natural course. In the midst of the intensity, Naomi would encourage May to surrender to the experience. She would use touch and calm words; she would model breathing and resting.

She studied May. Would she resist or surrender? Long ago she stopped believing her own predictions about how each woman would respond to the greatest test of her life. But if she was forced to conjure a guess she expected May would surrender with grace to the unstoppable force of nature.

Hours later, May stood by the bed, rocking from side to side during a strong pain. Tendrils of dark hair stuck to her shiny face. Naomi stood behind May, pressing into the cave between her spine and pelvic bones. Hours of contractions attuned Naomi to May's pattern. She waited for the young woman to bleat like a goat, signaling the peak of the labor pain, and the moment Naomi should press as hard as she was able. The sound came, Naomi leaned in as May pushed hard against her fists; then the young woman leaned away with the waning contraction. May panted as the pain released its grip.

Naomi heard a slight pop and a splash.

May shouted, "Oh, dear Lord. Oh, dear Lord. What is happening to me?!"

Naomi stepped back and looked between the two white calves below the hospital gown. A dark puddle marred the linoleum. Labor was moving along . . . and the dark smear told her the baby might not be handling it well.

With calm in her voice that belied her concern, Naomi said, "Your waters have broken—a wonderful sign that you are closer. I'd like to take a listen while you are in bed, if you don't mind."

May's glassy and confused eyes stared at Naomi. The baby might not have time for Naomi to wait for a reply. She gently tugged May until the young woman crawled onto the mattress in front of her. She lay curled on her right side.

Naomi grabbed the wooden tool that would allow her to listen to the baby's heartbeat. She pressed the larger opening of the Pinard horn low over May's uterus and leaned over, placing her ear against the smaller opening. She closed her eyes to block out all stimulation, allowing her to concentrate on the subtle sound entering her ear.

Whoosh . . . whoosh . . . whoosh.

The familiar sound of a fetal heartbeat registered—but too slow.

"May, let's get you on your other side. To see if baby likes it better."

"Is she . . . ?"

Naomi didn't reply, but pulled at May's arm to turn her over to her left side.

She leaned over May's belly again with the Pinard horn and concentrated. Whoosh. Whoosh. Whoosh. Whoosh. Naomi exhaled in relief. That was better.

"The baby," Naomi explained, "is happy like this. I'm sorry, but you won't—"

"Aaahhhh," May shouted. "Ahh, ahh, ahh . . ."

Naomi listened through the contraction, juggling the horn and pressing against May's lower back to provide a small measure of comfort. The baby's heart rate slowed, slowed, slowed . . . as the pressure built. Naomi's heart beat hard, waiting for the uterus to release. When it ended, the swoosh of the baby's heart came closer, closer, closer until it sprang back to normal; Naomi exhaled in relief.

"Is the baby okay?" May asked, fear in her voice.

Naomi nodded and smiled in reassurance. Naomi learned long ago not to say more than was necessary at this point in labor. By all she could assess this baby was doing well enough in this position, but there was so much she could not measure. In a few hours they would know the outcome of this birth. She'd seen what seemed to be perfectly normal births end with a blue baby that never took a breath or too much bright-red blood come after the placenta. Most births ended with a baby and mother separated into two whole and healthy beings, but she could not predict which ones would not have that outcome.

The contractions kept coming and coming, pain Naomi was glad to see, though it was so rough on a laboring mother. May moaned with each one, handling the intensity as well as any woman could. Naomi was impressed with the young woman's strength and calm.

Hours passed with May lying on her side as her cervix slowly was opened by the force of nature. Naomi gave her sips of water, wiped her brow, and listened through the horn. All was going as well as could be wished for. The baby's heart rate dipping with the contractions and accelerating during the rests. Naomi looked for the telltale signs that this baby was ready for May to join her will to the contractions.

"Dear God. Dear God!" May exclaimed.

She grabbed Naomi's hand and squeezed hard. She stared right into Naomi's eyes, May's colored eyes wide and filled with panic.

"Tell my Momma and Nana Lisbeth I love them," she whispered. "And I'm sorry."

Naomi took a deep breath. She smiled, just a little, showing her calm in the face of May's distress.

"You will tell them yourself," she soothed. "This is all normal. You will get through this and see them soon. Are you feeling pressure? Like you wish you could use the toilet?"

May nodded. "I'm sorry. I can't hold it in anymore."

"Don't hold it in," Naomi explained. "That's your baby ready to come out. You help now. You use your muscles to push."

"Really?"

"Yes."

When the next contraction came, May grunted and pushed along with it.

"I'm going to see what's going on from your other end," Naomi said.

She released May's hand to look between her legs.

"I'm going to place my fingers inside you," she explained, though it was likely May would hardly notice at this point in labor. She didn't have to go far to feel the head. She felt around the fontanel. This was a great position. It likely wouldn't be long.

Another contraction came; May pushed with it, and Naomi felt the head move downward. May's instincts and her body were going to get this baby out soon.

"I'm going to find another midwife to join us. It's much easier with two once the little one arrives," Naomi said.

"Stay with me," May begged.

"I'll only go to the doorway, to the bell in the hall." Naomi rubbed May's leg. "You can see me the entire time."

Naomi sounded for assistance and then returned to May.

"Your baby . . ."—she corrected herself—"this baby is going to be here very soon."

Nurse Hand, Naomi's favorite colleague, came into the room. She readied a blanket, suction bulb, and scissors. Then she stood by as May continued pushing this baby into the world.

"I can see the head," Nurse Hand said to May. "Would you like to reach down to touch it?"

May shook her head. With the next contraction Naomi used her fingers to stretch the taut fold of skin around the baby's scalp. The dark-haired head slowly emerged, further and further until Naomi could see a bit of forehead. The labor pain ended, leaving the baby's head partway out.

The bluish tint on the baby's skin alarmed Naomi.

"May, you are nearly there. The head is almost entirely out. With the next wave I want you to use every ounce of strength you have." Naomi looked at Nurse Hand, her eyes wide, telegraphing the nature of the situation.

"This is it, May," Naomi said. "Your last pain. Keep the pressure strong."

May inhaled and joined her muscles to the force of her body. Naomi used her forefingers and her thumbs, stretching the skin around the head with all her might. When she released, the baby's head slid through the tight opening. The whole head was out. She tugged at the baby as the contraction stopped.

"Keep going, keep pushing," she instructed.

May did as she was told, while Naomi pulled at the base of the neck; one shoulder emerged and then the other rushed out, followed by the entire body.

Naomi turned the baby over and rubbed the limp, blue body. Suddenly the infant jerked and took a breath. Her lungs filling with air, she cried in life.

Naomi smiled. "A girl. You gave birth to a girl."

She rested the slippery baby on the bed between May's legs. She smeared off the mixture of vernix, meconium, blood, and amniotic fluid. Nurse Hand passed her sharp, sterile scissors. Naomi waited for the cord to stop pulsing to cut it—separating this newborn and May. Then she wrapped the tiny baby in a clean cloth, ready to pass her to Nurse Hand. May reached out for the bundle, her instinct strong, despite the fact she would be giving this child to a new mother. Naomi placed the baby in May's outstretched arms. May's eyes glowed, wonder and joy poured out, as she gazed at the infant.

Naomi returned her attention to the delivery of the placenta, grateful Nurse Hand was able to attend to May and the newborn child. Fortunately, it came quickly and complete with a safe amount of bleeding. She finished her duties between May's legs, and returned her attention to May's mind and heart.

Naomi explained, "Most babies are awake and hungry for this hour or so right after delivery—and then they sleep off the ordeal. We want to get food in her while she's awake."

May nodded.

"I can give her a bottle in this room, you may give her a bottle in here, or you can send her to the nursery," Naomi said.

May's lower jaw quivered. Naomi felt tears push at her own eyes. For some women, the ones who just wanted to be away from the newborns, this was an easy decision, but May looked torn. Naomi patted the young woman's hand.

May said, "I will feed her"—her voice broke high—"this one time."

Nurse Hand gave a nod, left, and returned with a bottle.

Naomi gave May as much privacy as she could while staying in the small room. She made herself look busy tidying up though there was little left to do.

May spoke to the little baby, almost too quietly to hear. "I want you to have the best life possible. I know God will find you a good mom and dad who can give you more than I can by myself. I love you and will think of you every day, for always.

"Naomi," May called.

Naomi turned around. Tears poured down May's cheeks. Naomi's heart clenched in sympathy. This was the most painful choice a woman could make—raise a child you didn't believe you could adequately care for or surrender a child you already loved to another family.

"Will you please say a prayer over her," May pleaded. "Then I'll be ready to say . . . goodbye."

Naomi swallowed and nodded. She crossed to the bed, placed one hand on May's shoulder and one on the bundle of baby. She bowed her head, closed her eyes, and took a deep breath.

"Dear God, in the name of Jesus we pray for your mercy and love. Please look over this baby in need of your care. Find her the most wonderful home where she will be cherished and loved—and given guidance to become a good servant to You and to all of mankind.

Bring peace to May's heart and assure her of your unending forgiveness and unending goodness. Amen."

"Amen," May repeated. "Thank you." She looked at Naomi. "She will be well taken care of, right?"

Naomi nodded. "We screen our families very well. There's a barren mother longing to hold a baby in her arms, and this baby is the answer to her fervent prayers. God works in mysterious ways. We cannot understand the whole; we can only do our best to listen to Him for our next step on our path."

Naomi sounded more certain than she felt. It was her job to notice what each patient desired most and give her the evidence that it was the right choice. She could have just as easily assured May she would be the best mother for this baby, regardless of her marital status. Naomi believed it was best for children to grow up in a family where they are wanted. Only May knew if she wanted this baby.

"Can I give . . ." May's voice broke. She cleared her throat and blinked back tears. "May I write a short note for her?"

Naomi replied, "Yes, I will get you a card."

When Naomi returned May was staring down at the baby. One finger gently traced the infant's eyebrows, chin, and earlobe. Naomi was the same with her own three children. Each a miracle and yet ordinary. Somehow they grew inside her. Their bodies and her body knowing what to do.

Naomi handed the card and a fountain pen to May. The young woman took the paper and wrote without hesitation. She must have been thinking it through for a while. Naomi resisted the urge to read it without permission.

May blew on the words to dry the ink.

The young woman read it out loud: "'I loved you from the beginning. Your new family will give you a better life than I ever could. May Wagner.' Does that sound right?"

"It's a lovely sentiment," Naomi said. "And I should have told you that you cannot sign it. No identifying information is allowed. I apologize."

Naomi handed May another card. She always brought several, as it was rare that they only used one. May wrote the note again—without her signature. The green-and-yellow blanket she'd finished crocheting while laboring was spread over her legs. The tiny baby lay in the middle of it. May took one corner and wrapped it over the baby's left shoulder and then wrapped another over the right. May laid the card on the sleeping child's chest.

May placed her hand on the card and closed her eyes, and her lips moved—in a silent blessing, a prayer, or a message. The bottom of the cotton blanket was just long enough to fold over and tuck around, completing the swaddle.

May lifted the baby, and kissed each of her cheeks and her forehead. "Goodbye. I love you."

She held the baby out. Naomi's heart twisted in shared sorrow. She took the baby from May's arms and carried her to the nursery. Sometimes decisions that were right were still painful.

Less than an hour later, Dr. Briggs barged into the quiet room. The old white man regularly offended Naomi. He was certain his understanding of medicine provided the best and only course of action, but he put no value on the complexity of the human heart. His science skills were commendable, but his compassion was lacking and his arrogance was both infuriating and occasionally dangerous.

Without introduction or pause, he spoke from halfway between the doorway and the bed, nearly shouting to make his point: "The baby has defects that will make it unsuitable for placement with a family. We will be transferring it to the home for the feebleminded.

You need to be sterilized so you do not bring more defective children into the world."

And then he left.

Naomi's stomach lurched so hard she feared she might vomit. She swallowed back her bile, and stared at the young woman recovering from her labors. The doctor's words were harsh—and untrustworthy. Naomi examined the baby at birth and saw nothing grossly amiss. The infant took the bottle with ease, her face was well shaped, and she appeared typical in every way.

"Is that . . . ? What?" May stammered. Then she sobbed. Tears streamed from the young woman's eyes. Naomi placed an arm around her. May leaned against her and cried.

When her tears ran out she leaned away. "Is the doctor speaking of the home in Jack London's story?"

Naomi nodded.

"It's not a good place, is it?"

Naomi shook her head. "I don't . . . I don't." She took a deep breath. Should she be honest with her young cousin? This would be one of the most impactful decisions of her life; Naomi didn't wish to have an undue influence.

May begged, "Please, tell me the truth."

"Are you certain you want to hear what I believe?" Naomi asked.

May nodded, fear in her eyes.

"I couldn't condemn any human to that life," Naomi spoke plainly. They didn't have enough qualified staff to provide basic human kindness to those with mental defects and epilepsy. The people in that home were treated like animals. The recent inclination to send away babies that were deemed unfit for society was horrifying, unethical, and unkind.

May took in a shaky breath.

"Can you bring the baby back to me? I want to see what's wrong with her," May said. Then she started to cry again. "It's my fault. I tried to . . . I used Mrs. Sanger's methods."

Understanding, and nausea, settled on Naomi. "Oh, I see." Anger burning her heart like a fire under a cauldron. She supported Mrs. Sanger's mission but not her unproven, and too often harmful, methods. *Dear God, forgive May for whatever harm she may have brought to this baby.*

CHAPTER 8

MAY

March 1916

May sat up in bed. She smoothed the pillow around her. Adrenaline made her heart pound fast and hard as she waited for Naomi to return with the baby. She must see what was wrong before making this decision.

Naomi held the newborn swaddled in the green-and-yellow crocheted blanket. May's heart leapt. She reached out her arms, eager to hold the bundle.

The little one was asleep, her face calm and beautiful. She looked perfect. May's shoulders dropped and her heart opened as she rested the little one against her chest. She smelled lovely.

Kindly, but with a hint of pity, Naomi said, "Would you like me to show you what the doctor found?"

May nodded. Her heart racing again, tears pushed at her eyes.

Naomi laid the baby on May's lap and unwrapped the swaddle. She slid her thumbs into the baby's hands and pulled her arms outward. The one on the left twisted just a little inward.

"Do you see the difference?" Naomi asked.

May swallowed and nodded.

"The legs are the same," Naomi explained. "There's a challenge on the left side."

"Is that all?" May asked.

"And she had a seizure while the doctor was examining her."

"She's epileptic?!" May heard the panic and pain in her own voice.

"As far as I am concerned it is too soon to tell. Some babies have one seizure at birth, but never again," Naomi declared. "However, it's most likely she will continue having them."

May felt as if she might vomit. She stared at the little girl's body. It was smooth and soft, like the finest silk. Was she really so damaged that she could not be cared for by a family? Her mind raced through her options. There must be something she could do besides surrender this baby to the doctor and go on with her life.

Perhaps in San Francisco there was someone who might help her place the baby in a new home. The little girl stirred. Her shoulders wiggled, her head turned from side to side, and her eyes opened, sliding in two different directions. Something was very wrong. The muddy-colored orbs looked inward, then uncrossed, and the baby looked right into May's eyes. May's heart swelled; she felt fiercely protective.

May questioned Naomi. "Can he really know she would be a horrible burden?"

Naomi shook her head. "Some men think you can measure value with numbers and scales and . . ." Naomi stopped herself, as if she'd spoken too frankly.

May reached for her hand. "Cousin Naomi, I value your opinion. I don't want to be foolish."

Naomi took a deep breath. "I think you will have to ask yourself what you can live with. Next year . . . in five years. What will be harder to live with: Being a mother to this baby? Or not being her mother?"

A chill shot down May's spine. She shook it off, but the shadow of it remained. "That is the question, isn't it?"

Naomi said, "No one really knows what she will be like. Will she walk? Will she talk? Will she have blue eyes? What is her favorite color? Do you want to be there to find out? Can you love her, regardless of what skills and abilities she has?"

May swallowed hard.

"If you will resent her, hate her, she might be better off without you," Naomi stated, "but—"

"Hate her?" May interrupted. That was absurd. Hate was the furthest emotion from her. Fear, confusion, yearning, yes, but not hate. May clarified, "I could never hate her."

The rude doctor intruded into the room, speaking at the threshold. Fury bubbled up from her chest.

"I understand you are questioning my diagnosis. I assure you I am well qualified and very experienced. This baby is damaged. We will not ruin our reputation by attempting to place her with a family. You have no other option but the Napa home for—"

May hugged the warm, precious being against her body. Without thinking she replied, "There is always another option. I am taking her home with me!"

Surprised to hear herself, she looked at her cousin. Naomi nodded, approval in her eyes.

May gazed at the baby. Did she mean it? *Am I going to be your mother?* Love and joy washed over her. Somehow, faced with this added complication she was suddenly certain this was the right answer.

"This is my daughter." May stared at the doctor. "It doesn't matter that she is different from other babies. I will take her home with me where I will care for her."

The doctor shook his head and looked at her with a combination of pity and contempt. He stormed out of the room without a word.

A peaceful certainty settled on her and her heart swelled with love.

She kissed the baby's head and pulled her up until they were cuddled cheek to cheek.

"I'm your momma, little one," she whispered into the baby's cheek. "I'm yours. And you are mine."

May's peace was short lived. Fear rushed in. She'd have to be honest with Momma and Nana—face their reaction to this sudden news. She might have to find a new home. Forever, she would be an unwed mother and this baby would be illegitimate.

Suddenly the baby wiggled her head from side to side, burrowing into May's neck. She bobbed her little head around. May's heart raced—was this a seizure?

"Looks like she's hungry," Naomi said. "Would you like to nurse her?"

"It's not too late?" May suddenly longed for the experience.

"She's less than a day old," Naomi said. "I think your body knows what to do to get her what she needs."

May gave an eager nod. Naomi encouraged her to open her robe and placed the baby across her bare body. May held the infant, steadying her head, while Naomi pulled the girl's arms out until they hugged her bosom. The baby bobbed her head from side to side and up and down, opened her mouth wide, and landed right where she belonged. May exclaimed at the strong sensation.

"That's just fine," Naomi said. "She knows just what to do. We will leave her like this for a while and then give it a go on the other side."

May gazed at the girl. She looked so normal. Naomi patted May's arm.

"Try to release your shoulders, or you will have a sore back soon."

May exhaled. She took in a deep breath and relaxed her muscles. Her mind and body were a jumble. "I can't quite believe what I've done. Do you believe I made the right choice?"

"None of us knows what God gives us when we have a baby. I can't predict this little one's future, but I've seen babies so sickly they don't have the strength to eat, and yet they grow up to be lovely adults. She doesn't look weak to me," Naomi said. "She may be different in some way, but she's got spirit. I predict you two are going to be just fine."

"Thank you." Gratitude filled May. "Can you . . . If you have the time, can you ask Nana Lisbeth to visit me tomorrow, explain the situation to her so she can help me plan how to talk to Momma?"

"Are you afraid Sadie is going to be disappointed in you?"

May nodded, her throat too tight to speak.

Naomi said, "Your mother knows as well as anyone that life does not always go according to our desires or plans. She provided you with a good home without your father."

"He died," May replied. "My mother was married before I was born. She didn't make a foolish mistake that would change her life forever."

May paused. Looking down at her daughter she felt a thrill at the sight and feel of this baby. A week ago this little being was a mistake to get past, but at this moment May felt the most powerful joy for her existence. She didn't even care that John had abandoned her.

Naomi said, "I think she will welcome this baby with her whole heart—once she gets past the shock. You will have to give her time to adjust. I'll telephone Lisbeth to tell her the exciting news that she's a great-grandmother."

May smiled, her eyes moist, and she nodded. They'd all been suddenly transformed, taken a giant step along the path of life even though they didn't know it yet. Momma was a grandma, and May was a mother.

"You'll feed her every couple of hours for these first few weeks. It will feel constant—that's how it's supposed to be while she's getting used to being on the outside," Naomi explained. "You haven't had much experience caring for a newborn, have you?"

"Only Matthias," May replied. "Since I moved in with them I've become quite adept at swaddling, diaper changes, and lullabies. He's amazing." She smiled and then shrugged. "That's it; I don't have a big family."

"I imagine the second cousins will grow up together."

"What do I do when she has . . . ?" May's throat closed. She cleared it. "A fit."

Naomi nodded. "They can look terribly dangerous, but there's nothing to do but wait it out. When she is very young there's no fear of injury from falling down."

May nodded.

"Hold her or lay her on a bed . . . Keep her from taking a tumble."

May swallowed. "Did you see it, before?"

Naomi shook her head. "Nurse Hand told me her left side seized. The jerking started at her hand and made its way down to her foot. She believed it lasted less than two minutes."

Jerking. That word struck hard. She looked down at the unnamed baby. She imagined holding her through such an ordeal. May nodded.

Naomi showed her how to break the seal to protect against injury before switching to the other breast. The infant eagerly latched to her right side. May felt a rush of well-being and love flood through her. She'd never felt so much devotion. She gazed at the baby's beautiful face. What would she be called?

"How did you choose Maggie's name?" May asked Naomi. "It seems a huge responsibility to decide that for her."

Naomi smiled. "Long before she was born, I'd decided I would name my first daughter after my sister Margaret. She died when I was seventeen."

May nodded.

"I didn't know we would call her Maggie until I saw her little face. With each child I just knew what was right. Like God whispered it into my ear for them. You'll know when you hear it."

Naomi continued. "I'm going home now. Nurse Bowen will help you with anything you need."

"Thank you, Naomi. For your kindness. For your wisdom. And for your confidence in me."

"You are strong, May. From the moment you were born, I've seen that in you. You are a fighter."

May nodded. She looked down at her daughter. She'd be fighting for her from now on.

At the end of the day, the night nurse offered to take the baby to the nursery to give May a rest.

"I'd prefer for her to be with me," May replied. "Is that foolish?"

The petite young woman smiled and shook her head. "No. That's perfectly delightful. I'll bring you a cradle in case you need it. But she can just stay right with you as long as you like. Ring your bell should you need anything."

May was dozing with the baby on her chest when she heard the door open again. She kept her eyes closed, hoping the nurse would leave without disturbing her. She didn't need anything but rest. But instead of the sound of the door closing she heard the nurse walk to her side. May took in a deep breath and forced her eyes to open.

Nana's face was inches away; her bright eyes stared at the little baby. May's heart leapt, and adrenaline poured through her, waking her up entirely.

"Oh, May!" Nana Lisbeth said. Tears streamed down her thin, pale cheeks.

"I'm sorry to disappoint you, Nana," May whispered. Shame pressed on the new mother's lungs.

"Oh, May," Nana Lisbeth said again. "I am sorry, so sorry, you carried this burden alone. It must have been terribly painful to bear this secret, for months. Hiding this, hiding *her*, from us."

May nodded.

"She's beautiful," Nana Lisbeth exclaimed. "May I hold her?"

Joy shot through May. She smiled through her tears and passed the precious bundle of baby to her grandmother.

"I cannot believe you came out so late," May said.

"For you? For her? I couldn't stay away once Naomi told me about my great-granddaughter!" Nana Lisbeth leaned over and kissed May's cheeks, twice on each side.

"Oh, Nana." May laughed. "Do you think Momma will accept her? Me? What I've done?"

Nana Lisbeth looked straight at May. In her clear, strong voice she said, "Your mother is utterly devoted to you. She will accept this baby with all the love possible."

"I believe she will be disappointed in me," May said in a hoarse whisper.

Nana Lisbeth shook her head. "Not disappointed in you; perhaps disappointed *for* you. She wants your life to be easier than hers." Nana Lisbeth stared off into the distance, lost in thought, then she spoke: "I think she will be most sad that you didn't come to her with your predicament."

May's heart dropped. "And you too?"

Nana Lisbeth took in a breath but didn't respond.

"I was certain I could take care of this without you two," May said. "Elena helped me."

"I imagined as much when I realized you were here. You moved in with them to hide your pregnancy?"

May nodded.

"I'm going to need a tremendous amount of help now. I can't keep being a burden to them." Shame flooded through May again as she realized the full weight of this decision. It felt impossible to provide for herself and for this baby.

"I know you like to be independent, but for her sake you need our help—at least to begin with."

May nodded; her grandmother was right.

"You must move back in with us," Nana Lisbeth said.

"Are you certain?" May asked.

"Of course. Your mother and I will both sleep better knowing we are doing what we can for you." Then her grandmother reassured her, "It will not have to be forever. In six months you can make another decision. But for now, you live with us."

"You sound like Auntie Diana!" May said.

Nana Lisbeth laughed. "After thirty years of being her family I suppose I'm becoming Greek too. Does she have a name?"

"I'm thinking of Kathryn Elizabeth," May said through a tight throat.

Nana Lisbeth teared up. Elizabeth was her given name, though she was called Lisbeth.

"I'm honored. Thank you. Kay Lynn Elizabeth," Nana Lisbeth repeated. "What an unusual and charming name."

"No, Nana. Kathryn," May said louder. "Kathryn Elizabeth."

"Excuse me," Nana Lisbeth said. "That is lovely too."

Kay Lynn. The name echoed in May's mind. It *was* charming, and unusual. She looked at the baby in Nana's arms.

"Are you Kathryn?" she asked the sleeping baby, "or Kay Lynn?"

The infant's eyes blinked open.

"She likes the name you gave her," May observed. She considered it, repeating it in her own mind several times: *Kay Lynn.* It felt right, as Naomi said—like God was whispering in her ear.

May declared, "Kay Lynn it is."

Nana Lisbeth smiled. "An unusual name for our unusual girl."

Our girl.

May imagined all the people she would have to face: Momma, Uncle Sam and Aunt Diana, her cousins, and her church. Would they accept Kay Lynn? Could she keep working? Where would they live? Who would care for her during the day? How ill would she be? Could anyone bear to take care of a sickly child? Question after question flooded her mind and overwhelmed her heart. She looked at Nana.

"How will I manage?" she asked, feeling the immense weight of this particular child's life.

"*We* will manage," Nana Lisbeth said. "One day at a time. Tonight you sleep as best as you can. You will feed her and change her napkins. In the morning you and I will face your mother together."

"Thank you." Gratitude sprang up in May. She'd never felt such a bubbling up of intense emotions of all kinds. Nana Lisbeth was a deep well of love and support. Knowing she would be at her side eased May's fear and multiplied her joy.

CHAPTER 9

MAY

March 1916

The next morning May cradled Kay Lynn in her arms, staring at her in wonder. She kissed her smooth cheeks. Devotion surged through May. Rationally, she should be terrified, but her heart was so bursting with love that she didn't feel anything but happiness.

"Ohhh my!" Auntie Diana exclaimed as she came through the door of the hospital room. Her brown eyes sparkled as she clapped her hands. Glee was all over her face. "Welcome, little one. Welcome."

May's heart swelled until it seemed it had to burst. She grinned at Auntie Diana. Never one to hold back, Auntie Diana was letting May know loud and clear her daughter, her Kay Lynn, was to be celebrated.

Nana, Momma, and Elena, holding Matthias, poured in behind her. May's chest hollowed out at the sight of Momma. She was trying to read her expression when Auntie Diana scooped up the baby and plunked her right into Momma's arms.

"Congratulations, Sadie! Now, you have to choose your grandmother name," Auntie Diana said, a challenge in her voice. "Nana Lisbeth and Bubbi are already taken."

Momma's eyes went wide, making her look like a doe startled by a hunter. Elena peered at the bundle with the sweetest smile.

She leaned over the bed for a hug. May clung to her cousin, grateful for the warmth and connection. The dream of the past day suddenly felt more real: she was a mother without a husband.

Elena pulled back. She stared at May, her eyes intense. She nodded, her lips pulled together in a tight, strong smile. May read it as respect and support.

May looked at Momma, who gazed at Kay Lynn with a mixed-up expression made of confusion, doubt, and wonder. May wanted to see love too, but there was nothing so simple on her mother's face.

"Elena has everything you need—except for milk!" Auntie Diana laughed. "You must provide that."

"It's true," Elena confirmed. "As you know, Matthias has outgrown all of his first clothes and his cradle."

"Thank you," May replied. She waited for Momma to say something.

Nana Lisbeth asked, "Did she eat well in the night?"

May nodded and kept studying her mother. Momma's silence was loud and condemning.

"What is wrong with her?" Momma finally asked.

Tears sprang to May's eyes. As she feared, her mother couldn't accept Kay Lynn.

"Sadie!" Aunt Diana exclaimed with a tsk. "Nothing is wrong with her. My niece is perfect just as God made her."

"I am not being critical," Momma defended, "simply practical. We must be prepared if we're to care for her properly."

Fiercely protective, May replied, "She's a baby, Momma. I will take care of her like any baby—feed her, change her, rock her to sleep. We don't know what she will require later. If she will walk, or talk, or be sickly. For now, she doesn't need anything special."

"Okay, then." Momma nodded. "That was what I needed to know. We can go to Elena's and get everything we need to set up a nursery in your room. It will be ready for you when you both come home."

May heard emotion in her mother's voice, but didn't know how to understand it.

"Cousin Naomi was truly your nurse?" Elena asked.

May nodded. They passed around the baby as she told the story of the birth.

After she finished, Nana Lisbeth said, emotion in her voice, "There was sad news in the newspaper this morning."

Worry swelled in May's throat.

Nana Lisbeth sighed. "Ishi died yesterday—pneumonia."

"Oh," May said as tears sprang up and poured down her cheeks. She looked down, embarrassed at her extreme display of emotion. She didn't realize she would care about his passing. Taking in a deep breath, she wiped her cheeks. Elena patted her shoulder.

"Thank you for telling me, Nana." She gazed at the old woman's tear-filled eyes.

Auntie Diana said, "A precious soul leaving earth on the same day a new one arrives."

May thought back to his kind and wise face. He was curious and unafraid despite all the pain and suffering rained upon him. He was content in the most beautiful way—not seeming to desire anything besides what was right in front of him.

"I was honored to know him—if only a little," May said. "And I hope to have a measure of his resilience."

Her family nodded. May looked at her daughter and considered the question currently weighing on her heart.

"I have to decide her last name," May shared.

"Of course . . . ," Elena said, "the birth certificate."

"The nurse encouraged me to fill in John as the father," she explained. "Fortunately there's no box to indicate that we are unwed."

"Thank God there are no legal scarlet letters here!" Auntie Diana declared.

May sucked in her breath. Leave it to Diana to say the unpleasant truth out loud. May was embarking on an unconventional path. She couldn't know how difficult a terrain it would be. Society was changing, the term *bastard* was considered outdated, but there were going to be whispers and stares, and even barriers.

"Has John come to see her?" Auntie Diana asked.

May looked at her aunt. She bit her lip and explained, "He doesn't know about her and I do not plan to tell him."

Her aunt nodded, but May couldn't read her attitude.

May explained, "I didn't intend to raise her, but now . . ." She let the sentence trail.

Now she was entirely responsible for Kay Lynn. Picturing their entire future was overwhelming; she would focus on today.

May considered each name: *Kay Lynn Elizabeth Wagner* or *Kay Lynn Elizabeth Barrow*. John hadn't earned the privilege to share a name with this child.

"I want us to have the same last name," she declared. "Wagner!"

May studied her mother holding the baby. A small, satisfied smile flitted across her features.

Nana Lisbeth declared, "Kay Lynn Elizabeth Wagner it is. Welcome to our family, little one." Nana rubbed the sweet spot in the middle of Kay Lynn's forehead, like she was baptizing her with invisible holy water.

"We should go home so we can prepare for your homecoming," Momma announced. She passed Kay Lynn into May's arms and said, "I cannot believe you are a mother—and I am a grandmother." She paused and blinked back tears. She stroked the baby's cheek. "Her face is lovely."

And then she left the room without waiting for the others.

Nana Lisbeth whispered in May's ear as they hugged goodbye: "Give her time. She's afraid for you, and for the baby, but it comes out as anger."

May nodded with a tight smile.

"We'll be back tomorrow to get you two home," Nana Lisbeth reassured.

"Thank you, Nana."

Aunt Diana said, "Every baby is a blessing—do not let anyone tell you otherwise."

"I am happy Matthias will have a cousin so close to his age who lives nearby," Elena said.

"Me too," May said. "And thank you, for everything!"

"You two!" Auntie Diana said. "I cannot believe you left me out."

"Oh, Mitta!" Elena said. "You don't get to be in the middle of everything."

"But I can try," Auntie Diana said. She kissed Kay Lynn on the top of her head and gave the new mother a careful, one-armed hug. She cupped May's chin with her hand and looked intensely into her niece's eyes.

"This is going to be hard," she declared. "And *you* are strong enough to do it. And *we* are right here supporting you—and her. I'm proud of you."

A wave of emotion ran up May's spine, and water burned her eyes.

"Thank you, Auntie." She swallowed. There was more to say but May's throat was too tight to speak. She was overwhelmed with the responsibility, wary of facing a shaming world, and uncertain about providing for Kay Lynn, and also deeply grateful for her supportive family. She wouldn't be facing this situation alone. Joy and insecurity, odd companions, swirled through her in equal measure.

CHAPTER 10

NAOMI

May 1916

Naomi walked from Mrs. de Hart's home toward the trolley stop after the NAACP meeting. It was a lovely spring day. She admired a tree with bright-pink flowers that contrasted with dark plum-colored leaves. It looked a bit like a cherry, but the bark was the wrong color. She'd have to ask about it next time she saw Mrs. de Hart.

With time to spare before she was expected at home, Naomi decided to keep walking down Telegraph Avenue to Fifty-Second Street to call on May and baby Kay Lynn. Since the delivery almost two months ago she'd only visited once, arriving with Gramma Jordan and a hand-knit cap.

"What a lovely surprise," Lisbeth said with a huge grin after she opened the door. "Come in. May and Kay Lynn are napping, and Sadie is still at work. Do you have time for tea?"

"That would be lovely," Naomi replied.

They sat in the small kitchen nook that looked out on their lovely back garden. Naomi could make out starts of tomatoes, lettuces, beans, and some sort of squash.

"How are you all settling in to this change?" Naomi asked.

Lisbeth drew in her lips and seesawed her head side to side.

"You remember," the white-haired woman said. "Becoming a mother is a jolt to the system like no other, really. So much love. So much worry. I reassure May that we'll face whatever comes, and there is no need to borrow trouble, but like most new mothers she has a hard time knowing what's to be expected—especially after the doctor told her Kay Lynn would be an undue burden to any family."

"Is the baby eating well?" Naomi asked.

"Yes," Lisbeth laughed. "She is a champion."

Naomi shook her head. "When the doctor said she was defective I was so angry. I cannot understand how you could look at a baby as lovely as she is and believe she has no value."

Lisbeth pulled her lips into a tight, sad smile and replied, "Some people measure value in all the wrong ways."

"Any more seizures?" Naomi asked.

"None," Lisbeth replied. "Truly she seems like any baby I have ever been around. Actually she's more social than many. Her lopsided grin is delightful!"

Naomi smiled. "You appreciate having a baby in the house, don't you?"

"I do," Lisbeth confirmed with a huge grin, and her blue eyes crinkled up. "I would not wish being a mother without a husband on any of my granddaughters. However, I will find joy where it is. Kay Lynn is a delight." Changing the subject, Lisbeth asked, "Are you in North Oakland simply to call on us?"

"No," Naomi said. "I attended the NAACP executive meeting at Mrs. de Hart's home."

"Thank you," Lisbeth replied, "for leading that fight. I'm so sorry we need such an organization, but I'm a proud supporter. We held a membership drive at church in February, and I gladly paid my dues and encouraged everyone to do the same."

"Thank you in return," Naomi said and squeezed her hand. Changing the subject back to domestic concerns, Naomi asked in a low voice, "How is Sadie adjusting?"

Lisbeth made the same uncertain expression with a pulled-in face and head tilt.

"She and I now share a bed," Lisbeth replied. "May and Kay Lynn have the other room. We thought this two-room bungalow would be just for Sadie and me—with four it *is* a bit crowded. And we are blessed to have this house."

Lisbeth paused and shrugged. "Life most often goes in unexpected ways."

The great-grandmother continued, "Sadie frets in the night about whether to offer assistance or not. She's uncertain about what May prefers. Sadie doesn't want to intrude nor for May to feel abandoned. On a few occasions she has sent me in."

"Oh, dear," Naomi said, feeling compassion for Sadie.

A cry and footsteps sounded in the other half of the house.

"They're awake," Lisbeth announced. She rose to fill a glass of water from the tap at the sink. Lisbeth opened the door to a built-in cabinet that had open slats instead of wood in the back. She took out two apples.

"What an unusual cupboard," Naomi remarked.

"I thought this Berkeley Cooler was the strangest thing when we first moved in," Lisbeth explained as she sliced the apples. "Air from the outside comes through the vents to keep eggs, vegetables, and fruit fresh. It doesn't replace an icebox, but it works quite well."

"Shall we?" Lisbeth gestured and carried the snack to May.

The young woman sat on the couch with Kay Lynn at her breast. Naomi was pleased to see the pair looking calm and confident, a good indication that Kay Lynn was healthy. Very sick babies displayed difficulty with eating from the start.

"Naomi!" May beamed. "What a delight. Thank you for coming."

Naomi kissed the young woman's cheek and sat down. "I was in the neighborhood and took a chance that I would be welcome. I wanted to see this little one. She looks like she is doing well—and you too."

May smiled at her daughter with so much love in her eyes.

"When you two are done, I should love to hold Kay Lynn if you don't mind," Naomi asked. "I have the opportunity to hold many newborns, but not so many babies when they are older. I'm in no rush to be a grandmother, but I do love the feel of a little one in my arms."

Lisbeth piped in, "If you ask just right she may let you change her napkin!"

Naomi laughed. In time she got her chance to hold Kay Lynn and take her for a clean diaper. At the changing table she looked her over. Kay Lynn's left arm continued to be pulled in and a bit twisted. Her left leg seemed slightly unusual as well. Naomi picked up a red rattle and held it in front of the girl. Her eyes slid in and out until she focused on the object. Naomi slowly moved it to the right and Kay's eyes followed it. Then she moved it back to the middle and the left and the baby tracked it as well as you would want in a baby this age.

"Aren't you a clever girl," Naomi said.

Kay Lynn grinned up at Naomi and held her gaze. Lisbeth was correct: Kay Lynn's social skills were impressive. Naomi laughed at the notion of a baby being advanced. The sparkle in Kay Lynn's eyes showed she was aware and on target. Naomi's quick assessment confirmed her belief that while this baby had some differences, she was unlikely to be an "undue burden" as Dr. Briggs labeled her.

Naomi returned to the living room, kissed the little girl's head, and passed her back to May.

"She's delightful." Naomi smiled.

"Not so charming in the middle of the night, but at least I can nap when she does," May replied.

"These days are hard, but pass soon enough," Naomi said.

She hugged them each farewell and left for home. The new tower, the Campanile, at the University of California was a striking landmark rising to an elegant point. She'd never walked on the campus. Perhaps she would do that after their next meeting.

Naomi stood on Telegraph Avenue, waiting for the train to take her downtown. A few bicycles and many cars passed her, but she didn't see a single horse and carriage. Only a few years ago this thoroughfare had many—along with their unpleasant smell. Technology was changing everything.

Directly across the street, a real estate agent's sign hung in front of a stately house with two front doors, one of the many duplexes that dotted Telegraph Avenue.

MUST BE SOLD. PRICE REDUCED. FLEXIBLE TERMS OFFERED.

Inquire at 1723 Broadway

Naomi's heart suddenly raced. The building was painted her favorite shade of caramel brown with a cream trim. The wooden windows were painted dark brown in the Victorian style, but this was a modern Edwardian, built since the turn of the century.

Traveling south on the train down Telegraph she kept thinking of the building. Duplexes were significantly less expensive than freestanding homes, and this one advertised terms. It was in that wonderful neighborhood close to their cousins and her dear friend. She could walk to Mrs. de Hart's home for their meetings. Perhaps this was their means of owning a home. By the time the trolley crossed Fortieth Street, she'd decided to step off the train at Eighteenth. There was no harm in making an inquiry.

"May I help you?" A petite white woman sat at a small table in front of the door.

"I'd like to inquire about the property at 5518-20 Telegraph in the Santa Fe Tract."

"Just a moment," the young woman said. "I'll let Mr. Davis know you are here."

"Hello, Mrs. . . . ?" A bald white man emerged through a door and bellowed with his hand out. "Welcome. Welcome. Come into my office."

She shook and replied, "Mrs. Smith. Mrs. Willie Smith."

"That is a fine property you are inquiring about. Only eight years old and in excellent condition. It's made from sturdy redwood to last for a lifetime—yours and your children's if you choose to give them an inheritance. Unfortunate circumstances for the current owners make this a great opportunity for you"—he leaned in and dropped his voice—"if you can act quickly."

She sat across from him, her heart pounding in anticipation.

He continued talking. "The price last year would have been $5,000 for both units. But now it is only $4,200."

Her stomach dropped. She didn't have close to that amount in savings.

"Do not let the amount daunt you," he boomed after reading her reaction. "We can work out a mutually beneficial arrangement, I am sure." The man continued, "Have you heard about terms? Instead of making a single payment for the investment of a lifetime, you can pay over five or even ten years with a down payment of 25 percent and only a small rate of interest accrued."

He rushed on without pause as if this information was more important than breathing. "The down payment would be $1,050. Payments over five years would be . . ." He paused to look at his sheet. "You are in luck. We have a special interest rate of only 6 percent guaranteed on that building. As a duplex it's a good investment, so our associates have offered us that special. Over five years the payment is only $62.83 per month."

$62.83 per month! That was far out of their ability to pay. She was foolish even to inquire. She clenched her lips together and started to rise.

He looked up at her, made a quick evaluation, and said, "Over ten years it would be $37.14. At only a slightly higher rate, 7 percent." *$37.14? Could that be possible?*

His voice lowered. "Do you have such a down payment: $1,050?"

She nodded. It was nearly their entire savings, but they did have that amount in their bank account.

His voice brightened again. "If you rent the other flat out you can make $22.00 per month. That would make it nearly pay for itself!"

Naomi nodded slowly. She did the math in her head. It was less than they paid in rent at the moment. The impossible suddenly seemed possible.

"Do you have children, Mrs. Smith?" he inquired.

She nodded. "Three."

"Boys and girls?" he pressed.

She nodded.

"These are three-bedroom flats. One for the boys. One for the girls. One for you and your husband. The lovely, modern kitchen in the back that has lots of natural light from the garden. You can grow your own food and cook nutritious meals for your precious, little children."

She didn't tell him her "precious, little children" were taller than her.

"Does it have a gas stove?" she asked.

"Of course," he said. "Would you like to see it? Let's go right now before anyone else makes an inquiry and snatches it up. It's only a death in the family that has forced them to sell. A home in a desirable neighborhood accessible to Berkeley and Oakland on the Key Route system is most attractive. You cannot lose money on property like this. It's just not possible."

He rose without waiting for an answer. "Come. I'll get the keys."

Mr. Davis led her to a shiny Studebaker and opened the passenger door for Naomi. She slid onto a leather seat as comfortable as the finest couch. She rubbed it with her fingers. This was her first time in an automobile, though she didn't say so for fear of appearing unsophisticated.

She'd been in trucks and on the trolley often, so the speed was not a shock to her system, but this felt like traveling in a living room rather than a freight train. They zoomed up Broadway, getting back to the building on Telegraph Avenue in less than ten minutes. It truly was close to downtown. Her heart raced from the anticipation of seeing a home she might be able to purchase as well as from the exhilarating ride.

"Would you prefer the upstairs flat or the lower one?" he asked.

"I'd like to be off the garden," Naomi replied.

He nodded and walked to the door on the left. It opened into a bright living room with three large windows in a bay. The hardwood floors were polished to a shine. Bright-green tile surrounded a gas fireplace.

"It's not electrified, but there are gas fixtures in every room. And the price of electrification is dropping every year. Soon installing it will pay for itself," he explained.

He walked through the redwood-paneled dining room to the kitchen. "It comes with the icebox and the gas stove—a huge cost savings to you. And it has a water heater! Do you live in an old Victorian with the sink in a separate room from the stove?" he asked.

"Yes," she replied.

"Every housewife says this is a huge improvement," he declared. "I'm sure you will agree. This kitchen will change your life for the better."

She nodded, her heart pounding with desire. This home was perfect. Coved ceilings, built-in cabinetry, and modern appliances—for hardly more than they were paying now.

"There is a separate space for laundry . . . and"—he opened the back door—"your garden."

The lot was enormous. Plenty of space to grow so much of their food. Gramma Jordan could live upstairs with Mrs. King, just as they did now. Surely, they would prefer the fresh air and this large yard to their old, cramped flat in West Oakland.

The three bedrooms were off a private hallway and each had a built-in closet. The modern bathroom had white tile on the floor and around the tub. The shower plumbing was behind the tiled walls.

"I can tell you love this home," he said. "Do I have a sale?"

This home was far larger than Mrs. de Hart's and somehow cost less.

"I would like it very much," she replied. "I will speak with my husband about it as soon as he is home. He's a train man and will be back in Oakland in seven days."

Mr. Davis shook his head. "This incredible bargain will be gone in less than a week. I should have asked you if you could make a decision today before we came. I'm sorry I wasted your time."

He made an empathetic face and walked toward the front door. Naomi's hopes were dashed to pieces.

"I won't show you the upstairs as there's no point if you cannot make the purchase without your husband's approval," he said over his shoulder, ". . . unless you wish to see it."

She wanted this home with an urgency she only ever felt once before: when marrying Willie. Naomi was so certain God intended him to be her husband that she did it despite her mother's disapproval because Willie was passing for white. Her mother's dismay was so great she sabotaged their plans, but didn't succeed. Naomi had been right then; Willie was a good man and fine husband.

"I would," she declared, "like to see it."

God was showing her this home. Their family's future would be secure if they owned this property.

"Duplexes do not come open for sale very often, do they?" she asked, confirming her strong feeling with information.

"No. They are such a good investment that even when people move from them they let them out for income. You cannot go wrong investing in Oakland real estate. It is not possible to lose money."

"My husband does not need to sign?" she questioned.

"Women in California, even married ones, can enter into contracts," he replied. "You might be surprised how often I sell directly to a woman."

She was hesitant to bring up race, as he'd shown no prejudice, but needed to be certain.

"And there are no barriers because of my color?" she asked, longing to hear an answer that would get her this home.

"Oakland has no racial restrictions when it comes to Negroes. Only limitations where the Chinese, Japanese, and foreigners may buy," he explained.

She nodded, grateful for herself, but unsettled on behalf of others. She considered. Was she actually going to do this without Willie's knowledge or agreement? He knew she wanted this more than any other goal. Whenever she raised the question he practically challenged her to find a home they could afford to purchase.

Her head cautioned her to wait, but her gut told her to leap. This was her home, her future, and her children's security. She just knew it in her heart.

"I will take it, Mr. Davis. You have yourself a sale!"

CHAPTER 11

NAOMI

May 1916

"Willie, please don't be angry with me," Naomi started. A week later he was home for only one night; he needed to know about the new flat before he left in the morning. After all these years of marriage she understood he didn't easily agree to changes ahead of time, but once they happened he was fine—and often grateful. She'd ease him into this transition by first letting him know they were moving. Once he saw the duplex, and loved it as much as she did, she'd tell him she'd bought it for them.

Her husband sighed. He gave her that look—the one that said, "You did something you know I won't like and now you want me to be calm." He raised his graying eyebrows and shook his head.

"Do I want to know what you've done?" he teased, but there was a weary caution in it too.

He used to find her certainty and ambition endearing; now he seemed tired by it.

"Perhaps not"—she paused, taking in a deep breath to calm her racing heart—"but I can't keep this from you because you would notice that we'd moved next time you returned."

His eyes opened, but otherwise his face held its expression. The loud beating of her heart filled her ears. She studied his face, but he gave her nothing.

"You are moving?"

"*We* are moving," she corrected him, "to the Santa Fe neighborhood."

"I have to live within walking distance of the station," he responded in a low growl. "You know that."

"The proximity guideline is not being enforced. The home is on Telegraph Avenue on the Key Route so you can get to work easily. It has a large yard for a garden, it's close to nice stores, and Idora Park is only blocks away."

"You know I don't want to live in the suburbs," he reminded her. "I like our home, the neighborhood. I'm comfortable here even though it's old and run down."

She nodded.

"Have you signed a contract?"

"Yes."

"Can you get out of it?"

"No."

"Then there's nothing to speak about, is there?" He stood up.

"Willie . . ."

He held up a finger. "This has been my home for many years. I may not sleep here as often as you do, but when I'm tired and lonely it's comforting to know I will come back to you and to this house."

She nodded.

"I'm going to need a minute." He stared at her.

She nodded again. When Willie was upset it was best to say less rather than more. She needed to give him a chance to get used to the idea. He would come around; she was confident of that. Surely he'd understand owning their own home would provide them, and their children, with security for life.

Ten days later, Joseph carried one of the final crates in his arms. Her last night in this home was behind her; tonight they would sleep in their new apartment at the duplex. The change had all happened so fast it was hard for Naomi to take it in. Ten days ago she spotted the sale sign and now they would be living just a few blocks away from Lisbeth, Sadie, May, and Kay Lynn.

Willie hadn't had a chance to see it. He didn't ask any more questions about their new home; she didn't even get a chance to tell him that she'd bought it. Willie left with an air of resigned disappointment. Naomi wished he was excited for this change, but it was hard for him to be exuberant about an idea. She prayed she was right about this being a great opportunity for their family.

"Ma," Joseph challenged. "Why you look so sad? You've been wanting this move forever. Today's a happy day!"

"All three of my babies were born here," she told her son. "We had so many precious moments. Just because I'm happy to go doesn't mean I can't be sad too. This was a great home for us."

Joseph kissed her cheek and said, "Maybe it's a Mama thing—or just you, but I can't wait. Idora Park here I come!"

Naomi laughed. She took one last walk through the empty house. In each room a cascade of memories poured through her mind— Cedric learning to walk, Maggie baking her first pie, Joseph sounding out his first word, Willie leading prayer. Their conversations, laughter, and tears still vibrated in these walls.

In her empty bedroom she pulled a pencil from her skirt pocket and knelt in the corner. She didn't know why, but she had felt the urge to write their names, put down proof they'd lived here.

Willie. Naomi. Cedric. Joseph. Maggie.

When she stood up she could barely make it out. It would likely get painted over as soon as tomorrow, but she would know it was there each time she thought of it, or drove by.

At the front door she stopped, and turned around. She gazed at the empty living room, held up her hand, and prayed, "Lord, thank you for this house that we made into a home. May it be a good shelter for the family that comes after us."

Naomi walked to the truck filled with their worldly goods. Sam, Sadie's brother, was behind the steering wheel ready to drive away. He had kindly offered the use of his and Diana's motortruck, which they gladly accepted.

She smiled at her children sitting in the truck bed.

"Maggie, do you have the crocus bulbs in a safe place?"

"Of course, Mama." Her daughter held up a burlap bag. "Right here!"

Naomi nodded and climbed into the passenger seat. Her heart was full of every emotion as she simultaneously drove away from home and toward home. It was a bittersweet day.

The next morning Naomi was unpacking in their new bedroom when Gramma Jordan walked in with a small wooden box Naomi hadn't set eyes on in many years. She gasped at the container of Grammy Mattie's small treasures.

"I came across this in the move," Gramma Jordan explained. "I've decided it's time to give it to you—and explain its contents to Maggie."

Naomi's heart rose into her throat and her mind protested both ideas. *You aren't so old. She's too young.*

But at fifteen, Maggie was a young woman, and needed to know the truth of their family history. Naomi nodded her consent. She and

Gramma Jordan exchanged a teary smile, knowing they were ending a measure of Maggie's innocence.

Naomi went to the door and called out to her daughter.

"Yes, Mama?" Her beautiful girl bounded into the room.

Gramma Jordan patted the cluttered bed and said, "Please sit, Magpie."

Naomi smiled at the endearing childhood term her mother had called her sister, and now her daughter.

Maggie looked between them. "You don't have more to say about marital relations, do you?"

"No, honey," Naomi laughed and continued, "This is some family history we are ready to tell you."

Maggie pulled in her bottom lip and nodded, her demeanor cautious, even wary. She knew enough of the world to be wary.

Gramma Jordan held the box carved with lilies in her hand. "This was my mother's. It holds your inheritance, good and bad. You need to know where you come from to get strength for where you are headed."

Maggie nodded.

Naomi blinked and felt a single tear run down her cheek. She took Maggie's hand and squeezed. Her heart beat fast; this was a painful part of mothering.

"An ugly truth is better than a beautiful lie," Naomi told her daughter. "Here's some evidence of the ugly truth in our family."

"It's okay, Mama," she reassured her. "I want to know."

Gramma Jordan opened the box, revealing a jumble of items: Grammy Mattie's single shell, a newspaper clipping, a metal eagle, fabric, and a bone.

The old woman pulled out the newspaper clipping.

"This is an account of Uncle Page's lynching." Gramma Jordan's voice was measured and calm, belying the emotion Naomi knew ran deep. "He was your Grampy Booker's brother. The information in the paper is a lie. He did not attack a white woman; he was publicly murdered as a warning and a threat for the audacity of owning a successful business and staying registered to vote."

Maggie swallowed and reached for the paper. She read the story, wiping away tears and shaking her head from side to side.

"Gramma Jordan . . . ," she started. "I don't. I don't. I don't know what to say. You were a little girl, Mama?"

Naomi nodded.

"You knew him?"

Naomi nodded. "Very well." Her voice broke. Tears streamed down her cheeks. "He was the closest of family . . . like Gramma Jordan is to you."

Maggie inhaled hard and nodded. Gramma Jordan sighed. They let the quiet be.

In time Maggie broke the silence. "I'm ready for you to keep going. There's much more in that box."

"This is the remains of your great-great-grandfather's toe," Gramma Jordan held up a bone.

Maggie's eyes got big in surprise and then her whole face pulled inward in disgust.

Gramma Jordan continued, "Grampy Booker's mother gave it to me before she died. It was taken off of him when he ran. I don't know the year or how old he was or any other details."

Naomi patted Maggie's arm. She nodded, encouraging her grandmother to continue.

Gramma Jordan pulled out the small eagle.

"You know I have this pain from a broken bone?" she asked as she rubbed the spot on her forearm.

Maggie nodded.

"My mama made us go back to Fair Oaks, the plantation in Virginia, to get her cousin Sarah after the war. You remember that story? This is the top of the owner's, Mr. Richards's, walking stick."

Maggie nodded.

"He'd struck and killed my Auntie Rebecca, Sarah's mom, with this eagle. After the Emancipation Proclamation Mr. Richards sold her granddaughters. The proclamation was a law only in name because there was no means to enforce it, which meant cruel men with weapons forced children into wagons and drove them away from their mothers."

Gramma Jordan pulled out the string with the shell. "This—"

"Wait," Maggie interrupted. "What happened to those little girls?" Maggie teared up. "Did they . . . Did you get them back?"

Gramma Jordan teared up too. "We found Ella, but we never found Sophia."

Her face filled with confusion and disbelief, Maggie looked between her mother and her grandmother. Finally she spoke: "Mama, that's horrid, so very sad. How can people be so cruel?"

Maggie was looking to Naomi for an answer to a very large, spiritual question. Naomi sighed, and considered her answer carefully.

"I suspect they cannot allow themselves any sympathy, otherwise they couldn't be so inhumane," Naomi said. "That kind of evil comes at a price to your soul."

Maggie stared at the bed. Once again they let the silence be.

"Gramma Jordan, you stood against that wrong—that's how you got your broken bone?" Maggie asked, her voice filled with emotion. "*That* stick hit your arm when you saved Grammy Mattie?"

"Yes. Mr. Richards swung it at Mama and I put my arm in the way."

"You were a true heroine!" Maggie said.

Gramma Jordan replied, "I'd never seen my Mama so fierce. She twisted the stick from that awful man's hands, knocking him to the ground, and then broke it in two on the side of the wagon."

"How old were you, Gramma Jordan?"

Naomi watched her mother consider for a few moments and then eventually say, "Twenty."

So young. Naomi heard that story many, many times, but she'd never thought of her mother as nearly a child in the previous tellings.

"That's amazing, Gramma Jordan," Maggie said. "*You* were amazing. Did you stay in touch with Ella?"

Gramma Jordan nodded. "Occasional notes passed between us. She died about ten years back, but I think she made a good life for herself in Virginia."

"But you rescued them?"

"Not everyone wants to escape their life," Gramma Jordan said. "We assumed she'd be happier in Chicago because we were, but she missed her home and decided to go back. That was what she chose to do with her freedom."

Maggie took a deep breath. Naomi did the same. That was enough pain for one day.

"Shall we finish the box another time?" Naomi asked, feeling protective of Maggie.

Her daughter shook her head. "I'd like to keep going, please."

"The most unpleasant parts are done," Gramma Jordan said.

Naomi nodded.

"I recognize the shell from Africa, passed down from our ancestors," Maggie said. "I have the one you gave me on my bureau."

"This is the one my Mama wore around her neck," Gramma Jordan explained. "She died before we came to California, but she knew we were moving here. She told me not to bury it with her, but rather throw it in the Pacific Ocean to tell our ancestors that we all got free."

"And you can't bear to part with it?" Maggie asked. "Gramma Jordan, we have to go do that!"

Naomi sighed.

"What?" Maggie asked and her face fell. "Do you have another tragic story?"

"You know we have worked for women's suffrage since before you were born," Gramma Jordan explained. "How can I tell the ancestors we are *all* free when some of Mattie's granddaughters can't vote? We can in California, but your cousins in Virginia and Michigan don't have the franchise."

"When the Congress passes the women's suffrage amendment can we toss it in the Pacific?" Maggie asked.

Naomi replied, "That's only the start. After Congress approves it, two-thirds of the states must ratify it before it is the law in the entire nation."

Maggie made a face. "Is that ever going to happen? Why doesn't every woman just move to states where they can vote?"

Naomi laughed. "You believe we can convince every woman to abandon states that won't give them a voice. You can start the campaign. Can you imagine all those states and territories with no women?"

Gramma Jordan declared, "And twelve with so many!"

Maggie grinned and replied, "I suppose it is better to work for the vote for women everywhere rather than ask women to abandon their homes."

Maggie smiled so sweetly at Naomi that her heart sang. These were the most tragic of stories, but her daughter seemed to be finding the strength and connection in them that she hoped for.

The box was empty save for a layer of very old fabric. Gramma Jordan carefully pulled it out by the corners and unfolded it to reveal an embroidered little red shoe.

"Auntie Lisbeth made this for me when I was born—back on the plantation. She was only a child, ten or twelve years old. In a strange way she loved me. She cared for my mother as dearly as she cared for anyone in that place. And my mother loved her. Some of that devotion got poured onto me. I keep this to remind me that love can be made—even in the most painful of circumstances."

Maggie stroked the faded threads.

"That is very sweet, Gramma Jordan."

Gramma Jordan cupped her bony hands around Maggie's face. Tears sprang to Naomi's eyes.

Staring at her granddaughter intently, Naomi's mama said, "These objects are to remind you of how strong your foremothers were and how determined they were to give you the best life possible. We have been fighting for you for generations. And you owe it to your granddaughters to fight for their future freedom."

Naomi's mother continued, "Don't believe lies anyone says about you. There is always hope for a better tomorrow; fighting for what matters to you is just as important as winning that fight. And always remember there is love to be found, even in the most painful of circumstances."

"I will, Gramma Jordan," Maggie replied. Then she looked at Naomi and said, "I will, Mama. I will always remember. Thank you for sharing these things with me."

Naomi took her daughter's hand and her mother's. They did the same, making a circle of three strong women. They'd walked Maggie across a threshold into womanhood. Naomi could not protect her daughter from the ugliness and pain of the world, but she could pass on the faith and strength that she'd gotten from her ancestors.

A week later Naomi sat on the platform watching Willie's train pull in. Handsome in his uniform, he hung out the open door, grinning as the squeal of the brakes brought it to a stop. He startled when he saw her, made a curious expression with his face, and winked. A sweet signal that he had come around, or at least was trying.

Then Willie went to work. He jumped down and put the steps out for the first-class customers. He spoke to each person as they disembarked, using their names and wishing them well.

Naomi noted his calm and kind attention. One by one, the passengers expressed adoration and gratitude. He'd made many admirers. Between nearly every handshake he placed his hand into his pocket—leaving the tips that were the largest part of his income. Willie was good at his job.

When the last passenger left, he came over.

"Why Naomi Smith, what brings you here?" he asked with a smile.

"I've come to take my husband to his new home," she sang back.

His face tightened. "It's done?" he asked.

Naomi nodded.

"Okay," he said, but she couldn't read his emotion. Angry, sad, resentful. It was hard to tell. She took in a breath to calm herself. *He'll be fine, even grateful, soon.*

"I'll finish cleaning up and be back."

They avoided speaking about their new home on the walk to the trolley. He told her about an enormous thunderstorm they passed through on the return trip. They didn't wait long for the streetcar that took them up Sixteenth Street to Broadway and then turned onto Telegraph Avenue. Willie would not even need to change cars.

"Have you met the neighbor yet?" Willie asked, finally bringing up their new home.

Naomi nodded. "On the day I was born."

Willie furrowed his brow.

"Gramma Jordan and Mrs. King stay there," Naomi explained, keeping her voice cheerful.

"Both units were open at the same time?" her husband wondered.

Naomi's heart raced. She'd wanted him to see the duplex before revealing she'd purchased it, but now she couldn't delay telling him.

"Willie, we own the property, both floors." She exhaled and then blurted out, "I bought it for us."

"You are joking," Willie laughed. "You cannot afford to buy a home!"

"*We* can afford it . . . by taking out a loan."

Her husband's face went red. "Naomi Smith, what have you done?!"

"Willie, mortgages are very, very common these days. I am certain we will be fine. I used our savings for a down payment. We will pay the balance over ten years—$37.14 a month. Then it will be ours free and clear!"

Willie hung his head down and swung it from side to side. Naomi couldn't tell what he was thinking or feeling.

She rushed on with the explanation, desperate to make him understand. "Gramma Jordan and Mrs. King each give us $9.00 a month. That is nearly half the payment."

He stayed bent over, staring at the floor of the trolley. She swallowed her arguments and forced herself to just let him be.

Finally he looked up and said, "You are something, Naomi Smith. I don't know why I am surprised after all these years."

"We won't be sorry!" she declared, hoping her enthusiasm was welcome. "This will be a good home for us—and an investment in our future security."

"You really don't mind living near all these white people?"

"They have been nothing but kind and welcoming, no hint of animosity. I assure you."

His lips pulled up. It was nearly a smile.

Naomi said, "Your auntie and cousin live less than three blocks from here. Maybe we will see Lisbeth and Sadie more than twice in a decade," she exaggerated.

"How much is that payment?" he asked.

Naomi repeated the number.

"That's less than our rent!" he exclaimed.

She responded, "The repairs and assessments make it a bit more, but in ten years we will own it free and clear."

"You should have been a businesswoman, Naomi. I don't know how you pulled this off. Have you been consulting with Madam C. J. Walker?" he teased.

Naomi smiled. "I'm taking our future into our own hands, like she advocates."

Willie said, "I hope it all works out for us."

It wasn't a rousing endorsement, but it wasn't condemnation.

After a few minutes of silence he asked, "Does that make us landlords?!"

Naomi laughed. "It's not much land to lord over, but I suppose so."

As she expected, Willie was warming up to this change. He was gone for work most of the time, so they were both accustomed to him following her lead and trusting her to make good decisions on behalf of their family.

"Landlord!" she repeated with a laugh. "Perhaps I'll call you Lord and you can call me Lady from now on."

They got off the trolley at Fifty-Second and Telegraph Avenue.

"Lisbeth and Sadie are just up this street," she said. "Do you recognize the area?"

Willie nodded and said, "The trees are nice."

"Here's the produce market and the butcher." Naomi pointed. "And the newsstand."

"Convenient," he replied.

"Very," Naomi confirmed. "Can you see Sather Tower, the Campanile?"

He shrugged.

"The tall tower," she explained. "That is the University of California."

"So close," he said.

"Yes. They have concerts and lectures. Mrs. de Hart says it's lovely to walk along Strawberry Creek. And Idora Park is only a few blocks from us."

She stopped at 5518-20 Telegraph Avenue. Her heart sped up as she watched for Willie's reaction.

"It's huge!" he said, his eyes wide in surprise. "We really *own* this?"

Naomi breathed out relief and breathed in pride. "My understanding is that the bank owns most of it," she bantered. "But in May 1925, we can burn our mortgage."

Naomi took Willie on a tour through their new home, and their new investment. He was not nearly as excited about the kitchen as she was, but delighted in gas heat in the living room.

Naomi walked him into the yard.

"This is really all ours?"

"And Gramma Jordan's too. Mrs. King isn't so keen on it, though I'm sure she will make use of it from time to time," she said.

"Joseph and I can make us a table for eating out here when the weather is nice," he suggested.

"That would be lovely," Naomi agreed.

"Can I hang a hammock between the apple trees?" he asked.

"Of course, husband," she replied.

His eyes grew moist.

"Thank you, Naomi." He looked at her. He shook his head. "You are truly amazing. I don't tell you enough, but marrying you was the best decision of my life."

Naomi's heart burst and she covered her mouth with her hand. She blinked back happy tears and hugged Willie tight. Pressed against his chest, she declared, "Me too, Willie. I feel the same way about you."

CHAPTER 12

MAY

July 1916

Exhaustion was a heavy blanket clouding May's mind and spirit. For the third night in a row Kay Lynn had woken up many times. From teething, gas, hunger? May didn't know. She wished her daughter could tell her what was wrong, but at four months old, speech was a long way off—if ever, because of Kay Lynn's disabilities. Their doctor said they would only know what her capacities would be with time. Thankfully she never seized again. The only indication that something might be different about her was that her right hand reached for objects and her left was still in a fist like a tiny newborn's. Nana was utterly certain there would be nothing "stopping her Kay Lynn from a rich and full life."

Kay Lynn was content enough during the day, which actually gave May less compassion for the girl in the middle of the night. Nana Lisbeth assured her night waking was a common development around four months. She recommended feeding the baby more often in the day and starting rice cereal, which might help her sleep better in the night.

Kay Lynn took right to the mushy meal when she was offered it at lunch. Now there was a new routine. When the adults were eating breakfast, lunch, and dinner, Kay Lynn was having her cereal. She'd yet to sleep better at night, but Momma said it might take a few days for her body to adjust.

May patted Kay Lynn's back to get her down for her after-lunch nap. Desperately tired, May yearned to lie down next to her daughter on their bed. She looked at the shelf above their dresser. Only two clean diapers left. She *must* do a washing today. She sighed and forced herself to stay sitting upright but let her eyes slide closed. Once Kay Lynn was taking the long breaths of sleep May stood up. Tears of frustration and exhaustion companioned her as she carried the heavy basket to the laundry porch.

May was hardly managing their life as it was. Each time she considered adding work she became overwhelmed. Momma and Nana Lisbeth were not pressuring her—but she wanted a solution that did not require her to be entirely dependent on her mother. She blinked back tears.

A knock at the front door interrupted her before she finished filling the washtub. Fortunately she wasn't arm deep in this messy process.

A stranger with gray hair and a weathered face stood on the front porch. He looked her up and down, as if he were deciding who she was, though she was certain they had never met. Before she questioned him he asked, "Are you May Wagner?"

He spoke with an accent—European of some kind.

She nodded.

"I am Heinrich Wagner." He paused, searching for a reaction. When it didn't come he continued, "Your father."

Her chest constricted as if she'd been struck, making her so light-headed she steadied herself on the frame lest she fall.

From the entryway behind her Momma's voice muffled through the buzz in her ears: "Heinrich?!"

"Hello, Sadie," he replied, his voice deep. "Are you so sad to see me after all these years?"

"Why have you come?" Panic filled Momma's voice.

Outraged, May demanded, "You are not surprised to see him alive?!"

"You told her I was dead?" The man, who was nothing like the father in her heart and mind, laughed. "That seems fitting."

May stepped back into the entryway, looking between them. Momma was pale, her hand covering her heart. The man, his hat in his hand, looked cautious and yet cocky.

"It has been over twenty years, Heinrich!" Momma challenged, "Why have you come now?"

"I need you to sign—for my American citizenship." He waved a paper at her.

Momma took in a loud breath. May gestured with her arm to invite him in, but her mother was a fortress wall blocking his path.

Momma hissed, "Why would I do that for you?"

"We will both get our American citizenship. You understand that you became German when you married me? Who wants to be a German living in America in these times, right?"

Momma stared at the ground. A loud silence filled the room as she considered his question.

May's heart pounded fiercely, her head pounded. Questions lined up: *Where have you been? Why did you leave? How could you . . .*

Finally Momma broke the tension. "Leave the paper with me. Come back tomorrow for your answer."

He gave a single nod, handed over the paper, and departed. Momma dismissed him without giving May the opportunity to invite him in. She glared at her mother.

Momma declared, "There's a good explanation."

May looked at her mother, but she seemed a stranger. Fury exploded in May. *Momma lied to me.*

Behind Momma's shoulder, Nana Lisbeth watched, pity on her face. May stared into her grandmother's eyes and challenged, "You knew too?"

Nana Lisbeth bit her lip and gave the smallest of nods. May looked between the two women. Her family; the people she trusted. She thought she knew them, knew herself, but she'd been wrong, very wrong. They were liars and she didn't know who she was.

May suddenly wanted to slap her mother's face; she'd never been this angry in her life. She spun around and went into her room, where Kay Lynn was asleep on the bed. She paced, waiting for the overwhelming surge of emotion to wane.

"May, please hear me out," Momma demanded through the door—raising more fury in May.

"I don't trust anything you have to say!" May screamed back. She sounded like a childish maniac to her own ear. Kay Lynn woke with a loud cry, her scream adding to the chaos. Exhausted and confused, May wasn't in any state to listen to an explanation for Nana Lisbeth and Momma's deceit. She had to leave before she said or did something she would regret forever. She tied her screaming baby to her chest, packed up a few belongings, and stormed out of their room.

"May?" Momma pleaded, her eyes darting to the bag in May's hand, "What are you doing?"

"I am going to Elena and Peter's," May hissed at her mother. "Do not come for me."

When May arrived at her cousin's home the house was empty. She let herself in and sat at the kitchen table. She was calmly feeding

Kay Lynn by the time Elena walked in carrying a bag of groceries in each hand and with Matthias tied to her back. Elena's eyebrow rose in question.

May blurted out, "My father is alive! He came over and my mother made him leave before I could ask him anything or he could get to know me. Can we stay here until I am calm?"

"Of course." Her cousin replied without hesitation. Then she asked, "Did you have any notion he might be alive?"

"No," May replied. "Did you?"

One side of Elena's lip drew up.

Outrage exploded in May. "What?!"

"I was young when he left so I hardly remember him. You moved in with us, but then he returned. Soon after he left again and never came back. A few years ago Tina remarked there wasn't a funeral, which left an odd question in my mind."

Outraged that Elena had suspected he might be alive, May glared at her cousin. Had they all known? And kept it from her?

"Why? Why didn't you tell me?"

Elena defended herself. "How could I accuse Aunt Sadie and Nana Lisbeth of lying? Years and years after he left? I had no evidence. Just that one comment from Tina. Truly I didn't *know* anything."

Questions swirled in May's mind. She couldn't settle on one. *You are not who you thought you were* pounded in her mind.

Elena asked, "Why did he come back *now*? What's he like?"

May teared up. "He didn't act anything like the father I dreamed of. And my mother chased him off so quickly that I didn't get to ask him a single question."

May got quiet. She replayed the scene in her mind. It happened so fast that she didn't easily remember the conversation, only her flood of emotion. Had her mother actually chased him off? Or had he left when he got his question answered?

Finally May explained, "He asked her to sign papers so they could both become United States citizens. Apparently, they are still married. When do you suppose they last saw each other?"

Elena thought for a moment and then asked, "You were born in 1894?"

May nodded.

"You were not walking when he returned. I can't say if your mother saw him since then, but I think summer of '95 was the last time I saw him."

"Momma said, 'Over twenty years without a word.' Why would he abandon us?" May asked.

"I don't know." Elena shrugged then reassured, "But you are welcome to stay here while you solve your mystery."

"Thank you," May replied. She was grateful to Elena for her generosity, and yet frustrated to need a place to stay once again. Elena smiled back and stood up to work on supper. She placed a bag of green beans, a cutting board, and a knife in front of May.

May gazed at Kay Lynn. Could her anger get into her daughter through her breast milk? What a strange thought. Kay Lynn grinned up at her, causing thin milky liquid to stream out the corners of her lips. May smiled back. She would do *anything* for Kay Lynn. Didn't her mother feel the same way?

She sat Kay Lynn up and kissed her sweet cheeks. They grinned at each other. There was nothing as delightful as Kay Lynn's smiles. May rubbed her daughter's back to bring up a bubble. Elena laughed when it came out loud and long.

"That girl can burp like an old man!" Elena declared.

May laughed too. She tied Kay Lynn on her to free up her hands and got to work washing the vegetables.

As the soothing, warm water ran over her hands, May was struck hard by the realization that no one else could solve this situation for her, nor did anyone else care as much as she did. Elena was supportive and kind, as she'd been when May was pregnant, but she wasn't very affected by the return of May's father, Heinrich. May was alone—yet not alone—as she faced her life. She wished, not for the first time, for a husband. Not John himself, but a companion for life's decisions.

Elena interrupted May's thoughts. "Full warning: Leonardo is coming for supper tomorrow night."

Leonardo. May hadn't seen him since they graduated from high school. She squinted her eyes and pursed her lips at her cousin.

"We didn't know you would be here when we extended the invitation," Elena said defensively. "You can be somewhere else, but I am not going to cancel because you are staying with us. Peter arranged it with him days ago."

May took in a deep breath. She was being self-absorbed.

"You will be nice to him," Elena commanded.

"Of course!" May said, offended at her cousin's suggestion that she would be rude. "He has done nothing to cause me to be otherwise. And I imagine he's way past his infatuation with me by now."

She looked down at the top of Kay Lynn, asleep in her wrap on May's chest. Her sweet, full lips were shiny, her light-brown hair was pasted to her scalp.

She didn't regret her daughter, but she'd been naïve about her ability to conjure up a life entirely different from her mother's. The weight of her situation pressed hard on her. She didn't know how she was going to support herself. Living with her mother was not a permanent solution, nor was relying on her cousin.

May kissed Kay Lynn's warm scalp. "We will make our way— together. Somehow. I promise."

She blinked away the moisture in her eyes, grabbed her bag, and brought it to the room off the kitchen. They wouldn't stay permanently, but May was enormously grateful to have somewhere to be for the time being.

The next morning Nana Lisbeth walked into the kitchen while May was cleaning up from breakfast. Elena and Peter had left for work with Uncle Sam and Auntie Diana at the produce market, so Kay Lynn and May were alone in the house.

"Your mother sent me to make certain you are both safe . . . and ask if you need anything," Nana Lisbeth said.

"I need to know the truth about my father!" May hissed at her grandmother. She sounded horrible even to her own ears, but she didn't regret being angry.

Nana Lisbeth took Kay Lynn out of the high chair and cuddled with her at the table.

Her voice measured, she replied, "I agree that your mother should have told you long ago."

"Why didn't you?!" May challenged.

"It was her decision," Nana Lisbeth said.

"Why did he leave?" May asked.

Nana's face constricted . . . in thought? In pain? It was hard to know. She shook her head.

"It still is her decision," Nana Lisbeth replied, then requested, "Ask *her* directly, please. She knows she needs to tell you."

May's ears buzzed in anger. She simply wanted to know the truth about *her own* life. Her emotion must have shown.

Sympathy in her voice, Nana Lisbeth said, "I know she wanted you to believe he cherished you, not that he abandoned you. Her decision may have been misplaced, but her hope was to protect you."

May swallowed hard. She felt ill. "Protect me from what?"

Nana Lisbeth sighed. May stared at her grandmother, her eyes demanding an answer.

Nana Lisbeth exhaled. "You will be facing the same question, all too soon." Nana Lisbeth gestured at the baby on her lap. "When do you tell Kay Lynn the truth? What story will you tell her?"

May's heart pounded. She suddenly considered the situation from her vantage as a mother, rather than as the child.

"Is it your mother's place to tell her?" Nana Lisbeth questioned. "Mine? Elena's? Or yours?"

May sat down. Tears stung her eyes.

"We decided long ago to allow your mother to make her own decision when it came to informing you about Heinrich."

We. That word seemed a strong wall holding back a menace. Her family discussed this? Did she *want* to know the truth about her own father? Was she strong enough to know? May's heart softened.

"Thank you for coming all this way, Nana. You know you could have just telephoned," May said.

"Your mother would not have rested until I saw you both with my own eyes. She wants to telephone or call on you tomorrow," Nana Lisbeth said, "but only if you agree."

May sighed. She didn't know what she wanted.

"Do you need some time to think about it?" Nana Lisbeth asked.

Somehow her grandmother always knew what was in her heart. She nodded.

Nana Lisbeth patted her hand. "Would you like company? Or to be alone?"

May wished she knew what she wanted—for today, from her mother, for their future. It was all a jumble of thoughts and feelings.

May looked at her grandmother and shrugged.

"I'm going to visit with Matthew. You two can walk with me. We don't even have to talk, but the fresh air might do you some good."

Being outside did sound nice. May nodded. Nana Lisbeth took Kay Lynn for a clean diaper. May packed dried fruit and they left the house, strolling in a comfortable silence for an hour—from Broadway up Piedmont and into Mountain View Cemetery. May hadn't walked such a distance in some time—since before Kay Lynn was born. Nana Lisbeth was right; it felt good to be in the world, to remember it still went on despite her confusion and despair. Her life had narrowed since she'd become a mother. She kissed the top of Kay Lynn's head.

Entering the cemetery felt like walking into her own history. As a child May and her cousins came here nearly every week with Nana Lisbeth. It was a delightful afternoon activity. Sometime during high school May stopped going on these visits. Too occupied with her own life to consider death, it had been several years since May called on Grampa Matthew with Nana Lisbeth.

The memorial park was familiar, and she felt like she should know how to get to Grampa's grave, but she would not have been able to find it on her own. In contrast, Nana Lisbeth went confidently to it, winding her way through a maze of old markers. Nana Lisbeth placed a bright-yellow daisy she picked along the way against the double headstone.

MATTHEW JOHNSON

BORN FEBRUARY 5TH, 1835 CHARLES CITY, VIRGINIA

DIED MAY 13TH, 1890 OAKLAND, CALIFORNIA

BELOVED FRIEND, FATHER, HUSBAND

The blank space waiting for Nana Lisbeth stabbed May in the heart. Someday her grandmother would be under there, rather than standing beside May. As a child she'd somehow missed that painful reminder of mortality right in front of her.

Nana Lisbeth rested a bony hand on the top of the headstone; her white-haired head bent over and her mouth moved, in private prayer with God or a conversation with her husband. May felt honored to be watching this tender moment—and a little embarrassed to be intruding. After a few minutes Nana Lisbeth kissed her fingers and touched the top of the stone. Tears filled May's eyes. Grampa Matthew died twenty-six years ago—and somehow he was still a comfort to Nana. May wanted that kind of love in her life, and would never have it. She brushed away a tear.

"Would you like to talk to him?"

May's heart jolted at the question.

"He's very good at listening," Nana Lisbeth joked.

Could she find comfort in talking to the grandfather who died before she was born?

Nana Lisbeth explained, "It isn't necessary to touch the headstone when you speak to him. You can talk to him from anywhere because *he* is not here—he is everywhere. However, I find I feel his presence best in this place. It has more to do with me than with him."

May felt she was being let in on a secret. She walked forward and touched the top of the gray stone. She rubbed Kay Lynn's back with the other. Her daughter would need to eat soon, but she was still asleep.

Grampa Matthew? Just the words felt strange in May's thoughts. Cousin Tina was four when he died, and she was the only one of them who remembered him and used that name as if it meant an actual person. For May he'd been a two-dimensional image from photographs and a character in stories. She conjured a picture of him. He *was* her grandfather too, inside her in some way even though she never met him.

Grampa Matthew, she thought again. *Help. Please help me.* Tears spilled over onto her cheeks. She waited. She took some deep breaths with her eyes closed. She waited for more words, more desire, but nothing came. She needed help, but she didn't know anything more than that.

Like her Nana, she kissed her fingers and placed them on the stone in a silent benediction. Her heart felt full, but not relieved. He might be listening, but she couldn't hear him speaking.

Nana Lisbeth walked to a bench and sat down. May followed. She untied Kay Lynn and fed her before she'd fully woken. No one was near so she didn't need to cover up in any way. It was lovely to sit in the warm sun, next to her grandmother while holding her daughter. Suddenly she was overcome with thoughts and feelings.

"Nana. How could I have been so foolish not to realize my mother didn't love my father? I made up a story that she cared so much she could not bear to mention him, but that was not the case. I see all the evidence so clearly now."

May continued, "I found a photo of him when I was five or so. I hid it under my mattress. At night I would talk to him. Sometimes I took it out to study it, searching for me in his features."

Nana Lisbeth nodded.

May asked, "You knew it was there?"

"I found it one day when I changed your bedsheets." Emotion in her voice, the old woman said, "I told Sadie. I implored her to speak of him to you. It didn't seem right that you didn't know anything about Heinrich besides his name. But . . . I do not know what she was afraid of, but she didn't."

"And now I am just like her with a baby and no husband. How will we survive? I can't go back to the university." The thought of walking into her department laid a heavy blanket of humiliation on her heart. "How did this become my life?"

Nana Lisbeth replied, "When you're a child you believe your parents know a special truth about the world, that they know what is right, and that life unfolds in a predictable manner.

"That understanding does not get shaken unless something very dramatic happens. Then you see your parents are fallible humans making imperfect choices given their circumstances. There are no crystal balls like the witch had. In truth we are all much more like the great and powerful Wizard of Oz. We are people pretending we have more skills than we do."

Nana Lisbeth kept speaking. "We are Unitarians—and as such we do not believe in predestination. Our free will gives us choices—and we must live with the results of them."

The two women and the baby sat in the warm sun in silence. May looked around at the gravestones. Each of these was a life. Some short, some long. The few words on each marker left out more than they told.

Nana Lisbeth broke the silence. "May, I know this is not the life you expected. However, it is the life you have. Try to see the joy in it even while you mourn what you've lost."

"Nana, you had a great love," May said. "You do not know how lucky you are."

"My life with Matthew was not only love; we had our struggles, I assure you," Nana Lisbeth snapped. "Our marriage didn't come from luck. It was born from a painful choice to leave the only home I'd ever known."

May felt appropriately chastised. Nana's family hadn't approved of her marriage to Grampa. May didn't know any more details because no one spoke openly about it, but May knew that Nana was estranged from her family after their wedding.

May nodded and mouthed a silent apology. Nana Lisbeth patted her in acceptance.

"Nana, can I ask you a personal question?"

"You may ask, though I may not answer," her grandmother replied.

"How is Willie your nephew? He *is* colored isn't he?"

Nana Lisbeth scoffed, then bit her lip and replied, "It's a shameful part of our family history, so I don't speak of it, but I never intended it to be a secret from any of you grandchildren."

May nodded to encourage her to keep going.

"Willie's mother, Emily, was my half sister. My father forced intercourse on her mother. On the plantation it was a well-known secret the white men raped the colored hands."

May's throat closed tight and her head spun. She couldn't remember being told her Nana Lisbeth was the daughter of a plantation owner; she'd always known it. But she'd never thought about the specific horror of it.

"Oh, Nana Lisbeth, that is terrible," May responded.

Nana Lisbeth nodded, clearly upset, but wanting to say more.

"I'd been so naïve that I didn't question all the shades of workers— the enslaved." Nana Lisbeth blinked back tears. "I was so ashamed."

"Nana, it wasn't your fault. You were a child."

"May, from the age of twelve to the age of twenty-one, after Mattie escaped, Emily was my handmaid. She dressed me, combed my hair, and washed my clothes. She was going to be a wedding *gift* to me." Nana's voice was high and tight.

She exhaled. "I had eyes to see and ears to hear, but I chose to ignore the ugly truth hiding in front of me until I was forced to understand the evil of my situation."

May nodded, considered her words, and then finally said, "I'm glad you did."

"Sadie was not always an ideal mother," Nana Lisbeth said. "She has difficulty expressing her loving feelings and lived primarily with the fear she would not be able to provide you what you need. I believe you can have more empathy for her challenges now, but never, ever, doubt her devotion to you."

May looked at Kay Lynn and nodded.

"I hope you will find a way to make peace with her," Nana Lisbeth directed.

"Me too, Nana," May said. "I just . . . I'm afraid if I see her while I am this angry I will say something I regret and we will not be able to forgive one another."

Nana Lisbeth nodded.

"But tell her I love her and I need some time before I see her. She can understand that, can't she?" May's voice broke. "Can't you?"

Nana's blue eyes softened. She nodded slowly. "You are wise not to speak from fury. Could you manage a telephone conversation?"

May exhaled, considering Nana's request. She nodded once. "Tell her I will call at ten o'clock tomorrow morning."

The ends of Nana's lips pulled up into a small, tender smile of approval.

May mouthed, *Thank you.* She sat back and leaned her head against her grandmother's shoulder. She didn't have any more answers to the pile of uncertainty, but she felt calmer, as if she gained space and time to make sense of her mother's deception and create a decent, if not easy, life for Kay Lynn.

Back at Peter and Elena's home, May was somber as they prepared for supper with Leonardo. Fortunately, Elena didn't attempt to cheer her spirits. She left May to her own thoughts and allowed her to pound her confusion into a loaf of sourdough. Kneading dough was soothing.

By the time Leonardo knocked at the door she was ready to face company. May greeted him in the dining room with a smile; she carried Kay Lynn in one arm and a plate of roasted chicken in the other.

"Hello, Leonardo."

Leonardo was more handsome than he'd been in high school. He'd filled out, so his features fit his face, and he carried himself with more confidence. His dark-brown eyes stared at her, his eyebrows drawn in confusion. Then recognition dawned and he beamed at her.

"May? May Wagner?" he exclaimed. His eyes moved to Kay Lynn, and his brows rose in question.

"Yes," May replied. "*My* daughter."

"Congratulations! No one told me you were wed."

May's heart constricted. She wasn't practiced at this yet. She'd been to church with Kay Lynn; thankfully news of her situation was spread by gossip to her fellow congregants. People who didn't approve stayed away. And those who supported her were kindly enthusiastic in welcoming Kay Lynn.

May shook her head. "I'm . . . I didn't. I'm not married." She stared right at him, perhaps with more of a challenge than she'd like.

He looked confused for another moment and then nodded.

"Congratulations on becoming a mother," he said, his tone warm and genuine. "It's nice to see you."

"Thank you," she replied, relieved at his gracious response. Leonardo was a very kind man.

Elena was correct that Peter hadn't gossiped with his extended family. Men didn't seem to readily share this sort of news.

Her cousin came in with the braised greens and mashed potatoes. "Sit! We are ready to eat," she declared.

Peter put Matthias in the high chair. May balanced Kay Lynn on her lap. Peter reached out his hands for grace. Leonardo offered Kay Lynn his hand and smiled at her. She studied his face intently. Then she reached out, wrapping her pudgy fingers around his thumb, and gave him a huge, toothless grin.

Peter declared, "She approves of you."

Leonardo looked at Kay Lynn and wiggled their joined hands.

He replied, "The feeling is mutual."

May smiled at the pair. They gave thanks for the food and the gathered company, in a combination of Greek Orthodox and Unitarian grace that served the spirit of this home.

For the first time that day, May felt genuine joy and peace. She didn't know what their future would hold; the uncertainty loomed large, but there were still opportunities for peaceful moments of gratitude.

The conversation immediately turned to the upcoming election. Peter looked at May. "Have you registered to vote?"

May nodded. "Of course! My family would disown me if I didn't."

"The women of California will tip the election away from Wilson." Elena snorted. "Can you imagine his face when he learns we women voted him out of office?"

Leonardo laughed. "I wish I shared your confidence. Everyone I know says they are voting for Hughes—but I suspect some may actually vote for Wilson because they don't want to go to war."

Peter sighed. "I assure you I am not voting for Wilson," he said emphatically. "However, I sympathize with those who will."

"What?!" Elena sat forward and challenged her husband. "How can you say that about a man who has no regard for *my* rights as a citizen—or the rights of anyone who is not a rich white man."

"If Hughes wins, men will be sent by the boatload to Europe—guaranteed," Peter said. "I read speculation that there will be a draft."

Elena sat back with a sigh; the outrage in her face transformed into worry. She looked between Peter and Leonardo.

"I'd hate for anyone to go to war," May said. "I'm holding out hope we will send weapons to the Allies, but no soldiers." She shrugged. May couldn't consider voting for Wilson, but if he won, the United States staying out of the war would be a consolation.

May asked about their stance on prohibition. "Are any of you in favor of Proposition 1?"

The three shook their heads in unison.

"Me either," May said. "Prohibiting alcohol will cause more problems than it solves."

Kay Lynn's hand suddenly darted for the mashed potatoes. May pushed the plate out of the way just in time to avoid a mess.

"That was a first!" May declared.

Kay Lynn was changing so fast it was hard to keep up with her.

"May I hold her?" Leonardo asked.

"You like to hold babies?" May asked.

He flushed and nodded. "Perhaps not very manly, but yes. I have so many sisters and brothers that there was always a baby needing carrying."

May smiled and handed over Kay Lynn. She studied her daughter to make sure she approved. Leonardo held up a clean spoon. Kay Lynn reached for it and got it to her mouth.

"She'll be ready for mashed potatoes soon," Elena declared.

May looked between Peter and Leonardo. "You two are cousins? From your father's side?"

Leonardo laughed and shook his head. "We are so-called cousins because our fathers came from the same village. They didn't even know each other in Greece. But here? They are suddenly brothers!"

Peter said, "Every man older than me who speaks Greek is my *uncle*. I don't believe I share ancestors with any of them."

The whole table laughed. May envied their large community. She'd always been jealous of her cousins for having each other as well as a mother and a father, and her mother's relatives. Her family had been so small, just her and Momma. Nana Lisbeth too, but she wasn't the same as having a father and siblings.

She felt an overwhelming stab of jealousy. Elena and Peter would make a family with many children. They'd have large, loud celebrations where she and Kay Lynn would be welcome. She should be grateful, but she only felt insecure and envious. The evening was going so well and suddenly she was upset. Her strong, erratic emotions were exhausting. May pasted on a smile and continued with the conversation, forcing herself to hide her deep, humiliating feelings, hoping not to ruin the pleasant evening.

As promised May walked to Aunt Diana and Uncle Sam's the next morning to call Momma. Not so long ago only the very wealthy on Nob Hill could afford this way to communicate in an instant. Today May would have preferred living in the time when letters and telegrams were the only form in which news was delivered from a distance. She dreaded this conversation, fearing it would only make feelings worse between them.

"Hello?" Momma's voice came right after the first ring. She must have been waiting by their neighbor's telephone.

"Hi, Momma. It's May." She worked to keep her voice calm.

"Thank you for speaking with me," Momma said. She sounded tired.

May waited for her to continue, letting the silence build.

"Please come home?" Momma pleaded.

"How could you lie to me?" May heard the anger in her own voice. "For all those years?"

"I'm sorry, May. Truly I am," Momma said, her regret apparent. "I just wanted you to be comforted."

May exclaimed, "You believed my father being dead would be a solace to me?"

"It seemed kinder than the truth," her mother replied.

May's chest tightened. "That you didn't want me to know my father?!" May hissed into the phone. She restrained her voice, knowing that Aunt Diana was likely listening in from the next room.

"May, you don't know what he was like."

"Exactly. I do not know my father because *you* kept me from him for my entire life!"

Momma replied, "I thought it was a kindness when you were young. I intended to tell you when you were older, but I was afraid you would be angry. Please forgive me."

Rage exploded in May. Forgive, already? She could not bear to hear another word from her mother. It was immature, but she hung up, hoping it pained Momma's heart as much as this lie hurt her own soul.

Auntie Diana gave her a hug before she left but, thankfully, didn't try to talk with her.

Determined not to let her mother keep her from her routines any more than necessary, May went to church with Elena and Matthias the next day. Peter stayed home as he so often did. Because he attended two congregations, when he was absent he could leave the impression he was attending the other.

The beauty of the sanctuary was a balm to her soul. Her mother, grandmother, Uncle Sam, and Aunt Diana were already sitting in a row. She let Elena slide in first so she could be further away from Momma. She settled Kay Lynn on her lap and took in the stillness of the sanctuary, hoping it would soothe her spirits.

Elena leaned over and whispered in her ear, "Your mom wants to hold Kay Lynn, if you don't mind."

May looked at her daughter. It wasn't fair to punish her for her mother's mistake. She nodded and passed the baby to Elena. She watched as her daughter was transferred from person to person, getting kisses and hugs as she went. May's spirits rose seeing love being poured upon Kay Lynn.

Thank you, her mother mouthed. May nodded, fury, gratitude, sorrow swirling in her. Momma looked exhausted. Neither of them slept enough since Kay Lynn was born. She'd lost weight and sleep, working at the store during the day and in the evenings at home. Momma helped without a single word of judgment. She and Nana Lisbeth had kept them all fed and clean for months. May *was* enormously grateful for Momma's efforts.

And yet she felt very far from forgiving her mother for lying about her father for her entire life. She looked around the sanctuary. Who in this room knew the truth about her life and kept it from her? A cyclone of shame and embarrassment twisted in her chest.

The worship began with a favorite hymn: "Amazing Grace." Rather than being a comfort the words taunted her:

> I once was lost but now am found
> Was blind but now I see

Now that she was no longer blind, May was lost. Would grace ever lead her home again?

CHAPTER 13

MAY

July 1916

Two days later, May was preparing lunch in Elena's kitchen when she heard the front door open and shut. Surprised because she wasn't expecting anyone, she called out, "Hello?"

Auntie Diana walked through the doorway. The fear and sorrow in her eyes were alarming.

She spoke in a rush: "Lisbeth telephoned with horrible news: Sadie has tuberculosis."

A large stone dropped into May's stomach. She swallowed and blinked back tears. "How? What happened?"

"She collapsed when she got out of bed this morning. The doctor detected a high heart rate and congestion in her lungs. Sadie doesn't have the cough, and for now her fever is low, though it may go up."

The blood rushing through May's head made it hard to hear. The image of Momma holding and cuddling Kay Lynn at church filled her mind.

"How long has she . . . Is she contagious?"

Auntie Diana sighed and shrugged. "She must have been infected on Sunday, but you know it's not easily passed."

"How long . . . When will she be better?" May could not face the alternative. How often did people survive tuberculosis? Half the time?

"May"—Aunt Diana's voice broke—"we will only know in time."

"I must go to her," May declared.

Aunt Diana sighed.

May teared up. "Did Nana Lisbeth tell you to keep me away?"

Her auntie shook her head and pulled in her lips. "You have to know there's a risk of infection—to you and to Kay Lynn. The doctor wants to send Sadie away to a sanatorium, but Lisbeth insists she's going to do the care."

May felt tears on her cheek. "What should I do?"

"I cannot tell you the best choice for you and your daughter. For me?" Auntie Diana pulled a handkerchief out of her pocket and held it over her face. "Uncle Sam is waiting in the truck out front. We are going there right now."

May's heart wrenched. If it were only her she would have no hesitation, but she was making this decision for Kay Lynn too. She looked at her beloved baby, who recently mastered sitting up in a high chair. Her trusting daughter stared at her.

Then she pictured her mother in bed. She would be there for months, maybe even a year. Modern medical practices were making inroads against tuberculosis, but the cure was neither rapid nor guaranteed.

She couldn't imagine staying away for so long, leaving her mother's care only to Nana Lisbeth and Auntie Diana. The neighbors? Strangers?

"We're coming with you!" May declared.

Her aunt nodded like she knew that would be May's answer.

"I will wear two handkerchiefs at a time and keep Kay Lynn out of the sickroom." May wondered, "Do you agree?"

"I . . . Yes, that seems a good balance."

May nodded. She left Kay Lynn with Auntie Diana while she packed up their things. They were moving back home, because her mother and her grandmother needed her.

Kay Lynn sat on May's lap in the bed of the truck as they pulled up to their house. *Home. I'm home.* A wave of longing washed over her. May had been too attached to her anger to feel anything else toward home in the five days she was away. Uncle Sam helped her climb out of the truck, and they walked past Nana's beautiful flowers. Strangely, some of the white carnations were tinged with scarlet.

"You go first. I'll stay with Kay Lynn," Aunt Diana directed.

Anxious to see her mother, May walked toward Momma's room, and then remembered she needed to cover her face. In the linen closet she found the bag of old clothes, waiting to be repurposed for quilts. She tore her favorite skirt from high school into rectangles. After several mishaps she looked in the mirror. She looked like a terrified robber. It was hard to breathe from the layers of fabric or tight lungs—or both.

May opened the door. Surprisingly, the room was bright and airy. The windows were entirely open and the curtains wide apart. Momma's eyes were closed and her forehead was damp. Nana Lisbeth stood up from the chair at her side.

She hugged May and whispered, "I'm glad you came."

May nodded. "I couldn't stay away."

Nana Lisbeth pointed to the chair. "I'll leave you two."

Momma blinked open glassy eyes. "Oh, May. You are here. You shouldn't be . . . Kay Lynn?"

"I have two masks, Momma. And I will wash my hands when I leave."

Momma smiled and teared up. "Thank you." She struggled to inhale and then struggled to whisper, "I am sorry . . . about—"

"Shhhh," May interrupted her. "We are not going to speak of it now. It doesn't matter. I only care that you get better."

Momma nodded almost imperceptibly and her eyelids slowly drew down. May waited for her to open them again, but she didn't. Instead a soft wheezing filled the strangely cheery room. Momma was as weak as May had ever seen a person.

She wanted to take Momma's hand but feared it wasn't safe, so she decided she would hold it through a layer of fabric until she could learn the recommended health practices.

As May watched Momma sleep, her chest twitched with sorrow. Imagining Momma dying was more devastating than an unintended pregnancy, John dropping her, or the lie about her father. Yesterday she thought her situation was unbearable, but none of that mattered in comparison with losing her mother.

May let her tears flow; they fell onto the bedcover, making damp circles. She wasn't very practiced at it, but felt a prayer pour out of her.

God, please heal Sadie Wagner. She is wanted and loved and too young to die.

Maybe it was too much to ask. She wasn't even sure she believed in the sort of God who could choose to heal her mother or let her die, but it was a comfort—and made her understand why people pray for those they love and themselves.

May stayed in the room until her breasts became uncomfortably full. She left her mother sound asleep and found her family around the table in the kitchen. Kay Lynn flapped her arms and smiled at her return. May reached out to scoop up her daughter. Auntie Diana held up a hand to stop her. May paused and sighed. These new habits would take a while to learn.

She untied her masks and washed her hands thoroughly before cuddling with her girl. Kay Lynn arched her back, signaling she wanted to eat.

"Do you mind?" she asked. She'd never fed Kay Lynn in front of her uncle, but she didn't want to be alone right now.

Auntie Diana said, "He's seen it all—me, Tina, Elena—nothing makes him uncomfortable."

Uncle Sam nodded. "You go right ahead."

May nodded and fulfilled her daughter's need.

"I'm sure you already went over this. But could you tell me what the doctor said?" May's voice broke.

Suddenly aged, Nana was bent at the neck and her eyes were sunken. Was she sick too?

"Did the doctor check you?" May asked.

Nana Lisbeth nodded. "He listened to my chest. I am fine."

For now, May thought.

"Dr. Latham says only time will tell. Half of his patients recover and live for five or more years, though often it returns again."

Half do not hung unspoken in the air.

"Rest, milk, fresh air, and sunshine are the prescription for Sadie," Nana Lisbeth said.

May nodded.

"We must always wear masks in her sickroom, and then not touch our faces until we've washed our hands," she continued.

"I will make us as many masks as we need," Auntie Diana declared.

"What have you told the market?" Uncle Sam asked.

"Mrs. Jones kindly agreed to telephone that Sadie is ill, but they have not been told about the tuberculosis. Dr. Latham will inform the health department."

May felt unsettled at the mention of the health department. Her mother would now be one of the statistics reported in the *Oakland Tribune*. Oakland was proud of their low numbers for transmissible diseases. Sanitation and education were the key, but somehow her mother had been infected.

"How long . . . ?" She didn't even know how to ask.

"He couldn't tell me a prognosis except Sadie doesn't appear to be at immediate risk of death, though he cautioned it *could* change rapidly, but most likely not."

"There's a good reason TB used to be called consumption," Uncle Sam said. "It progresses so slowly most of the time." He placed his hand over May's. "Your mother is very strong. My sister is not going to be devoured by this disease."

May inhaled sharply. She nodded, grateful for the comforting words.

"Nana," Uncle Sam called, using the title for his mother bestowed by his children, "how are you set for money?"

Nana Lisbeth moved her head side to side and then shrugged. "We have savings; they won't last for a year, but we have time to sort that out."

"Nana, if Kay Lynn stays with you, I can work Momma's job at the market," May offered. She'd imagined she might find a position in an office once Kay Lynn was weaned, but working the market would keep them in food and keep the lights on. Kay Lynn was old enough to eat rice cereal if May couldn't take breaks to nurse her.

"You want to move back here?" Nana asked.

"If you agree," May replied.

Nana Lisbeth nodded. "Thank you. You two can take my room. I can sleep in the living room."

May took her hand. They would get through this together.

CHAPTER 14

NAOMI

November 1916

It was the night of the national election. By good fortune Willie was home for three nights in a row. The previous evening Naomi, Willie, and Gramma Jordan attended the Women's Party rally, expecting a celebration with like-minded people.

However, one man disturbed the gathering by proclaiming to be for women's suffrage but against expanding Negro suffrage. He proudly declared that as a Southerner he could not abide allowing Negro women in the South to get the vote.

He felt entitled to speak his mind, but the stomping and jeers from the crowd taught him otherwise: this modern city was not going to import Southern traditions when it came to the rights of women and Negroes. Naomi had never been more gratified to live in Oakland.

Over supper Naomi announced to Joseph and Maggie, "Your elders made the paper this evening."

"Front page of the *Tribune*," Gramma Jordan declared as she waved the newspaper in her hand.

Joseph said, "Hand it here."

He read the headline out loud:

BIG VOICE OF JONES HALTS RALLY

——

Brass Band, Shouting Men and Calling

Women Fail to Stem Oratorical Tide

Against Votes for Negroes in South States

——

Women's Party Allows One Man Floor:

Meeting Breaks Up in Disorder

When Hostile Shouts from Negroes Howl

"I'm proud of you, Ma and Pops," Maggie said.

"Thank you," Willie said.

Naomi beamed at her family gathered around the table—in the home that they *owned*. Each time she remembered that fact a shiver of pleasure traveled through her.

She missed Cedric, always, but reminded herself to delight in this moment. Willie was home for three nights. With Joseph graduating in May time together would become more and more rare. Like with Cedric, she wanted Joseph to work in Oakland, but he wanted a career that would keep him away most of the time too—not on the rails but in the US military.

As soon as he finished high school Joseph intended to enlist in the Twenty-Fourth Infantry. Back when he was eight years old he'd been charmed by a houseguest who stayed with them for a few nights. The man, a former buffalo soldier, spoke about the beauty of Yosemite and the camaraderie of the infantry.

His story about matching wits with ranchers in the national park was especially memorable. The white ranchers knew the colored soldiers could neither arrest them nor fine them for illegal grazing; the soldiers' only recourse was escorting the ranch hands and their cattle across the boundary of the park. They were caught and removed only to return again and again.

Until the soldiers came up with a most clever plan: they removed the ranch hands at the nearest park boundary, but drove the herd to the farthest side of the enormous park. It took many days for the ranch hands to reunite with their stock. And so the buffalo soldiers defeated the cattlemen. Naomi felt sure there was much the man wasn't saying about his experiences, but he spun such a great tale that her son's fondest dream was to become one of those strong, clever, and adventurous buffalo soldiers.

Naomi said, "Hughes is going to win, and that man who brought *The Birth of a Nation* to the White House will be gone. The politicians will learn that fueling the flames of hatred between the races and disregarding women's rights will not be tolerated in the twentieth century."

Willie implored, "From your lips to God's ears!"

"I saw May with Kay Lynn at the polls today," Naomi told her family. "She was voting for the first time. That baby is so dear. As precious and perfect as any you have ever seen. She seems to be getting blond curly hair!"

"Did she say how Sadie is doing this week?" Gramma Jordan asked.

Naomi shook her head. "May says she is neither better nor worse, which is a relief and a sorrow."

Willie said, "It's only been a few months; there's every reason to think she started resting soon enough to fully recover."

Gramma Jordan sighed. "I feel for them. I wish there was more to do besides bring them dinner."

"Your ham hock soup is the best medicine around." Naomi patted her mother's hand.

Joseph looked up from the paper and changed the topic: "I'm going on the roof after dark. Maybe I can see the screen at city hall and learn the election results tonight."

The *Oakland Tribune* was collecting election tallies by telegram from the Associated Press and United Press. Using modern technology they were going to flash the results on a large screen erected downtown. When a winner was determined they'd sound a boom loud enough to be heard throughout the city followed by color-coded fireworks. Blue sparks would declare Democrat Wilson the winner; green would be sent up for Republican Hughes.

Naomi said, "How will you get up there . . . and isn't it too high to be safe?"

"A ladder can reach from Gramma Jordan's back porch," Joseph replied.

Naomi looked at Willie. Would he back her up?

"Falling off a one-story roof isn't safer than falling off two stories," he told her. "We just have to be careful."

We. Willie was going up there too. She shook her head, but didn't say more.

"If you see anything interesting, I'll come up!" Maggie declared.

Willie added, "I want to experience this modern technology for myself."

"You join them too," Gramma Jordan encouraged Naomi. "Willie will make certain you are safe. You can shout down to me and Mrs. King what you see."

Naomi wondered if it was worth pushing past her fear to be with her children to celebrate a new era for their nation. She decided yes, she wanted to have that memorable experience for herself.

In the dark night, Willie held the ladder steady. Naomi gripped the rungs tight and her heart raced as she climbed up one at a time. At the top, Joseph gripped her hand as she stepped onto the roof. Once she'd taken a few steps up the slope and was well away from the edge she exhaled. Joseph walked her to a blanket spread out near the peak and pointed at the screen lit up in the distance. She nodded.

Naomi took in the spectacular view. San Francisco sparkled bright across the bay. A few lanterns bobbed in the dark water from boats traveling in the night, and a dim Marin barely showed past them to the north. She turned around to see houses lighting up the slopes of the Berkeley Hills, whereas to the south the hills in Oakland, with hardly any homes, were dark shadows in the sky. This was Naomi's first time on any roof; it was magical. She should have done this long ago.

The four of them huddled under blankets against the November chill. Images flashed on the screen. The words and numbers were often too small to read from this distance, but the name of a state in large letters with either an elephant or a donkey could be seen with their binoculars. They took turns watching and announcing winners as they were shown.

Joseph wrote down the results from each state. They shouted down to Gramma Jordan, but she grew tired of the wait and went inside. They agreed to pound on the roof to let her know if there was any important news. Willie explained the Electoral College to their children as they waited. The strange and convoluted system that chose the president was put in place to ensure more representation for the Southern states. Maggie was outraged as she understood the man with the most votes might not end up winning the presidency.

The outcome in many states was predictable and went as expected. California was not one of them. Their state, one of the few with the women's vote, was as likely to go for Wilson as for Hughes. Naomi prayed for an outline of California to flash with an elephant. She desperately wanted the nation to send a clear message that Wilson's hatred and hypocrisy would not be tolerated. He must be voted out of office in order to respectfully move forward as a country.

Naomi rested her head on Willie's shoulder as she stared at the screen. Her heart raced as she waited in anticipation; she felt like prey hiding from a hunter. When the pounding in her chest became too intense, she would look away from the screen and gaze at the nearly full moon. Its bright light gave her hope. It would continue to shine down on her regardless of who was president of the United States.

Hours later, the moon lit up a different place in the dark sky and they were still waiting to know the results in the two states that were going to decide the outcome: Minnesota and California. Their combined twenty-five Electoral College votes were pivotal. Naomi struggled to keep her eyes open. Maggie slept with her head in Naomi's lap.

"Should we give up?" Willie asked.

"Not me!" Joseph said. "I'm staying up here until it's light again."

Naomi shrugged. She'd so wanted to see the flashing fire: bright-green flames telling President Wilson to leave the White House.

Naomi wondered, "Do you believe the sound will wake us up in time to run to the window? Will the fireworks be high enough to make out from our bedrooms?"

"I don't know," Willie said. "But I do know my muscles are going to take hours to warm up. And my knowing won't change anything about the results."

Naomi nodded. "I'll go out for a paper first thing in the morning. We'll wake up to good news, right?"

He patted her leg. They all held on to hope for the right outcome. She nodded her consent and they gave up on knowing that night.

Naomi woke with a start, burning to know the outcome of the election. Willie slept next to her. She walked in the dawning morning to the corner store for a newspaper.

"They were just delivered!" The young clerk said, "The latest news is . . . there's no news." He held it up for her to read.

HUGHES HAS LEAD IN CALIFORNIA

SIX STATES HOLD POWER IMBALANCE

ANTI-PROHIBITIONISTS CLAIM VICTORY

This report, already hours old, confirmed the counts were heading in Hughes's direction but neither of the two states that mattered, California and Minnesota, were finished tallying votes. Naomi rushed home with the inconclusive but hopeful news.

The next morning Naomi delighted in the news that Minnesota had decided for Hughes. In contrast, the results from the rural California counties put Wilson, a Democrat, in the lead for president even though the Republican, Johnson, held a decisive 250,000 lead for governor of California. The Republican National Committee was suspicious of those results but there was no evidence of any wrongdoing. Naomi's hopes for a Hughes win were diminished, but not entirely dashed.

By Friday evening any embers of hope were thoroughly smothered. The California results were final and the Republican Party decided against requesting a recount. It was only three days since the election, but it felt an eternity. Nothing would change. That horrid Wilson was going to be the president again.

Gramma Jordan said, "My only consolation is President Wilson will keep us out of the European War, so we don't have to worry about our Joseph and Cedric."

Anger shot through Naomi, and she glared at her mother.

"I am not ready to hear that there is anything good about this outcome," she snapped. "That man who doesn't support my rights, as a woman or a colored person, will still be in the White House."

"But—" Gramma Jordan started.

Naomi interrupted her. "Nor do I believe he will keep the United States out of this war. The drums are beating hard; he will relent and my sons are going to be his cannon fodder."

Naomi exhaled. "I'm sorry, Ma. I know you do not want that hateful man as our president either. I just . . . I just. I'm angry and disappointed in my country. Will we ever learn to be one nation?"

CHAPTER 15

NAOMI

March 1917

The Poor Little Rich Girl was showing at the T & D Theatre in downtown Oakland. With four days off, Willie was taking Naomi for a night out. After the movie they'd dine at their favorite restaurant, the Golden Eagle Hotel, near their old home in West Oakland. It felt good to be dressed up and going out with her husband. Naomi didn't like that he slept more nights on a train than he did in their home, but it did make their time together more special.

A bit of bright yellow caught Naomi's eye as they walked by the front garden. She and Gramma Jordan had transplanted many of their favorite flowers from their old garden soon after they moved; it was too early to know which would make the transition. Naomi stopped, bent over to push aside the greenery, and a bright flower glowed up at them, even in the dusk.

Willie laughed. "Well, it must be home, if a yellow crocus has bloomed."

"Gramma Jordan wasn't confident they'd come up this year," Naomi said, "but look at it. It made itself right at home. Guess the move wasn't as big a shock as we thought it might be."

Willie laughed again. "Point made, wife."

On the trolley they discussed the news about the Zimmerman Telegram that was filling the papers. The German foreign minister had sent a note to the Mexican government offering financial and military support to invade the United States to retake Arizona, New Mexico, and Texas. Mexico denied any intention of waging war against their northern neighbor, but it raised tensions.

Willie ventured, "Now that Wilson has cut off all ties with Germany over this, it's just a matter of time before we declare on the side of England."

"They are going to draft our sons." Naomi sighed.

Willie nodded. "That seems to be what everyone thinks."

Naomi's stomach clenched. "Aren't you afraid for them?"

"Of course I am. But Cedric and Joseph are as strong and capable as any young men. They'll get tested and prove to themselves and the world what they can do. I'm going to encourage Cedric to follow Joseph's lead and become a buffalo soldier."

Naomi teared up. "Really?"

"Naomi, you know we want them in a well-established unit. Some of the officers are Negro."

She exhaled hard. There wasn't anything else to say. Willie was right and what she wanted wasn't going to change her sons' futures.

Minutes later they walked from the trolley stop on Telegraph to the theater on Broadway. Willie bought the tickets at the kiosk and handed them to the uniformed attendant guarding the front door. The young man took them and cleared his throat. "You can find a seat in the balcony."

"This film is popular—as you mentioned," Willie said.

They climbed the stairs, her arm looped through his, with their earlier conversation floating behind her, but it wasn't a heavy weight on her heart. She was determined not to borrow trouble. Willie led the way to two seats in the front row, not quite in the middle.

Naomi looked down at the main floor and saw many empty seats, not the crowd she expected. Fury shot through her. She and Willie exchanged a fierce look. Naomi stood, and he followed her back down the stairs. Her heart beat hard as she turned into the auditorium. The young attendant left his post to stop her. White customers stared as the scene unfolded.

"Upstairs only. It's a new policy"—he looked Willie up and down—"regardless of who you are accompanied by."

Anger exploded in Naomi. They'd watched movies in theaters for several years without such a boundary.

"We'll just get a refund then," Willie said, sounding calmer than Naomi thought he should.

"No refunds," the young man said, a challenge in his eyes. "Also our policy."

Willie took a slow, steady breath. Naomi squeezed his arm as hard as she could, pouring her rage into her fingers. Willie covered her hand and they left the theater. Shame seeped out of every pore as she walked past white patrons queued up for the show. A few of them whispered to each other. One man shook his head in sympathy for her—or maybe contempt.

Willie started to speak. She raised a hand to silence him.

"Not here. Not now," she hissed.

She held her head up high, though she must have fury on her face, determined to show dignity as they left. Naomi marched to the trolley stop. Willie pulled against her arm but she didn't stop.

"Naomi, let's keep our plans for supper out," Willie begged.

She froze, stared at him, incredulous, but at the pain in his eyes sympathy rose in her.

He whispered, his voice on the edge of tears, "I don't want to give them the power to ruin our whole evening."

Naomi exhaled. He was right. She nodded and walked toward Sixteenth Street. After a few steps she put her arm through his. Soon they'd be surrounded by colored people.

"Thank you," she said to her husband.

"For what?" he asked.

"Reminding me to fight for us"—her voice broke—"and for our children. Even in something as small as dinner out. They may bar us from their businesses, but they cannot stop me from living my life on my terms."

Willie patted her hand. "Now that sounds like my wife." He laughed.

"Tomorrow I'm going to Mr. Butler's to make certain the Northern California branch of the NAACP will add this to the list in our fight for our freedom." She shook her head. "Trying to segregate theaters in Oakland."

"Yes, you will!" Willie declared with a nod. "Yes, you will."

By the next organizing meeting of the NAACP, Mr. Butler opened the gathering with some splendid news.

"Mr. Richardson, in his first case after passing the bar, has obtained a stay against the segregation of theaters in Oakland," he exclaimed.

The group murmured their approval; Naomi joined in.

"Praise the Lord!" she proclaimed.

"Thank you, Mrs. Smith, for bringing this issue to our attention," Mr. Butler said.

Naomi was gratified by the praise, but more grateful for their success at barring the practice. They lost the fight to ban the showing of *The Birth of a Nation*, but they'd won this battle.

"We have shown we will not be humiliated and assigned second-class citizenship in the city of Oakland!" Mr. Butler declared.

"If only that were true. We chop the head off one evil snake, and another slithers in to take its place!" Mrs. de Hart said.

All eyes turned to the middle-aged woman.

"The Santa Fe Tract improvement board is voting on a resolution for land segregation," she explained. "If it is approved they will bring the proposal to the Oakland City Council."

Naomi's throat tightened.

"They wish to emulate the land segregation laws in Baltimore and Louisville?" Mr. Butler asked, his voice filled with dread.

"We must stand up to them!"

"We have to learn their plans."

"Can they force us to sell?" Naomi asked, on the verge of tears. She imagined telling Willie they were being chased out of their neighborhood. Would he forgive her if she lost all their savings? Could she forgive herself?

"I understand that is the intent with the laws in other states," Mr. Butler said. "The Supreme Court is hearing the case from the national NAACP."

"When will they argue and make a ruling?" Naomi asked.

"This term, but we don't know the precise dates," Mr. Butler explained.

"We can't wait for that," a voice to her left shouted out.

"When is the Santa Fe Tract meeting?" Naomi asked.

Mrs. de Hart replied, "In two weeks, on a Tuesday evening."

Naomi nodded. Willie would be home.

"I will ask my husband to attend. He's so light whites don't see he is colored," she offered. "Forewarned is forearmed." She swallowed her fear and sighed.

Mrs. Brown shook her head and said with sympathy, "You just bought your beautiful home in the Santa Fe Tract, didn't you?"

Naomi nodded. The sympathy caused her emotion to grow. She swallowed hard.

"We will fight them with everything we have," Mr. Butler declared. "Our friends on the city council will stand for our dignity."

Naomi wished she shared his confidence. She looked around the room at these finest of people. It was 1917! How could their lives be destroyed by hateful attitudes?

Two weeks later Naomi and Gramma Jordan waited for Willie and Lisbeth to return from the Santa Fe Tract Improvement Club. Lisbeth readily agreed to attend with him despite the stress of Sadie's illness. Though they were not the closest of families, they could count on one another in times of need. Naomi feared the worst when she saw Willie's and Lisbeth's pained demeanors.

"I have tea." Naomi led them to the kitchen, where Gramma Jordan was already seated.

At the wooden table, Willie sighed and shook his head. "It was as sickening as you might imagine."

Lisbeth nodded. "Their comments were bathed in polite language, but racial contempt is the basis for the proposal."

"Are they bringing a law for the city council to vote upon?" Gramma Jordan asked.

Looking near tears, Willie and Lisbeth both nodded.

Naomi exhaled hard.

"Lisbeth was the only person who spoke against. The only one," Willie said.

"How many were there?" Naomi asked.

"Fourteen men," Lisbeth said, "all strangers to me. Even though I live in the Santa Fe Tract, I wasn't given any notice of this meeting—except from you. These gentlemen . . . or rather hateful men . . . live close to Market Street. They have given themselves a name and act as if they are representing our entire neighborhood.

"They started this agitation because a white neighbor sold his house to a colored man. When the colored man rejected their suggestion that he move, they threatened him with creating a law to force him to sell."

"Orville Caldwell," Willie said in a quiet voice.

Naomi looked at him, her eyebrows drawn up in question.

"One hateful man is doing this, willing to ruin our lives because of his beliefs," her husband replied.

"He is only one man," Naomi said.

"The others were indifferent and approved his proposal without seeming to have his underlying animosity," Willie said. "Their indifference to our dignity somehow seems a worse slight than his passion."

"What law are they proposing?" Gramma Jordan asked.

Willie pulled out a folded piece of paper and read, "No colored person may live or own property in a block where there is a majority of white residents."

"What are the polite arguments?" Naomi asked, anger in her voice.

Willie read, from the same paper, "We have the right to maintain our property values from the deterioration that inevitably follows from mixing the races. There will be no burden restricted to either race. We will only provide a legal means of regulation of the conduct of men of either race who show a disposition to ignore and disregard the wishes of others."

Lisbeth took Gramma Jordan's hand and said, "Jordan, surely the city council will not approve!"

Naomi looked at their entwined hands: Lisbeth's bony with age spots and Gramma Jordan's still smooth, dark skin. So few white women cared enough about a colored woman to hold her hand in comfort.

Naomi shook her head slowly. She didn't share Lisbeth's naïve certainty. Dread filled her belly: she looked at her husband and said, "I'm sorry. I'm afraid I have lost us everything."

"Not everything, Naomi," he replied, tenderness in his voice. "We will always have each other. And our children." He looked at Gramma Jordan. "Our precious family. They can't take that from us."

Naomi sucked in her breath; he was right, their family mattered more than this home. Willie wasn't angry at her for them being in this position. She took her husband's hand and said, "Thank you, Willie."

He seemed to be forgiving her more easily than she would be able to forgive herself. She feared she'd reached too high and they'd all suffer because of her ambition.

WAR TO BE DECLARED

The headline screamed at Naomi. Her outrage and fear weren't diminished by the fact that she wasn't surprised. The news had been building toward this outcome for weeks. The increasing likelihood of the United States joining in the European War preoccupied their dinner conversations. Naomi was absolutely certain they should not send young men to die in foreign lands, but Congress wasn't going to take into account one colored woman's opinion. Nor were her sons. They were swept up in the fervor. Willie was likely too old to serve, but she wondered if he would go too if allowed.

Joseph stood behind her and read over her shoulder.

"April 2nd, 1917. Mark my word," he declared, excitement in his voice, "this day changes everything—gives me more options when I finish school. Paris here I come!"

"So long as you do graduate!" Naomi declared, hoping she kept the panic out of her voice.

"I will, Ma," Joseph said. "There's no way I'm going to let Cedric hold a high school diploma over me."

Naomi laughed. Sibling rivalry might work in her favor.

For four days the paper was filled with politicking and speculation, but no congressional vote. On the fifth, Naomi read the sickening headline:

WAR IS DECLARED

VOLUNTEERS ARE CALLED FOR

Volunteers were needed—120,000 single men age eighteen to twenty-five—or a draft would be instituted. No amount of maternal persuasion would stop her sons from jumping to the front of this line.

A blanket of dread draped over her heart. She picked up the paper and went over to her mother's flat to share the pain of this news. How long would the war last? she wondered, knowing that was how long this fear would be her constant companion.

CHAPTER 16

MAY

May 1917

May carried scarlet and white carnations into the kitchen. "I left the mottled ones growing," she told her grandmother with a scoff. "I don't know what they stand for."

She pinned two white flowers to her dress. One on her left shoulder to honor her mother and one on her right to signal her disapproval of the war. Now that it was here, she was against sending young men across an ocean to kill or be killed. Every unmarried man was preparing to leave his family behind to face horrific challenges. They were fortunate that married men were being allowed to stay home— for now.

May put on a mask and brought a scarlet carnation and a white one to the sickroom. Momma was asleep, her loud, shallow breathing filled the dim space. The sick woman wasn't nearly strong enough to attend church but would be happy to be part of the Mother's Day service in this way.

May set the flowers on the bedside. *For Lisbeth Johnson and for world peace.* Unwilling to disturb Momma's rest, she didn't take her hand. Instead she held her hands out and prayed silently in her heart and mind: *God, Spirit of Love, help us to find a cure for Sadie Wagner that she may have a long and healthy life.*

She wished there was more to do, but their doctor didn't have a cure. It would be months or years before this limbo was behind them. Momma was at once a ghost in their home and a living presence that demanded attention. May wanted it to be over, but not if it meant life without her mother. She took a deep breath.

"I love you, Momma," May whispered. Her mother's shallow breath filled her ears as she closed the door.

In the kitchen, Nana Lisbeth wore three carnations: two white for her deceased mothers, Mattie and Ann, and one white to protest the war. She was staying home to care for Momma but would participate from afar.

"F . . . f . . . ," Kay Lynn declared, pointing with a pudgy finger and with her eyebrows arched in glee.

A wave of love crashed over May at the sight of a scarlet carnation on Kay Lynn's dress. That flower was for her, for May, to honor that she was a mother now. So much had changed since this ritual last year.

"Yes, you have a carnation too!" May told her one-year-old. "Thank you, Nana." May hugged her grandmother and left with her daughter for Sunday worship and supper. It hurt to leave Momma behind, but it felt good to be going somewhere besides work at the market.

An envelope addressed to May Wagner rested on the table in the entryway when she returned home from work.

John's handwriting sent a jolt through her. Without removing her coat or setting down her pocketbook, she ripped it open.

May 18th, 1917

Dear May,
Last week, I was most surprised to see you carrying
a young child—who I can only presume to be ours. I
have often regretted how things ended between us, but
never more than on that day. I must speak with you.
I will return next Tuesday at noon with the greatest
hope that you will have lunch with me.
  Fondly yours,
  John

A twenty-dollar bill accompanied the note. May swallowed. Anger flooded through her, but if she were honest, there was longing too. She'd cried too many times over these months about him, or being an unwed mother, or simply feeling inadequate; she didn't know. She wanted him to regret his choice, change his mind, and beg her for forgiveness. But she didn't know if she wanted to give it to him or to welcome him into their lives.

May looked for Nana. She waved the envelope, a question in her eyes.

"He stopped by a few hours ago. He asked to see his child, but I refused," Nana Lisbeth said. "I did give him an envelope, paper, and pen."

May handed her the note to read. She watched her grandmother read the words from the man who betrayed her.

"Will you meet with him?" Nana Lisbeth asked.

May shook her head. Then shrugged. "What do you advise?" May asked.

"He is Kay Lynn's father," Nana Lisbeth said, an unspoken reminder in the tone of her voice.

She sighed. *Her* father had briefly intruded upon her life, causing an enormous rift between her and her mother—and then disappeared entirely again. She'd yet to ask Momma the painful truth about Heinrich. She didn't know who she was protecting—her mother, her father, or herself. But she wasn't willing to upset her extremely ill mother to hear the story.

Was John like Heinrich? Would Kay Lynn be better off knowing her father or being kept from him? Unlike her father, John didn't wait more than twenty years to return. She decided meeting him would not harm her daughter.

"I'll be at work on Tuesday at noon. Can you send him to the market when he returns?"

Nana Lisbeth nodded.

"And thank you for keeping him away from Kay Lynn . . . at least for now," May said.

"It's your decision," Nana Lisbeth reminded her.

May didn't realize what a burden that responsibility would seem.

May saw John through the front-window glass of the market. He'd scarcely changed in the nearly two years since she'd seen him. Still handsome, with his lovely brown hair and eyes; his teeth straight and white. Before he could step inside she came out with a jumble of emotions. She wanted to feel nothing toward him, but he made her heart race—in desire and fury in equal measure.

"Hello, John," she said, consciously keeping her voice even.

He leaned in to kiss her cheek, but she shook her head and stepped back.

"I'm glad to see you," he said; nerves showed in his shiny brow and his grip on his hat. She glanced at his hands, that she'd so dearly loved holding. "I thought we could eat at the Claremont?"

"I have fifteen minutes, then I must return to work," she said, rejecting his plan. "We can sit here while I eat *my* lunch on my break."

He nodded, looking well reprimanded and joined her on the low wall.

"You are a cashier?"

"Yes," she replied, leaving out any details.

"Why didn't you . . ." He sounded accusatory, then softened his tone. "I wish I'd known you kept the baby."

She raised an eyebrow to show her outrage.

"I thought we agreed . . . ," he said.

"Agreed?!" she questioned.

"You agreed to take care of the situation, did you not?" John replied, blinking in uncertainty.

Confusion and anger pounded in her. How could he have taken that from their brief conversation?

"I do not believe I owe you an explanation for my choices."

"The child is mine, yes?" he asked, staring at her intently.

"Of course."

"Please, tell me about him," he begged.

"*Her* name is Kay Lynn. She was born March seventeenth of last year."

"Saint Patrick's Day? That's memorable!" He smiled, looking right into her eyes. He was trying to make amends, to learn about their child.

"And not a bit of Irish in her," May replied, slipping into a familiar banter.

John nodded with a smile. "I should like to meet her."

May inhaled slowly. She swallowed. John stared at her with his dark caramel eyes—a similar color to Kay Lynn's. Would he accept her?

"She's not like other babies," she said.

"What do you mean?"

May swallowed. She studied John's face as she spoke. "I intended to adopt her out, but she seized soon after she was born; her left side is weak. The doctor recommended she go to Napa."

Kay Lynn still hadn't had another seizure, but she was just over a year. The doctor said she still might have more. Her left side didn't work like her right, but she sat up, crawled in her own fashion, and fed herself. She might never learn to walk without crutches or braces. Would she ever speak in full sentences? It was too soon to know, but she understood what she was told as well as most one-year-olds.

Nana Lisbeth was adamant there was nothing about Kay Lynn that would prevent her from living a full and beautiful life, and that the judgment of perfectionists or stares of strangers in the future didn't take away her inherent worth and dignity.

"She's an epileptic?" he asked, his eyebrows drawn in. Was that confusion or contempt?

Protectiveness rose in May. She bristled at the need to explain Kay Lynn to John, or prove her value to a person who should already love her. "I must return to work."

May stood up abruptly, turned her back to John, and left him on the wall. It felt good to be walking away from him this time.

A few days later there was another note in John's handwriting waiting for her when she arrived home after work.

> *May,*
> *I should very much like to meet our little Kay Lynn.*
> *Please telephone me at SR2223 so we can arrange a*
> *visit.*
> *John*

May exhaled. Confused and angry, but also curious, she slipped the letter in her pocket. She found her daughter in the kitchen watching from the high chair as Nana Lisbeth cooked supper. Kay Lynn squealed and a huge, crooked grin showed her utter delight when she saw her mother. May returned the sentiment by scooping up Kay Lynn and covering her with kisses. She'd never felt this way about anyone before and longed to do whatever was best for her child. Whether that meant including, or excluding, John from Kay Lynn's life, May hadn't decided.

"How's Momma today?" May asked.

"No change," Nana Lisbeth replied. "She slept most of the day as usual. She managed to drink her milk. She's preferring it warm."

Nana Lisbeth pointed to a pan on the stove. May returned Kay Lynn to the high chair, despite the girl's protest, filled a mug with warm milk, and brought it to her mother's sickroom.

A weak smile crossed Momma's face. She looked the same: thin, pale, and sleepy eyed. Momma sat up and put on a face mask. She nodded her thanks as May put the cup on the bedside table.

"I never heard about your visit with John." Momma's voice was quiet and weak.

May sat on the edge of the bed, her face covered by a mask too. She teared up—overwhelmed with the complexity.

"He asked to meet Kay Lynn," May said. "But I didn't care for his reaction when he learned about her seizure and weakness."

Momma nodded.

May felt queasy remembering the conversation. "The look on his face when I mentioned Napa . . . he was disgusted."

"Give yourself some time. You will discover the right choice for you—and Kay Lynn."

May studied her Momma's expression. They'd yet to speak of it, so May still didn't know the details, but Momma also faced a similar decision long ago. May wasn't going to strain the weak woman with a painful conversation. She certainly felt more empathy for Momma after finding herself in a similar situation.

"I'll let you rest," May said.

Momma looked relieved. This short conversation already tired her out.

"I'm going to ask the Chinese herbalist to come," May said.

Momma shook her head. "It is unproven and too much money."

"Leonardo is certain it cured his father," May said. "Elena and Peter wouldn't have passed on the suggestion if they didn't believe it as well. Please, Momma. If the roles were reversed you know you would call him for me or Nana Lisbeth, despite the expense."

Momma stared at May. She blinked a few times. Then finally gave a single nod.

Relieved, May nodded back. "Thank you, Momma. We *have* to know we tried everything." May's voice broke. Slowly losing her mother to this horrid disease was a constant arrow in her chest. *Consumption* was an accurate and vivid description of tuberculosis. Each day tiny bits of her mother were being used up without being replenished.

CHAPTER 17

MAY

June 1917

Kay Lynn sat up in the pram as they strolled the four blocks to Idora Park. John was already waiting for them by the entrance on Fifty-Sixth Street. He watched them approach, a bouquet of flowers in his hand. May's heart leapt. Despite his abandonment, she still felt a familiar tug toward him. Her gut told her to be wary of a man who could cast her aside so easily. Her mind was not as certain as either her heart or her gut. Was he hoping for marriage? If so, marrying John was practical, but only a wise choice if he treasured Kay Lynn.

"Thank you for coming," he said as he handed her the flowers. He didn't repeat the mistake of attempting to kiss her cheek.

John reached into his pockets and pulled out a shiny silver rattle and a tiny teddy bear. He arched an eyebrow in question. May nodded and he offered them to Kay Lynn. The girl pulled her face inward, looking scared or perhaps skeptical. She looked at May.

"It's okay," May reassured. "You can take them."

Kay Lynn looked back and forth between the presents and John. She took the rattle in her right hand.

He shook the teddy bear. "This too."

Kay Lynn put the rattle down and reached for the stuffed toy. Her right hand grasping it and her left fist balancing it, she hugged it close.

"She likes it," May remarked with a smile.

John was staring at Kay Lynn's twisted left arm. He shook his head clear and looked up at May.

"I'm so glad. The rattle is from my mother. I chose the bear."

Surprised, May questioned him. "Your *mother* knows about Kay Lynn?"

"Yes. Of course. She very much wants to meet her grandchild," he said.

Her grandchild. Those words rankled May. Mrs. Barrow hadn't earned the right to be Kay Lynn's grandmother. She shook off her annoyance and pasted on a smile. Irritation passed over John's features, but he also put on a calm face and gestured toward the park.

"Shall we?" he directed.

"Let's go see the carousel," May said to Kay Lynn in a singsong voice, feigning a delight she wished she felt.

The rest of the afternoon didn't raise such complicated feelings. John made a point of engaging with Kay Lynn, but he did not press himself upon her. The girl slowly warmed to him and was most excited by her first taste of vanilla ice cream. May believed he was earnest in his attempt to make amends, and she strove to set her hurt to one side, determined to give him a fair chance.

He walked them home, but didn't ask to come in. That was just as well. May was not yet ready to have him face Nana Lisbeth.

"My mother wants us to come to supper next Saturday," he said.

She rankled at the assumption that she would be willing.

It must have shown because John apologized.

"I'm sorry. Would you do us the honor of having supper with my parents next Saturday? You . . . and Kay Lynn. As I mentioned, Mother very much wants to meet her granddaughter."

"Have you told her . . . ? Does she know about Kay Lynn's handicaps?" May challenged.

John shook his head.

May sighed. "You tell her and then see if she still wants to meet her granddaughter."

"But you will, if she wants to?" He looked desperate.

May stared at John. Was she being put on display, again? Would Kay Lynn pass his family test? Rather than clarifying her path, today muddied it further. Her heart, head, and gut could not agree on his intentions or devotion.

May asked him, "John, what do you want?"

"Isn't it obvious?" he replied. "I want us to be a family. A proper family!"

"Truly?" she asked.

"Please?" John pleaded. He welled up. "I made a terrible, immature mistake. I panicked at the responsibility. But I was wrong. I deeply regret my actions. It will be the worst error of my life if we cannot be a family. You must forgive me."

Her heart softened and her eyes stung. She shut them hard and took a deep breath. He was saying everything she wished to hear, but she hesitated to agree—out of a schoolgirl desire to punish him or a mother's instinct to protect her daughter? She could not be certain. It would not be harmful to give her head and her heart more time to come to a clear decision.

"Speak to your mother. If she wants us to come, we will," May said.

Relief and a smile spread across his face. "Thank you. May, you won't regret this. We can continue where we left off, pretend this year did not happen."

"Nearly two years," May corrected him.

"Yes, two years," he agreed. "We can go on with our dream of a life together."

She nodded. "Goodbye."

He grabbed her hand and stared right into her eyes. "Thank you for a lovely day. See you next week. Goodbye."

Only once she was inside did she realize he didn't say goodbye to Kay Lynn.

A week later she and Kay Lynn were heading to the Barrows' home for lunch. As May requested, John had made a full disclosure to his mother. Kay Lynn's handicaps didn't diminish Mrs. Barrow's enthusiasm for meeting her granddaughter.

May's attitude was as muddled as ever. Uncertainty about the best course ahead was her companion as they ferried across the bay. The sun glistened on the water and the sky was bright blue. A touch of fog rose above the hills to the west, but it didn't yet chill the air over them. May never tired of the view coming into San Francisco. Kay Lynn seemed to be equally mesmerized by the journey.

John waved to them from the dock at the Ferry Building. He looked eager, young . . . and handsome. She'd matured in the two years while he still seemed youthful.

He flagged down a motor taxi so casually that it must be a common means of transportation for him. It was too dear for May and Kay Lynn to ride in an automobile. She didn't know anyone who had purchased one yet, though Uncle Sam and Aunt Diana bought a motortruck for the produce market.

Mrs. Barrow greeted her with a warm and enthusiastic hug in the living room. She teared up at Kay Lynn, cupping her cheek and saying, "Hello, precious darling."

She looked at May. "I wish to scoop her up, but I know the dangers of that move at this age." Her voice broke. "I'm sorry she does not know me already, but we have time to make up for that now, don't we?"

Mrs. Barrow turned to her son. "Hello, Jonathon."

May noted the lack of warmth. Apparently, Mrs. Barrow had yet to forgive him either.

Mr. Barrow greeted his son with a handshake, but only nodded with an odd expression at May and Kay Lynn. Any warmth from the Barrows would not come from him.

Over a plate of roast beef and mashed potatoes, they discussed the news of the day. Mr. Barrow quizzed John about his upcoming semester and the politics of the department. Toward the end of the meal Mrs. Barrow focused her attention on May and Kay Lynn, who sat in a high chair between them.

"What have your doctors told you about her condition? She does not seem too impaired."

May was surprised, but relieved, to have a frank conversation.

"When she was born the doctor declared she would have more seizures, but I have not seen one. I don't know if she classifies as an epileptic."

"She feeds herself," Mrs. Barrow noted.

"Oh, yes," May replied. "Her right hand does everything typically. Her left . . ." May shrugged.

"Up," Kay Lynn said, and she pulled at the fabric on her chest.

May stood up and pulled Kay Lynn out of the high chair.

"She can speak!" the older woman declared.

May laughed. "She gets her point across with very few words. *Up* means either pick me up or put me down."

"Why did she pull at her dress?"

May thought. "Oh! That means she's done eating . . . for taking off her bib, I think. She started doing it so long ago that I forget it's unique."

"She is a clever girl, not an imbecile at all!" Mrs. Barrow declared.

May hugged her daughter and kissed the top of her head. "Yes, she is."

"May I show you something?" Mrs. Barrow's eyes shined as she asked.

May nodded. The older woman left the men at the table and led May and Kay Lynn up the grand staircase to the second floor. She turned into a bedroom set up with a bed and a crib, toys and a rocker.

"This room is for her . . . and you. We will get her appointments with the best doctors in San Francisco. You can stay here when you are not in Marin. You and she will be a treasured part of our family," Mrs. Barrow said.

Surprised, and touched, by the intimate and generous invitation, she considered how to reply.

Before she'd mustered a response, Kay Lynn declared, "Up."

May put her down on the beautiful red Persian rug. She scooched right to the basket of toys, one arm and leg pulling along the other side as she sat on her bottom.

"She's so fast, though she looks a bit like a crab, doesn't she?"

May nodded.

Kay Lynn returned with a small doll, pulled herself up with May's skirt, and offered the toy to her mother.

"Thank you." May smiled at her daughter and took the toy. She walked to the bed and sat down, leaving Kay Lynn standing in the middle of the rug.

"She can walk?" Mrs. Barrow asked.

"While holding a hand," May explained. "She may need a brace or crutches to walk on her own. We will only know with time. So far her left hand isn't as dexterous as her right, but it helps. Her left side is weaker in general. That is the only way she seems different at the moment."

Mrs. Barrow spoke, confusion in her voice. "When John said she was nearly sent to the Napa home for imbeciles, I expected her to be, well . . ." Mrs. Barrow bit her lower lip. "I thought she would be less . . . developed, but she is as bright and delightful as any one-year-old I have ever met."

May looked at her precious Kay Lynn. She was the greatest delight to May, but for Mrs. Barrow to see that she was a treasure was immensely satisfying. May wondered how much to share with this woman, who was virtually a stranger, and yet could be a most important person in their lives.

"Sometimes I hug her close or smile at her across the room and my heart explodes at the notion she was nearly sent away . . . to live in those conditions." May shook her head to clear it of the thought.

"You have mothered her well," Mrs. Barrow declared.

May's chest caught at the compliment. "Thank you."

Mrs. Barrow offered a finger to Kay Lynn. The little girl scowled. She looked at May. May nodded her approval. Kay Lynn reached for the finger and toddled to the toy basket. Dropping down in front of it, she pulled out a ball and gave it to Mrs. Barrow with a charming smile.

Mrs. Barrow looked at May, tears glistening in her eyes. "My son made a terrible mistake. He told us nothing of it until a few weeks ago. I assure you we gave him our blessing to marry you two years ago, as well."

May hid the complex jumble of feelings Mrs. Barrow's statement raised. She had wondered if John had broken things off with her because his parent disapproved. She didn't know what hurt more, the idea that he capitulated to their demands—or his own lack of devotion to her.

As well hung in the air. John had not proposed marriage, but clearly his mother believed he had.

"She, and you, will have everything you need. For life," Mrs. Barrow rushed out.

May was hearing exactly what she'd thought she wanted. Security and a warm welcome should be what she desired, but even so, her heart didn't delight at these words.

"Thank you," May replied. "But the decision to marry is between John and me."

May didn't want to sound ungrateful or unkind, but she needed to be honest.

Mrs. Barrow nodded. "I understand. It's only . . ." Her eyes welled up. "Somehow, I love her already."

She smiled through tears. May believed her. She thought of her own mother, sick in bed, her future uncertain. Momma loved Kay Lynn immediately. As did May and Nana Lisbeth. If she and John had been married, Mrs. Barrow would have loved her all along too.

The older woman continued, "It's peculiar, but true. Her smile is quite like my Anne's when she was a baby." Mrs. Barrow raised the ghost of her daughter who died when John was ten years old. "This was her room." Her voice broke as she welled up with emotion.

May nodded and smoothed the comforter. Perhaps Anne slept under it. May looked at Kay Lynn, silky baby curls still swirled around her head. Simply imagining her death was an arrow to May's heart.

Kay Lynn grinned at her mother, pointed to the dolls in May's lap, and said, "Baby?"

Then she chomped her teeth with the sound she made for food and waved a toy spoon fisted in her hand.

"Yes, the baby is hungry," May said to her daughter. "Can you give her something to eat?"

Gripping the toy spoon, Kay Lynn walked three steps toward May and the baby doll.

"She did it!" May exclaimed. A surge of pride brought tears to her eyes. She looked at Mrs. Barrow. "Her first steps without assistance."

Mrs. Barrow clapped. "She approves of this room, I think."

Kay Lynn brought the spoon to the doll's lips. May wrapped her arm around her daughter and squeezed.

It seemed unfair that Mrs. Barrow was here for this eventful moment rather than Momma and Nana Lisbeth, who'd loved and supported them from the beginning.

Momma would get to see Kay Lynn walk, but what about all that came after? How long would Momma be ill, and when it was over would she be well or leave May forever? The pressure to entirely change their lives was overwhelming. She'd expected to be gratified by the sentiment to join John's family, but she only felt confused and irritated.

"My mother is utterly charmed by Kay Lynn," John said as they walked downhill to the Ferry Building. "I'm sure she told you."

"She did."

"She would like us to get married in their back garden, but I think we may want to do it in Marin," he said.

"I haven't agreed to marry you," she declared, fury in her voice at his presumption.

He stopped walking. "Of course." He looked at the ground. "I meant, should we get married, which I would like very much."

She let the silence be as they walked.

"I am Kay Lynn's father," John said, his voice a little heated. "Do you want her to grow up without a father as you did?"

May sucked in a breath. John didn't know that her father returned last year, very much alive, and then disappeared as soon as he got what he came for. John asked nothing about her life in the past two years. It seemed he wanted to pretend there was no breach.

He stopped suddenly. "Am I on her certificate of birth?"

"Yes," May replied.

He nodded with a small smile and stared off into the distance.

"What is her legal name?"

May let out a deep breath. "Kay Lynn Elizabeth Wagner."

A cloud of anger blew a shadow across his face. Then sorrow. "We can get that remedied," he stated.

She nodded, still confused about what she wanted, what was best for Kay Lynn, or what to say to this person who seemed more like a boy than a man.

"Will you please come to Marin? See my home . . . potentially our home." He looked adequately uncertain. Perhaps he realized he needed to court May in earnest. "On Saturday?"

"I work on Saturday."

"Sunday?"

"I have a family gathering at Elena's," she said.

"How are they?" he asked.

"Well," May replied. "She's pregnant with their second child, due in the fall."

"I always liked Elena and Peter," he said. "Salt of the earth." He stared off again, and then returned to his request: "When will you come to Marin?"

"I am off on Tuesday. Does that suit you?"

"I will make it so"—he smiled—"for you."

He was charming.

"You can stop working the moment we are engaged," he said. "I will take care of you and Kay Lynn from now on."

And my mother and Nana Lisbeth? she wondered. She wasn't ready to tell him that she was supporting the whole family since Momma fell ill.

He paid for her fare across the bay and waved to them as they floated back to Oakland.

On Sunday, after church, May sat on a couch in the living room at Peter and Elena's. Kay Lynn toddled away from her, a little rabbit in her right fist. She had abandoned her crab crawl entirely since those steps at the Barrows' a week ago. That day of firsts was also a last. May was struck by how often she was unaware of an ending while it was happening.

Kay Lynn finished her journey at Leonardo's knee. She offered him the rabbit, which he happily accepted. He picked her up and walked to May. Kay Lynn pointed, as if she were steering the way with her little pointer finger.

"Thank you," May said, and he sat beside her on the couch.

They were at Elena and Peter's for a birthday celebration . . . and a farewell party. Many of these young men had no choice except shipping off to war soon. Including Leonardo. The draft was turning lives upside down. May was glad to have an opportunity to speak with him . . . and wish him well. Kay Lynn stayed on his lap.

"She still likes you." May smiled.

"And I still like her," he replied with the sweetest smile. Then his face transformed into one of concern. "How is your mother?"

"You are kind to ask." He truly was a most thoughtful man. She considered her answer. "It's difficult to know. Some days she seems to be better. Others just the same."

"We can be grateful she's not worse, yes?" he inquired.

She nodded.

"Elena passed on my recommendation of Dr. Chan, right? He comes to your home. His needles are very small and don't hurt, despite the odd appearance. He also prescribed herbs. I'm confident he cured my father."

May nodded. "He's coming tomorrow to give her a treatment. We are willing to try almost anything at this point."

"Lenny!" Peter called from across the room.

"I'm being summoned," he said with a regretful smile.

"Lenny?" she repeated. "You go by Lenny now?"

"Leonardo Stephanopolis was turned down repeatedly," he explained. "Once Lenny Stevens applied for a job I got one almost immediately."

"That's unfair—being Greek should not interfere with your employment."

"Fair or not, it did." He shrugged. "I'm glad there was a simple solution for it. I don't mind being Lenny. Leonardo is a mouthful."

He set Kay Lynn on the couch, rubbed her curls, and walked away.

"Leo . . . Lenny," May called to him.

He turned back, his eyebrow rose in curiosity.

"I will hold you in my prayers. Every night," she said. Surprisingly, her voice broke. "Stay safe. Please."

His lips pulled into a sad smile. Looking at her intently, he nodded. Then he shrugged. "I wasn't going to stay safe, but since you asked, okay," he teased. She returned a bittersweet smile.

Leonardo was about to face the unfathomable. He didn't know where he would be sent or what horrors he might see, or commit. A shiver traveled down May's spine. She resisted the urge to flinch, to shake it off, until he'd turned around.

Elena walked up to May asking a question before she even sat down. "How did your visit to *Nob Hill* go?" She drew out the words to emphasize the posh neighborhood.

May leaned over Elena's belly. "Hello, baby," she sang to the little one.

Elena laughed and rubbed the spot over her womb.

"Well?" her cousin asked.

May seesawed her head from side to side as she pondered the question. "If I told you every detail you would think it went well. Mrs. Barrow was warm and thoughtful. She placed a high chair between the two of us and virtually ignored the men at the other end of the table. John seemed an outcast in his childhood home. Over lunch she made it clear they gave their blessing to marry me two years ago, that her son made a terrible mistake, and she was horrified when she found out he abandoned me even after learning I was carrying his child. She has set up a nursery for Kay Lynn and was delighted by her in all the ways you would want for a grandmother."

"That sounds encouraging," Elena said. "What is your concern?"

May sighed. "John wants me to see his home in Marin. He told me once we are engaged I can stop working and we can be married very quickly."

Elena kept listening, encouraging May to keep talking.

"He doesn't know Momma is sick. Or that I am the sole source of income for my family."

Elena drew her eyebrows in. "Why haven't you told him?"

"He hasn't asked, but I haven't offered the information either. I do not trust that he will agree to take care of Momma and Nana Lisbeth."

"What will you do if he won't?"

"I don't know." May shook her head. "Mrs. Barrow was utterly charmed by Kay Lynn. She offered to take her to a physiotherapist—to get her anything she needs. John does not seem to have given her much thought, though that is common for fathers, right?"

"Yes. Especially with daughters; especially when they are so young," Elena agreed. "You seem so doubtful, not excited at all."

"I do not trust him," May confessed, and she welled up, "but he is Kay Lynn's father. I don't know what to do."

"It has just been a few weeks since he reached out to you. Perhaps in time he can prove himself," Elena said. "When do you have to decide?"

"Soon. Never. I do not know."

"What will be best for Kay Lynn?"

"I wish I knew."

"And for you?" Her cousin asked with such tenderness that May teared up again.

May shook her head. A few years ago she was so certain John would be her perfect husband, and a great father. Now she believed they would be provided for, and be warmly welcomed by his mother, but she did not trust John. What was more foolish: marrying him or rejecting the security he could provide?

"I don't know that either," May told her cousin.

CHAPTER 18

NAOMI

June 1917

"Look at you, sons!" Willie appeared as if he would burst with pride.

Joseph and Cedric grinned as they showed off their new uniforms in the living room: Joseph in the Twenty-Fourth Infantry's tan; Cedric in the Tenth Cavalry's khaki. Willie was confident that enlisting right away in these well-respected, long-established colored units was better than waiting to be drafted into newly formed units without a history of courage and honor. Joseph couldn't be happier to have his childhood dream of being a buffalo soldier realized.

Naomi wasn't as certain this would be an excellent opportunity for their sons. She feared Joseph's dream would soon become a nightmare. For him and Cedric. She swallowed back her nausea and exhaled hard. She pasted on a smile, but her distress was obvious for all to see.

"Let's go," she declared, grabbing her purse and heading toward the door.

They were all well dressed for a family photo at a studio. Afterward they would attend the reception for the colored troops that Mrs. Tilghman organized at the Fifteenth Street AME church.

There would be flag waving, speeches, and celebrating, but Naomi didn't share any part of the excitement. She only felt dread and fear.

Joseph was being sent to Houston to patrol the border. The protests of the NAACP did nothing to change the government's decision to station the Twenty-Fourth Infantry in a former slave state. The army insisted the local citizens and police were going to respect the United States uniform, if not the man wearing it, but Naomi doubted the colored troops would be given the regard they deserved.

Cedric would be in Nogales, Arizona—also patrolling the Mexico border. Naomi didn't know enough about the desert city to feel assured of his treatment, but she feared it less than Houston with its history of mistreating colored people. However, Naomi's fears were irrelevant in this moment. Her sons were swept up in the patriotism of this time. Many colored people argued this war was an opportunity to advance their cause by demonstrating devotion to their nation.

A week later Naomi returned to the photography studio. She stood at the counter staring at the framed picture of her family. She was seated on a bench between Gramma Jordan and Willie. Cedric, Joseph, and Maggie stood behind them. All six faces had smiles, but she saw the fear in her own eyes. She'd tried to hide it, but it was obvious to anyone who looked carefully.

"Thank you," she said to the young Negro man, grateful he'd captured their family before the moment of upheaval.

He placed two more on the counter: two small prints of the same image. One for each son. She paid and went next door to finish her errands. As she walked in she saw a display of what she'd come for: pocket Bibles. She took two, leaving just three on the large table.

"These are selling quickly," the elegant saleswoman said. "What divisions?"

"Twenty-Fourth Infantry and Tenth Cavalry," Naomi replied to the now-familiar question.

"My son, James Dellums, will be in the Twenty-Fourth too," she said. "He's proud to be a buffalo soldier. Maybe they will watch out for each other—two Oakland boys, far from home."

"I'll tell my son Joseph Smith to look for your James," Naomi agreed.

She and this woman were bound in a club she never wanted to join.

Naomi came home to an empty house. She set the gold-framed image on the dining room table. One of the boys could hang it on the wall so Cedric and Joseph would be included in their family dinners no matter how far away they were. She wrote on the back of the small photos the words she'd been perfecting for days:

> *Take my love and the Lord's blessing*
> *with you wherever you go—for they*
> *are unwavering.*
> *And come home soon.*
>   *Your Ma*
> *PS. Do not equate kindness*
> *with weakness.*

She slipped a photo in each Bible, placed one on each of their pillows, and went into the kitchen to cook the last supper she could be certain they would share. She forced herself to take slow, steady breaths. The pain in her chest was only going to become worse. Tomorrow she would be forced to bear a new and greater burden of fear and sorrow.

Willie, Maggie, Cedric, and Joseph were already out the front door, ready to leave for the train station. Naomi fled upstairs, her heart racing in panic.

"You have to go without me," she told her mother.

Gramma Jordan argued, "Naomi, you have to be there."

"I can't; I will break down on that platform."

"You will hold my hand and squeeze as hard as you must, but your sons will see your face as they depart from home."

"I don't—"

Gramma Jordan interrupted. "You will regret it for the rest of your life if you are not there. You may have your breakdown once we return home."

Naomi considered her mother's words. *Regret.* If they never returned she'd know she missed her last minutes to be with her sons. She nodded and walked out the door of her mother's flat.

Cedric and Joseph looked handsome and mature in their uniforms, but still too young to be heading to war.

"You have your Bibles?" Naomi asked.

The boys, young men, nodded in unison. Joseph slid his finger into his breast pocket and pulled the top of it for her to see.

Cedric looked her in the eyes and said, "It's right here, Ma. Right over my heart."

Naomi swallowed hard and gave him a tight smile, grateful that her love and the Lord's words would be right there with him.

There was nothing else to say on the long journey to the train station. Maggie sat on one side, their arms linked. As promised Gramma Jordan held her other hand. Every once in a while Willie looked at her, nodding his assurance and respect. He saw her pain. But she was pushing past her despair, sending her sons off in love.

The station was packed with colored faces, young men in uniforms surrounded by family of all ages and hues. The men would go to Chicago and disperse for their training to Camp Funston in

Kansas, Camp Logan in Texas, or elsewhere. The boys, carrying identical duffel bags and similar uniforms, had become soldiers, no longer individuals.

The four of them made a circle around Joseph and Cedric. They each placed a hand on the young men. Naomi breathed in the warmth and energy of her beloved sons, and breathed out love into each of them.

Willie's voice was low but clear as he prayed:

"Dear Lord, watch over our precious sons. Keep them safe from enemies foreign and domestic. Help them to always have honor and dignity. Return them to us strong in body and spirit. In your name we pray. Amen."

Naomi's amen was in her head, her throat too tight to say a word. She hugged Cedric, then placed her hand on his cheek like he was a boy. *Bless you,* she mouthed. *I love you.* He stared right into her eyes, his sorrow matching hers.

"I love you too, Ma. Always. I'll be home before you know it." And then he moved on.

Joseph said, "Bye, Ma. I love you too!"

They hugged. He broke away, ready to go, looking more excited than was wise given what he was about to face. She held onto his arm.

He hadn't been on his own in the world or experienced the overt hatred that could cost him his life. She stared into his eyes, searching for words to keep her youngest son safe.

He interpreted her silence. "I will, Ma." His eyes shiny, he continued, "I'll think of you every day and ask myself what will make you and Pops proud."

And then both her sons were gone. Maggie remained on her right. Gramma Jordan on her left. Willie's hands rested on her shoulders, his cheek nestled against her head. Her remaining family a fortress around her, keeping her upright.

She searched the windows of the train. Surely Cedric and Joseph would join the boys waving out the portals. Up and down the cars she studied the young faces. Excitement was the overriding expression, though she saw sorrow too. Would she recognize her own sons now that they were made into soldiers? What if they were too far from each other for her to see them both?

Her heart raced and she swallowed against the boulder in her throat.

"There's Joseph!" Maggie pointed to the left toward the front of the train. Naomi hunted until she found him. His big smile lit up his face as he frantically waved. She raised her hand back in farewell. The train jerked. It was starting to go.

"Cedric?!" she exclaimed.

Shouts filled the air. It was so loud she could not hear Maggie right next to her. Naomi searched up and down the train while she continued waving, desperately wanting Cedric to see her wishing him goodbye. When she looked back at Joseph he was already gone. She scanned further down the track but could not make him out. She stared as the windows slowly moved past her, waving at the mass of boys, hoping to make out Cedric's face.

"Ceddie!" Maggie screamed.

There! Peeking out between the waving arms of his comrades were her son's sweet, brown eyes. She teared up and mouthed, *God bless you.* His eyes crinkled. Message received. She exhaled and watched his face disappear from sight like a leaf floating down a river.

"You can let it out now," Gramma Jordan said once they were home.

But somehow the fear and anger were so large Naomi didn't have tears. The wall she put up around her heart held fast. She shook her head.

"Shall we work in the garden?"

Naomi considered. Her spirit was exhausted; she longed to lie down, but she thought better of it and nodded at her mother. Taking to bed was not going to bring her sons back.

They were weeding around the tomatoes when Maggie shouted from the back porch. Mr. Butler was calling for her on Mr. Washington's phone.

Naomi exchanged a confused glance with her mother and walked down the block alone. It was foolish to fear there could possibly be bad news about her sons only a few hours after they'd departed, but still she pictured a derailed train or an outbreak of scarlet fever.

Mr. Butler's voice came through the line. "I wanted you to know about our success on this challenging day."

Naomi nodded, relief rushing through her.

"Father Wallace got a stay on the vote at the city council meeting," the man's deep voice declared. "Your home is safe."

Puzzled, Naomi thought until she remembered what he was speaking about. The Santa Fe Improvement Club's resolution on segregation was on the council agenda today. It was a pressing issue in her heart, but concern for her sons and their departure overshadowed it so entirely that she forgot this was the day they were taking up the question.

She replied, "Thank the Lord. That *is* wonderful. I appreciate you calling to let me know."

He continued, "Thank you and congratulations. Your good work is paying off."

"*Our* good work," she replied. "Please give him my gratitude."

"I will indeed," Mr. Butler replied. "See you at our next meeting if not before. Mrs. Tilghman wants us to take up supporting the colored troops as a regular agenda item."

"I agree," Naomi said. "We have to see that they are treated with dignity and respect—in Oakland as well as afar."

Naomi stopped in front of their house for a moment of gratitude. *Thank you, Lord, for protecting our home.* It would be here to welcome her Cedric and her Joseph when they returned. She went inside and into the dining room to the family photo.

She stood at the image, her palms out in a blessing, one directed at Joseph's precious face and the other at Cedric's. Naomi closed her eyes and prayed hard:

Dear Lord, watch over my sons. Place my love directly into their hearts that they may know their mother is praying for them and waiting for their safe return. Amen.

She opened her eyes and looked at their images—so grown up and yet somehow her babies too.

Her knees gave out and she let herself sink to the floor. Fear and sorrow exploded the wall in her chest and she let her tears flow. There was nothing she could do to protect her sons but pray.

They are in your hands, Lord. They are in your hands.

Her tears ran out, and she wiped her eyes. She found Willie and then her mother to deliver the good news. Together they could celebrate the joy set in the middle of this painful day. They'd saved their home on the day their sons were leaving to fight for their country.

CHAPTER 19

MAY

July 1917

"Sit with me," Nana Lisbeth directed.

May joined her grandmother at the dining room table.

"You are troubled?" Nana Lisbeth proclaimed, more of a statement than a question.

May nodded.

"About John returning to your life?" Nana Lisbeth confirmed.

May nodded again. Tears stung her eyes, and she blinked them away. For days she'd seesawed back and forth. Each time she landed on a decision she questioned it.

May replied, "Two years ago he was everything I ever dreamed of; it seemed the height of sophistication to marry a college professor."

"And now?" Nana Lisbeth wondered.

"I'm a jumble of uncertainty," May replied. "How can I know less when I've lived more?"

Kay Lynn toddled to her and raised her arms, wordlessly asking to climb onto her mother's lap. May smiled at her daughter and lifted her into her arms. She kissed the top of the little girl's head and rubbed her silky hair.

"You are asking yourself what is best for her?" Nana Lisbeth suggested.

May nodded. "How do I know? Marin is supposed to be lovely—country living near the city. It used to seem close to Oakland. But with Momma sick, it's too far. She might not . . ." May left the unthinkable sentiment unsaid, but her heart clenched tight at the thought of her mother's death. It was too much to bear.

"You make the best choice for you and Kay Lynn," Nana Lisbeth declared. "Your mother and I will be fine with whatever happens. Do you understand?"

May nodded but that didn't suddenly give her clarity. "I wish someone else could make this decision for me—and Kay Lynn."

"There are some choices we can only make for ourselves. And we make them without fully understanding the repercussions. I find when I sit quietly in prayer, there is a still, small voice that tells me what I truly want. Not what I should want, but somehow the right choice for me. Learn to trust that voice," Nana Lisbeth said.

"Do you think that is God talking?" May asked.

Nana Lisbeth shrugged. "I'm enough of a Unitarian that I'm not certain—nor do I care. Is it my own intuition? Is it the voice of God? As you just said, the more I've lived the less certain I've become. Does it matter what we call it? In another language or religion it has a different name, but I have learned to rely on it, whatever it is."

"I have agreed to visit San Rafael on Tuesday. At least I can see Marin County and my future home before I decide," May said. Her heart clenched. "You would never move there, would you?"

Nana Lisbeth sighed. "I will visit you and Kay Lynn." She smiled at her great-granddaughter. "But no, I would not move across the bay, so far from home, but that doesn't mean it's a mistake for you."

"But Momma . . . ," May questioned.

"When she's better, your Momma might join you," Nana Lisbeth said.

"But . . ."

"Diana will come. She has told me she will move here anytime we ask. Others can cover her work at the produce market."

May nodded. Of course her Aunt Diana would do whatever was necessary to take care of family.

Nana Lisbeth said, "I believe you need to have another conversation before you make a final decision."

May pulled in her eyebrows in a silent question.

"Your mother," Nana Lisbeth said. "Talk to Sadie. She had a terrible choice that affected your entire life's course. Hear her out before you make this decision on Kay Lynn's behalf."

May's heart raced. Nana Lisbeth was right, but she was scared about what she might learn. Would it reflect badly on her mother, her father, or both of them?

The pungent, earthy aroma from the warm cup of tea in May's hand filled her nostrils even with a mask on. The Chinese herbalist had left a pouch filled with roots, bark, and pods after he treated Momma a few days before. They simmered the dark mixture in water, filling the house with this smell. Momma said it tasted horrid, but they told themselves her cough was improved, though it was difficult to know for certain. Momma wasn't suddenly healed, but they still had hope it would cure her.

The open windows in the sickroom allowed in fresh air, the best remedy known to modern medicine. May set the cup on the bedside table and took Momma's thin elbow to help her sit up. A coughing fit bent the sick woman forward. May rubbed her back, to comfort her soul and perhaps calm her lungs. When the fit stopped, Momma rested against the pillows and May sat on the edge of the mattress.

"Momma, will you tell me the story"—May's voice shook as she asked—"about my father?"

May saw her mother take in a shaky breath. Her mother nodded and held up a hand. She wasn't ready to talk—from the illness or perhaps a reluctance to tell May the truth.

Eventually she spoke in a raspy voice. "He had a temper. If I ever crossed him he stopped talking to me."

May's eyes watered and Momma stopped talking.

"Keep going," May insisted.

"He tried to keep me away from my family. On occasion he would hit me," Momma said, her voice even quieter.

May leaned in to listen, her chest clenched in dismay.

"After every anger fit, he would apologize. He always had an explanation and he insisted it would not happen again, but it did.

"I thought I simply needed to be kinder, more patient, more compliant. I could accept how he treated me." Momma looked at May. She blinked her eyes and then hung her head. It seemed she was gathering her strength to say more.

"The day he turned against you . . ." Momma's eyes got hard and she shook her head. "One day he held you out a second-story window, threatening to drop you if I didn't obey him immediately. You were not yet a year old."

May's throat closed tight and her eyes opened wide. She swallowed hard.

"You know that I avoid Twelfth Street near Sam and Diana's? I can point to the window where it happened. He was crazed, demanding that we move to Hawaii, where you and I would be trapped by him— even though the journey there was a risk to your health because you were so premature."

Stunned, the horrific image of her own father holding her out of a window filled May's imagination; she pushed it out of her mind.

"For years I lived in terror he would return to take you from me," Momma whispered so quietly that May had to lean in to hear her. "When he didn't come back or write, I despaired that he did not care to see you again."

Silence filled the room. May sat upright to study her Momma's face.

"I never found the strength to tell you," Momma confessed, "though I always believed it was your right to know. What is the correct age to tell a little girl her father threatened to kill her? How was I supposed to inform you that your father abandoned you and never, not once, sent a letter asking about you? It was too easy to imagine your confusion and sorrow, and painfully difficult to contemplate disturbing you."

Momma fell silent, panting from the exertion of speaking so much. May watched the gingham curtain flutter in the breeze. Her chest held back an explosion of feelings. Momma was right, this was devastating. In her imagination he'd been perfect, exactly what she desired in a father at any moment.

"I took the coward's way." Momma's voice was weak. "Please believe me when I say I did it out of love and as a kindness."

May's eyes welled up.

Momma's bird-thin hand rested on her arm. "Can you forgive me?"

"Yes, I can," May replied. "I already have." And she meant it. Losing the idea of her father had ceased to be important after facing the very real possibility of losing her actual mother.

"Truly?" Momma asked, yearning on her face.

"Momma," May explained, "my situation, with John and Kay Lynn, has taught me that life is not as simple as I'd hoped. Hard times call for hard choices. How can I fault you for Heinrich's decisions?"

May took in a deep breath and said, "Momma. I'm so sorry you . . . I can't even imagine. The terror."

Momma nodded. She closed her eyes. "Sometimes the image intrudes and I see you falling from his hands." Momma bit her lip.

May took her Momma's hand. "I didn't; you protected me."

Momma nodded.

"Thank you," May said to her Momma, tears in both of their eyes. "For saving me. And for telling me the story."

A newfound respect for her mother's strength rose in May. Momma *had* fought to protect her daughter. May would as well. She didn't yet know their best future, but she'd see what John was offering before deciding their fate.

CHAPTER 20

NAOMI

August 1917

The house was dark and quiet by the time Naomi returned from work. As it went with babies, she was never certain if she would return by six for supper or late into the night, like today.

She was exhausted and jittery, the strange combination that seemed to accompany those precarious labors that might end in a death. When the baby finally emerged he was blue and flaccid—not able to take a breath on his own. Naomi's forceful exhalations right into his mouth eventually revived him. He might be slow for the rest of his life. Or his entry into the world might not leave a mark on him. Only time would tell.

Her stamina wasn't helped by the fact that sleep was getting harder and harder to come by. Heat waves from the change of life woke her even on cold, foggy nights. Once she was awake she fretted about her sons' well-being. Letters from Joseph and Cedric were of little comfort. Much could have changed between the time they wrote and when she read their words.

Naomi turned to prayers, but they weren't always effective in relieving her burden. Gramma Jordan told her the change of life could go on for years. She'd have to learn to live with this somehow, but it seemed an unfair burden to face such an intrusive internal disruption in a time of family crisis.

Naomi smiled at the plate covered with a blue cloth napkin. Maggie had made sure she would come home to a good meal.

She unpinned the scarlet carnation from her uniform and placed it in the food scrap bin. It would be put on the pile outside and in time turn into nutrition for their garden. Like many mothers with a son in the war, Naomi pinned a scarlet carnation to her clothes each morning to broadcast her pride and fear.

She looked out the window as she washed up. It was a clear night, not something she could count on in August. She wished on the three stars that made up the handle of the Big Dipper: *Keep Cedric and Joseph safe; Keep Cedric and Joseph safe; Keep Cedric and Joseph safe.*

The evening paper sat unopened next to the plate. Willie was away for work and Maggie didn't read it as she found the news depressing. Every day Naomi pored through the paper looking for names of dead and wounded soldiers stationed around the world, a terrifying and heartbreaking ritual. She began with a prayer that her sons would not be named and ended it by sending a blessing to the young men who were in the paper and their loved ones.

She also scanned every page, looking for any hints about the Negro troops. Most often she was rewarded with a sentence or two that told her where her sons were stationed or about their mission guarding the border with Mexico.

Naomi carried her plate and the newspaper to the dining room to eat with Joseph and Cedric. She opened the paper and her heart stopped cold at the headline.

RIOTING NEGRO TROOPS ORDERED FROM TEXAS

Her stomach clenched tight and her lungs contracted.

Dear God, Please protect my son.

She put her fork down and skimmed through the horrid account. The first paragraphs told her nothing about how Joseph might be faring. It explained that the Houston Chamber of Commerce had assured the War Department the Negro troops would be accorded respect, but trouble began on the day they arrived. Sixteen people were dead: thirteen white, one Mexican, and two Negro soldiers. Martial law was in place.

She scanned for one name: *Joseph Smith.* She flipped to page three and kept searching, her heart beating hard. A few names popped out, but not her son's. She breathed out in relief, but then felt a small measure of shame. *God bless the souls of those who died. And send your love to their families.*

She returned to the front page and read more slowly about the simmering conflict the NAACP warned about before the troops arrived in Houston. On the third page, in the second column, she read of the tipping point as recounted by Major K. S. Snow, the commanding officer of the Negro battalion:

> Thursday morning in Houston a police officer arrested a Negro woman and in doing so, I am informed, slapped her face. A soldier of the Twenty-Fourth, who had been drinking, remonstrated with the policeman for what he considers his unnecessary striking of her. The officer then began beating the soldier with his pistol.
>
> The man's face and head were badly cut by the pistol butt. He was arrested by the same officer and taken to the station, where he is now held.

Thursday afternoon, according to a report to me by Corporal Baltimore of my military police force, a soldier of my command was arrested by an officer. Corporal Baltimore, who was nearby wearing his military police badge, asked the policeman, purely for information, he says, about why the man was arrested.

The policeman told him it was none of his business. He then hit Corporal Baltimore on the head with his pistol butt. Corporal Baltimore ran up the street, the policeman firing at him as he fled. He took refuge in a house under a bed. The policeman followed, dragged him out, used further abusive language and struck him twice more with the pistol.

When the men in camp heard of these occurrences Thursday afternoon it excited them greatly and they made open threats of retaliation.

Naomi kept reading, nausea joining her pounding heart as she imagined the fear and pain of the scene. One hundred and fifty men were blamed for the violence. One hundred were arrested; fifty escaped. Was her Joseph one of them?

The pride of young men would be their undoing. They became so certain of their position that they harmed themselves in their own defense. She wanted to believe her Joseph would not have taken out his anger on innocent bystanders, but she knew he was as likely to go along with a crowd as anyone.

Her chin quivered. She heard a sound escape from her own chest. Naomi pressed her hand to her mouth, muffling herself, hoping to tamp down the emotion. She was tired from the long, hard birth and didn't have the reserves to keep her feelings inside. Tears streamed down her face. She surrendered to the overwhelming emotions, letting the sobs come.

She felt a hand on her shoulder. Maggie stood at her side. Naomi pointed at the newspaper. Her daughter read the article, fear and sorrow overtaking her face as she read.

"Oh, Ma. We must pray for Joseph . . . for all of them," Maggie said when she was finished. "He wouldn't have . . . ?"

Naomi shrugged. Her tears had run out. "He would give his life to defend his friends; you know he would."

"His name isn't in the paper," Maggie replied, wanting that to be the evidence Joseph was safe.

"There are two dead colored men and one hundred more arrested. Fifty are on the run. We don't know any of their names."

"What do we do?" Maggie asked.

"We do what too many women are doing right now. We wait and we pray."

Dear God, watch over our sons. I pray Joseph is safe from harm.

Naomi repeated that prayer each time panic rose in her throat. Every few minutes throughout the day she caught herself imagining the worst. She'd take a deep breath, say her prayer, and keep going.

She combed through the paper the next day for any news that could relieve her fears. There was nothing about the Negro troops on the front page. On page eight a letter to the editor stated that due to the mutual animosity between Negroes and whites in the South they should be kept separate.

Fury built in Naomi. There was no recognition of the history borne by Negroes, nor of the obligation of the government to protect the dignity and freedom of the colored men fighting for the United States.

The Sunday paper reported that the men were sent to New Mexico to be court-martialed by the military though twenty-five hundred citizens of Houston signed a petition to the federal government demanding the soldiers not be removed from Houston. At church there were prayers and speculation, but not much more information. Two families received telegrams with the words: I AM FINE. Naomi wished Joseph had the means to send her such reassurances. She longed for a letter from him.

Monday evening she feared she would have an actual fit when she read in the *Tribune* that more colored troops were being sent to Houston.

"Ma," Maggie said gently. "Are you certain it's in your best interest to read the news? It seems to upset you greatly and not offer you any useful information."

Naomi stared at her daughter. Maggie was correct; the news was more upsetting than reassuring, but if her son had to live through this trial, she was strong enough to be aware of it.

A week after she read about the troubles, a letter from Joseph arrived in the mail. Naomi's heart leapt at the sight of her son's bold script. Blood pounded through her temples as she tore open the letter she prayed was written since the conflict. Seven days was barely enough time for a letter to cross the nation.

> *Dear Ma and Pa,*
> *I am fine.*

Naomi closed her eyes, exhaled, and gave praise: *Thank you, Lord. You are great.* She sat at the table, wiped her eyes, and blinked until she could make out the words again.

> *Dear Ma and Pa,*
>
> *I am fine. I cannot say the same for all of my fellow soldiers. I don't have the luxury of going into detail. However, I want you to know the man who was arrested for defending the colored girl is an honorable person. The accounts say he was drunk, but he was not—only outraged at her treatment. He could not stand by and watch the abuse being rained upon her. Corporal Baltimore, the military police officer who inquired about the arrest, is the most fair, measured, and reliable man I have met. He feared for his very life even after he'd returned to our base.*
>
> *I do not condone the response of my fellow soldiers, but I do understand the anger. We have been humiliated and disrespected from the moment we arrived in Houston. Our United States uniforms mean nothing to the white men who are continually "putting us in our place." I thought I understood the depths of contempt for our race, but nothing has prepared me for this.*
>
> *One of the leaders of the rebellion is also named Joseph Smith. Do not fear that I am unsafe should you read his name in the newspaper. I remained at our base on August 24th and I am still here, doing my duty to my country even though it does not return the favor. I am showing the dignity of our race, in spite of the difficulties.*
>
> *As always I remain your dutiful and loving son,*
> *Joseph*
> *PS. Give my love to Gramma Jordan and Maggie.*

Naomi's hand trembled as she placed the letter on the table. She forced herself to take a few shaky breaths. Her body swirled with fury, relief, compassion, and fear. How could they compel her son to stay in a hostile situation in his very own nation? He'd signed up to fight Germans, to defend the ideals of America. And he was being forced to defend his dignity and safety from white Americans.

She folded up the letter, returned it to its envelope, and left it on the table for Willie to read when he came home that night. They would have two days to pray together for their sons, and she would sleep a little easier with him in their bed.

CHAPTER 21

MAY

August 1917

The house in San Rafael was beautiful, everything she and John dreamed of when they were courting. Or when she believed they were. Built in the arts and crafts style she adored, it had dark wood paneling and high coved ceilings. John's eyes shone in delight as he showed her through the four bedrooms and two bathrooms.

"There is room for a larger family, as you can see," he declared. "I'm only sad that you weren't able to decorate it yourself."

You only have yourself to blame, she thought, but didn't say out loud. Keeping her ambivalence hidden, she gave him a tight smile. She appreciated his enthusiasm, and loved this house, but was uncertain of the correct course for their future.

"I thought we could walk to my college, and then return for lunch," he suggested. "It is just ten minutes up Grand Avenue."

"Kay Lynn will be hungry at noon," May responded. "Can we return in time to eat by then?"

"Easily!" he declared. He reached his hands for Kay Lynn but she shook her head and clung to May. It was too soon.

May carried Kay Lynn up the hill. The toddler would have taken a long time to make this climb. Golden hills dotted with oaks rose around them. John spoke about the history of the college during the lovely walk to the campus and his office. He showed them around the campus until they came to an overlook with a view of the East Bay rising across the water.

May put Kay Lynn down and the girl spun around at her feet.

"What is she doing?" John asked.

May shrugged. "She likes to spin until she falls down. Apparently many one-year-olds think that is a delightful pastime."

John made a noncommittal face. He didn't seem to find Kay Lynn either charming or difficult. He wiped moisture from his brow and stepped very close to May.

He grabbed her hand. "This is everything we dreamed of. A home on a hill overlooking the bay close to a professorship for me."

He got down on one knee and held a ring out to her. "May Wagner, please do me the honor of becoming my wife."

Stunned, May stared at the large sapphire stone. Kay Lynn reached for the bright-blue jewel in his fingers. John pulled it away from the little girl's reach, took May's hand, and slid the ring onto her left finger. He grinned up at her, stood, and leaned in. Before his lips landed on hers, Kay Lynn shot between them and raised her arms.

"Up!" the girl demanded.

May bent over, rebuffing John's kiss, and swung Kay Lynn onto her hip. The girl grabbed for the shiny jewel on May's hand.

"Careful!" John said. "Don't let her remove it. It's a family ring from the Victorian era—my father's mother's."

John nodded and grinned at her. He seemed to think she'd consented to marry him. She considered challenging his presumption, but since she hadn't decided *against* being his wife she left his interpretation of events to stand. She did not owe him honesty about her doubts.

He offered his arm. May took it with a sigh. This *should* make her heart sing, not be unsettled. As they walked back to the house she tried to sort through her hesitancy.

John brought her to the kitchen, pointed to bread, cheese, and fruit, and directed May to slice it. He seemed to believe they would just carry on, as if these two years were inconsequential. Kay Lynn stood at her legs whimpering. It was nearly twelve thirty. Going against their family rules May handed Kay Lynn a piece of cheese. Kay Lynn eating while standing was preferable to tears from hunger.

"You can tender your resignation now," John declared when they were seated around the table.

May furrowed her brow.

"Surely you do not intend to work at a market in Berkeley," he said. "I've been assuming we will marry soon—this week or next. We have to decide where. As I said, Mother believes San Francisco, but I think this yard is fitting." He waved to the window facing the back garden.

May felt her throat close. She questioned how honest to be with John about her mother, her anger at him, and her hesitation to move to Marin.

"You don't expect a large church wedding?" He stared at her, looking incredulous.

"My mother is very ill," May said.

"So she can't attend," John said with a slow nod. "I'm sorry."

"I'm the sole income provider," she explained.

His eyebrows drew inward, then he went pale.

"You support your mother and your grandmother?"

She nodded.

"How long has your mother been ill?"

"Since June 1916."

"What does she have?!"

"Tuberculosis."

His eyes widened and he lost more color. He cleared his throat. "Why didn't you tell me before now," he challenged.

The muscles around her heart constricted. "You didn't ask about them." She heard the anger in her own voice. She took a breath to settle herself. "You haven't asked me about my life. You seem to assume that nothing changed for me, though I can't fathom how you could hold that notion."

He stared at the table—in thought or emotion, she couldn't tell. Finally breaking the silence, he asked, "How much?"

"Excuse me?"

"How much income do they need?" he asked. "I'll ask Mother and Father to give them an allowance . . . to replace your wages."

It seemed so very strange to share personal details, but if they were to be married he needed to know. She said the number. He nodded.

"Just until your mother is better?" he asked.

"If she gets better." May swallowed hard.

He nodded, his face pinched inward in pain. "Your grandmother can be taken in by family should . . ."

I am her family, May thought. But she nodded and replied, "Uncle Sam and Aunt Diana would welcome her."

"It's all settled then," he said, his lips pulled into an uncertain smile. "Or nearly so. I'm confident Mother and Father will consent as they are eager for our marriage to happen—extremely eager. When shall we do this? And where—here or in San Francisco?" he asked. Then he thought for a moment and added, "If you want your mother to be there we can do it in Oakland," sounding strangely confused and proud of his suggestion.

"Let me think about what will work best," May replied. "I would like Momma to be there, but she doesn't have much stamina. Perhaps my backyard so she can watch out the window."

As she spoke dread filled her heart. Did she feel ill at the prospect of marrying him, leaving home, or abandoning her mother? She looked at John. She wished she shared his confidence in this step. She pasted on a smile and nodded. She needed to give this decision more thought, much more consideration, but she wasn't going to share her uncertainty with him.

"You accepted his proposal?" Nana Lisbeth asked when she got home.

Puzzled by Nana Lisbeth's assumption, May pulled her eyebrows in. Nana Lisbeth took May's left hand and pointed to the engagement ring.

May sighed. "He placed this on my finger without waiting for my reply. It happened so fast that it's a blur. I should have prepared myself for the question, but I didn't, or rather, I didn't know my answer to that question."

"You sound uncertain," Nana Lisbeth asserted.

"Nana Lisbeth, I don't want to be his duty. He didn't want to marry me two years ago. I fear he's only doing this because he is a father. I want to be loved." May's voice broke. Tears pushed at her eyes. "Am I a silly schoolgirl to want that?"

Nana Lisbeth patted her hand. "I don't believe so. The person you marry has the most significant impact on your life. It's better to be alone than to be with a man who does not treasure you."

May nodded.

"Do you love him?" Nana Lisbeth asked.

"I can't tell. Perhaps I love the memory of loving him. Or I love who I thought he was."

Nana Lisbeth nodded.

May continued, sharing the truth she'd kept hidden in her soul: "I do not trust him, and I don't know if I will ever again, but he is Kay

Lynn's father. His family has the resources to give her everything she needs, doctors and physiotherapy."

Nana Lisbeth pursed her lips, considering for a moment. A comfortable silence filled the room.

Then she broke the quiet. "I nearly married someone else instead of your grandfather."

"You did?!" Grampa Matthew and Nana Lisbeth's marriage seemed destined by fate.

"Yes," Nana Lisbeth confirmed. "In our small world along the James River, Edward Cunningham was the best catch—as you say—but he was not kind or interesting. I felt I was a possession, not a person, to him. And he was cruel . . ." Nana stopped, considering her words, and continued, "in the manner we spoke of in the cemetery."

Uncle Willie's conception, May remembered and said, "Oh!"

Nana Lisbeth continued, "So I broke off the engagement—causing a life-changing scandal. My mother couldn't forgive me for bringing shame on her, but I never regretted my choice to marry a good man over a good husband."

"What about a good father? Does Kay Lynn deserve to know her father?" May asked.

Nana Lisbeth pulled her lips in. "This may sound very modern of me, however, I'm not certain her father has to be your husband."

A buzz of confusion burst through May's head. Her dismay must have shown because Nana Lisbeth patted her hand.

"I wish someone could tell me the right path forward," May said. She shook her head and made a face. "I know! You are going to say I have to listen to my 'still, small voice' inside."

"Whatever you choose, there will be losses and gains," Nana Lisbeth said. "That is the nature of life. We pick one path, which means cutting off all the other choices. Sometimes I hope the Hindus are correct and we get to have more than one chance to be on earth."

"Oh, Nana Lisbeth," May said. "Me too."

Both Kay Lynn and Momma were napping, giving May the space to listen for the "still, small voice" Nana Lisbeth talked about. Ideally she'd hear a shout, as she had when she knew she *had* to be Kay Lynn's mother, but she would appreciate any volume if it provided clarity.

She sat at the edge of the bed near her sleeping daughter. May wasn't practiced at direct prayer, but it could not do any harm—and it might help. She closed her eyes, took in a breath, and asked God, *What should I do?*

She waited, listening for a voice, her own or God's. Kay Lynn's breathing joined the question. May noticed her own heartbeat, her own breath, and the sound of the birds in the trees, but no answer.

Should I marry John?

Instantly her throat closed and she felt as if she might cry.

Should I stay in Oakland? She breathed the question deep into her lungs.

May's shoulders dropped and her heart opened. A chill traveled down her spine.

I don't want to marry John.

She searched for her body's response. Nothing.

I am not going to marry John.

Peace, tinged with sorrow, settled on her.

"I am not going to marry John," she said. Suddenly she felt free, a weight lifted off her. She had her answer. The still, small voice had spoken softly, but clearly.

May opened her eyes and looked at Kay Lynn, asleep next to her on their bed. She placed her hand on her daughter's sweet head. She took in a deep breath and then exhaled.

"Little girl, it's going to be you and me . . . with love and help from our family."

It would be a harder life, financially and socially. Kay Lynn would live with the burden of being born out of wedlock. But with certain clarity, May knew this was the right choice for them both. She rubbed her daughter's blond curls. Love and devotion welled up in her. She would do anything to protect her daughter. Her still, small voice was telling her this was the way.

"Kay Lynn," she told her sleeping toddler, "you aren't going to live with your mother and father. But you will have a whole family to love you. And I promise to tell you the truth."

May's throat closed.

She cleared it and whispered, "I will tell you the story of your father as best as I can. I promise."

The next day she opened the door to John. He expected to spend the day at Idora Park, perhaps planning their wedding. May's heart was in her throat, but her mind was still set. This was the right decision for them.

"You look lovely, as always!" John said with a charming smile. No wonder she fell in love with him three years ago.

"John, let's sit on the bench," she directed. "I have something to tell you."

His face drew in and he nodded. Surely he knew what was coming.

On the bench in the front garden, sitting side by side, she took in a steadying breath. She'd rehearsed her words, but starting was painful.

"Those are most unusual carnations." He pointed. "They can't decide if they are white or red."

May nodded. "Nana Lisbeth planted white ones and scarlet ones a few years back, for us to wear for Mother's Day. Scarlet to honor a living mother and white to honor a deceased mother. Somehow they mixed up, so many of the white carnations are tinged scarlet. With so many women wearing scarlet carnations to show pride for the sons in the war, she thinks it fitting in this wartime: scarlet for courage and white for mourning. It's all blended together right now, isn't it?"

He nodded. She studied his face.

"You know what I'm going to say?" she asked.

He nodded again. May took in a breath. She didn't *have* to say it out loud. Would it simply be cruel? Was he hurt? She couldn't tell.

"I will not be marrying you," she declared, retrieving the ring from her pocket. She took his fist, uncurled his warm fingers, and set the jewelry in his palm. He left his hand open, the sign of their potential engagement glimmered in the sun. She looked at his face again.

With sudden clarity she asked, "You are relieved?"

He teared up and nodded for the third time.

Relief surged in her. She laughed quietly. They sat in silence.

Eventually, he looked at her and whispered, "My mother will be . . . very disappointed."

May nodded. He really was a child still.

"She pressed you into proposing to me, didn't she?"

"It wasn't so much pressure as her certainty. I was confused, overwhelmed and . . ." John looked at her. "I just want to run from our mistake."

Mistake. There was a time May had thought Kay Lynn was a mistake too. Now her daughter was her greatest delight and motivation.

May broke their silence. "I am happy for Kay Lynn to spend time with any of you. She will always know you are her father."

He wiped an eye.

"I wanted to be . . ." He shrugged. "Ready?" He continued, "I nearly convinced myself that I was."

May exhaled hard. His reaction was a deep affirmation that merging their lives with John's would have been a grave mistake. Still, a sadness settled in her heart. Some part of her must have hoped he would protest by declaring his affection and devotion to them both.

She closed her eyes and took in a deep breath to settle her nerves. She felt the sun on her skin, warm and comforting. Opening her eyes she looked at the scarlet-tinged carnations mixed in with purple statice and orange poppies.

Courage and mourning.

John rose.

"Goodbye then," he said.

May replied, "I wish you the best, John, always." And she meant it, truly.

She watched him walk away down the sidewalk, getting smaller and smaller. Would he be a part of Kay Lynn's life? It seemed unlikely. He didn't ask after her when she was just steps away inside the house. May doubted he would make an effort to know his wonderful daughter—just like her own father. Fate was strange—repeating a pattern she was determined to end.

But now she had to accept she would be like her own mother, fending for her daughter as best as she could without a husband.

May took the pruners from the pot and cut one of the mottled carnations. Like her life, it was mixed up. She knew she'd made the right choice, though she wished it were otherwise. John was not the man she or Kay Lynn needed. In the kitchen she placed the carnation in a bud vase and carried it to their room to remind her of her own courage as well as the sadness of this day.

CHAPTER 22

NAOMI

October 1917

"What a delightful surprise," Naomi declared at the sight of her cousin-in-law standing on the front porch. "Can you visit over tea and lemon-poppy seed cake?"

"That would be lovely," Lisbeth agreed, her white hair pulled back in a chignon.

Settled at the kitchen table, Lisbeth asked, "Have you any news from Cedric and Joseph?"

Naomi shrugged. She wrapped her hands around the tin cup full of warm, soothing liquid. "I tell myself they are fine, since I have not heard otherwise," she said. "But I do not trust that they are. Can any of us?"

Lisbeth nodded. "Mrs. Sanger prefaces her family limitation pamphlet with the admonition to stop having babies to supply the millions of soldiers and sailors to fight battles for financiers and the ruling class. I'm so grateful my sons and grandsons are the wrong ages for this war. Then I am embarrassed to be so very selfish as to be relieved when others are suffering greatly."

Lisbeth looked at Naomi, tears in her eyes. "The time when Matthew was gone for the war was the hardest in my life. I could scarcely breathe, let alone sleep or eat, for those many months." She took Naomi's hand. "It took years from both of our lives."

Naomi's breath caught at the frank conversation about the pain she lived with. She nodded.

"I imagine the constant terror you have for your sons." Lisbeth's voice tightened with sorrow. "They are young and so kind . . ." She stopped speaking suddenly. She closed her eyes and took in a deep, slow breath, transforming dismay into calm and said, "They are on my prayer list—every day."

Afraid of a dam burst, Naomi blinked to keep back tears. She mouthed, *Thank you*. Suddenly she felt the too-familiar wave of heat travel out from her chest. She slipped off her cardigan, revealing her bare arms. She wiped sweat from her upper lip.

"Change of life surge?" Lisbeth asked.

Naomi replied, "It seems entirely unfair to have my temperature be so erratic. I feel as if I cannot even depend on my own body."

"I'm grateful those days are behind me," Lisbeth said. "It took a few years, but once it was over I delighted in the freedom."

"Lord, I am ready for that!" Naomi declared.

Lisbeth smiled and then changed the subject. "Sadly, I come with troubling news." She sighed, and her lips turned down into a frown.

Imagining sorrowful news about Sadie, Naomi asked, "Should I get my mother?"

Lisbeth shook her head. "Jordan can hear this from you: the Santa Fe Improvement Club is being troublesome again."

Naomi's stomach balled up like an angry fist.

Lisbeth explained, "I continued to attend their meetings because I do not trust Mr. Caldwell and Mr. Johnson, who has joined him in leading this unjust crusade. Unfortunately, I was correct to be concerned. They are bringing a modified ordinance to the city council.

It will make it a crime for a colored person to live in a neighborhood block if 75 percent of the residents are white, as well as the reverse: no white person can live in a block that is 75 percent colored. He claims that makes it equal and fair for all."

"If it passes we will be forced back to West Oakland!" Naomi declared.

"Mr. Johnson asserts it won't apply to those who are currently residing in the neighborhood," Lisbeth replied. "Apparently members of the city council have already expressed their reluctance to force the sale of homes. This horrible ordinance is his compromise."

Furious, Naomi rebutted, "I'm supposed to be thankful to be the last colored family to move into this block?"

"I wish I could protect you from this," Lisbeth replied, sorrow in her voice.

Naomi exhaled, working to get her anger under control. The lack of sleep and concern about her sons were not Lisbeth's fault. She took in a calming breath before she spoke to the elderly woman.

"Lisbeth, thank you for going to the meetings. And for the warning. I'll take this to the NAACP steering team this week."

It was a quick walk to Mrs. de Hart's home for the meeting. Naomi looked at the dark silhouette of Sather Tower on the campus. Leaves on the young maple trees on Telegraph Avenue were just hinting at a turn on this fall evening. She wondered if her sons saw any of the familiar signs of autumn in Houston or Nogales.

Shame mixed with fury coursed through her veins as she imagined telling the committee about the ordinance before the Oakland council. She'd like to keep her composure, but it would be difficult. The indignity of fighting this domestic battle while her sons were in uniform on behalf of the nation put her on edge.

Reverend Coleman, the editor of the *Oakland Sunshine* as well as the pastor of the North Oakland Baptist church, opened their gathering with a prayer. It calmed Naomi to remember that their work was on behalf of something so much bigger than themselves.

When it was time she relayed what she learned from Lisbeth. She teared up; they could hear her emotion, but she kept her composure well enough.

Mrs. de Hart exclaimed, "Dear Lord! Will it never end?"

Mr. Butler replied, "We must make our arguments to the city council. We have friends there who will use our words to make our case."

Naomi said, "We must say it is discriminatory, oppressive, and unnecessary for the public welfare." She wrote down her own words.

"It's not a good use of the police," Mrs. Tilghman added. "Nor does it provide equal protection. This goes against the Fourteenth Amendment of the Constitution!"

Naomi added Mrs. Tilghman's thoughts to her paper.

The group continued to generate their arguments with great enthusiasm and vigor until Mr. Jones cleared his throat.

"I am sorry to bring up an obstruction. I agree with everything you have said wholeheartedly and . . ." Mr. Jones looked pained. He continued, "East Saint Louis is on my mind. I fear if we fight this ordinance West Oakland and colored people may be targeted."

The circle grew silent. He referred to an instance of mass violence that occurred when colored people built businesses and stood up for their rights. White mobs viciously attacked colored people and buildings in that community, and neither the National Guard nor the local police intervened.

Anger exploded in Naomi's chest. "We cannot let fear prevent us from doing what is just," she countered. "If we do, then we have already lost all hope of a better future for our children."

Pastor Coleman agreed. "Though we may wander for *more* than forty years, we must keep moving toward the promised land."

Mrs. Tilghman said, "I agree. However, we must not be foolish. We have to keep a lookout for any signs of trouble, come together, and protect ourselves."

The group nodded. Naomi was grateful that her convictions were supported by these good people; the Northern California Branch of the NAACP was not going to let small-minded men force segregation of the races in Oakland without a fight.

They continued their discussion, raising various arguments, and finally settled on an angle of patriotism and respectability. Naomi did much of the writing, bringing all their ideas together.

Mr. Butler agreed to take their plea to his friend on the city council. Pastor Coleman would submit their letter to the *Tribune* under his name. Time would tell if their efforts would win this battle, and perhaps the war.

Two days later Maggie yelled from the kitchen, "Ma, you did it!"

Delicious smells greeted Naomi after her unusually short workday. No babies were ready to make an appearance. Maggie waved the paper at Naomi, a huge grin on her face. She dropped it on the table and pointed repeatedly to a headline on the front page.

ORDINANCE FOR SEGREGATION LOST

Joy shot through Naomi. She continued to read.

Declaring the proposed initiative ordinance seeking to create districts for the segregation of residences of Colored people to be unconstitutional, an opinion rendered by Assistant City Attorney H. L. Hagan was adopted by the council today as its reason for refusal to pass the ordinance. The proponents of the measure have threatened to circulate petitions for placing the ordinance on the ballot at the next regular election.

She exhaled hard. These men would never give up.

The opinion of the city attorney regarding the ordinance is:

"That it is not a valid exercise of police power. It is unjust, unreasonable, oppressive, burdensome, arbitrary, discriminatory, and unnecessary to the public welfare."

She teared up. The city attorney used her arguments.

"It is unconstitutional in that it assigns separate residence districts solely on the basis of color; it denies certain persons equal protection of the laws; it denies certain persons the inherent right to acquire, enjoy, and dispose of property."

The ordinances was [sic] proposed by Orville P. Caldwell and a number of residents in the Santa Fe district.

Naomi sat in the chair with a sigh.
"It's good, right, Ma?" Maggie asked.

Naomi nodded. It *was* good, but it was only a temporary reprieve that could be wiped away in the next election. They were going to put her value to a public vote. The majority of white voters might not vote to protect the dignity and rights of colored people. Which of her neighbors secretly wished her gone, if not from overt hostility then for their own economic reasons? Who felt she diminished their property value and wanted her to leave the neighborhood?

Maggie said, "Pastor Coleman's letter was printed in the *Tribune* today too. You can tell he is a newspaperman himself by his clear and persuasive writing. Did you help with the arguments?"

Naomi nodded.

Maggie turned the pages of the newspaper on the table until she came to page ten and pointed to a column toward the right. Naomi read it through to the end.

PROTEST AND PLEA

To the Editor of the *Tribune*:

As a citizen of this city and State I desire to enter a most solemn protest to the constant agitation of the question of the right of the Colored people to live in any section of the city where they can find a decent home within their means.

To begin, we have no country but this; it is ours by every inherent right of birth and blood. We are not aliens; we were born here. Our fathers and mothers were born here. We know no flag but the Stars and Stripes. For it the blood of our forebears was shed that luster might be added to its stars and color to its stripes. From the commons of Boston to the plains of Carizal our blood has freely run and our sons are answering the call of Uncle Sam to go across the sea and fight side by side with every man that freedom on land and sea may be the common heritage of all. And now it is distressing to many of us to have our freedom of the right to live in the city of Oakland questioned.

I would emphasize a fact that is daily overlooked. There are no traitors to the interest of this country among us. No disturbers of the industrial peace. Every black man works peaceably for his white employer and if he belongs to a union controlled by white men he is the last one to walk out. He works for a low wage and never grumbles when discharged but takes it as hard luck and goes on smiling and hopefully looking for another job. He will not join the I.W.W. because he is a peace-loving and law-abiding citizen. No anarchists, no Nihilists among the negro race. You can enter any public gathering composed wholly of colored Americans and feel safe as in the company of one's own best friends, for not infernal machines are among them nor are there any bomb throwers to be found. Their patriotism and loyalty are never questioned; would that much could be said of every man who lives under the protection of our flag.

There is an effort being put forward, presumably by the Santa Fe Improvement Club, to force segregation of the colored residents of Oakland. I want to call attention to the unfairness of the plan. And the hardships it will work on some of the most self-sacrificing and patriotic citizens among its people. This Santa Fe

Improvement Club proposes to make it a crime for any colored family to live in a block where 75 percent of the residents are white. That will mean in every section of Oakland there will have to be a change of residence for all the negroes. And where shall we go? In the bay? For the much-talked-of West Oakland would not give us a home. In not one block in all this can be found 75 per cent [*sic*] colored.

If this proposition goes on the ballot we have no way to vote it down without the aid of the true white American who knows the Black American never fails nor falters when white America is imperiled or threatened. Ask Roosevelt who saved the day in Cuba. Ask General Pershing if the colored soldiers can be depended upon. Do you want us to be ever loyal and patriotic and then would you forever humiliate and crush us because we are but one in ten and our skin is dark? Will you give us aid and encouragement to live clean, decent Christian lives serving the God your fathers taught us to serve?

G. C. COLEMAN

Pastor North Oakland Baptist Church

It *was* a good letter. Naomi was proud to be one of the people who drafted it.

"Ma, relish the success of this day. You worked so hard for it." Maggie patted Naomi's shoulder.

Naomi sighed. Maggie was right. This was a good day, but the many threats from all around only seemed postponed, not obliterated.

A few days later she was proved right. Dismay and indignation rose as she read the letter in rebuttal to Pastor Coleman. These men were not going to rest until they'd found a way to segregate the races. The Fourteenth Amendment to the Constitution should make these sentiments distasteful to all Americans—and yet these arguments were given respect simply by being presented in the *Oakland Tribune.*

THE PROPOSED SEGREGATION.

To the Editor of the Tribune:

Rev. G. C. Coleman of the North Oakland Baptist church has written some able articles for the press regarding the proposed segregation ordinance that citizens of North Oakland feel should be adopted as the best means of preventing any further ill-feeling between the parties involved. Unfortunately, however, the gentleman has based all his writings upon misinformation, and I crave your indulgence for space in your columns to set forth the salient points of the measure.

Section 1 provides in part, "and that nothing herein contained shall be construed or operate to prevent any person who, at the date of the passage of this ordinance, shall have acquired a legal right to occupy, as a residence, any building or portion thereof, whether by devise, purchase, lease or other contract, from exercising such legal right, etc., etc."

This means that the adoption of this ordinance compels "no man, white or Colored, to move," as stated by Mr. Coleman.

The ordinance applies only to blocks peopled entirely by white or Colored people. It does not apply to mixed blocks. That is, blocks in which reside both white and Colored people. In other words, it imposes no burdens whatever upon people of either race. But it does provide a legal means of regulating the conduct of men of either race who show a disposition to ignore and disregard the wishes of others.

Passing over without comment Mr. Coleman's references to the disloyalty of our citizens of the Santa Fe District, I will state briefly that reason why this ordinance is proposed at this time: Several weeks ago a non-resident owner named Moylan, sold a house to a Colored man named Norton, I believe. This house is located on Market Street, near Fifty-Fifth Street. On either side is a modest, tasty home occupied by white people who objected to the change from a white to a Colored occupant. They referred the matter to the Santa Fe Improvement Association and asked for assistance in adjusting the affair. A committee was appointed to, if possible, induce the Colored man to sell to a white man, this being deemed the fairest way to settle the matter. A buyer was found who offered the Colored man $150 for his bargain. The offer was rejected with scorn, coupled with the statement that "he would live in that house and all the devils in h—I couldn't stop him." He also made the further statement that "if there is one funeral there'll be two."

The committee reported and under the circumstances it was decided to secure, if possible, a law that would compel such men as Mr. Norton to respect other people's rights to maintain their property values invested in their homes from certain deterioration that invariable [*sic*] follows such cases.

Other Colored men are trying to buy or rent in our district. If we cannot secure legal protection by the passage of an ordinance as proposed, it will not be for lack of earnest effort to do so.

Like our Colored brothers, we are American citizens and proud of our flag. Many of our boys are either on the firing line in France or preparing for such duty. But we feel that we are only asking from our Colored brother the same right and privileges that we must and will grant to him.

Yours truly,

H. A. Johnson

"Ma, you cannot let the newspaper upset you so much!" Maggie declared. "I think you should stop getting the *Oakland Tribune*. The *Oakland Sunshine* can keep you apprised of events without causing you such distress."

Naomi pursed her lips and shook her head. She replied to her daughter, "I must know my enemies' plans and their arguments."

Maggie looked doubtful.

Naomi asked, "Do you understand that we only have our home because we organized?" Maggie shrugged. Then she nodded.

Naomi continued, trying to keep her voice calm, "If we were not paying attention they would have passed a law last spring forcing us to sell—at an extremely reduced price. We would have lost *all* of our savings and our ability to give you a good future. I am going to fight them with the resources I have—including reading the painful parts of the paper—for you and your brothers."

Maggie sighed and smiled. "Thank you, Ma." Then she teared up. "I wish you didn't have to pay attention to mean-spirited men."

"Me too, baby," Naomi said. "I hope we'll get this settled now, so you won't have to keep up this battle. The Civil War ended fifty years ago. I would have hoped we'd moved past these conversations by now."

A few days later Naomi was greeted by a joyous headline in the *Oakland Tribune*.

SEGREGATION ILLEGAL

She read through the article.

> When the United States Supreme Court on Monday reversed the decision of Kentucky courts and held that the segregation by legislative enactment of residents a community according to race was contrary to

the federal Constitution and could not legally be carried out, it paved the way for the speedy settlement of many distressing agitations. The Kentucky case arose out of the passage of an ordinance by the city of Louisville which sought to establish separate districts for the white and Negro residents. This ordinance was identical, in spirit at least, with ordinances enacted in many other cities of the South, and in some communities north of the Mason and Dixon line.

Recently the discussion of a segregated district for Oakland has been introduced and an ordinance prepared for enactment by the city council. The decision of the Supreme Court makes it necessary to seek some other method of attaining this object.

Naomi's heart sank low. The *Tribune was* advocating for segregated districts.

Regardless of what the arguments of prejudice, practical expediency and conservation of property values may have been, race and class segregation is morally indefensible. And when enforced after a mixed residential district has been established, it inevitably has worked for injustice. It is not surprising therefore to see the court declare it illegal.

Restricted and exclusive resident districts may be created by other and legal means, if these are adopted in time. Cooperation of property owners and contractual

> provision made at the time of sale of land and home
> have proved effective instruments of exclusion.

Effective instruments of exclusion. Those words made her ill. The *Tribune* was advocating for race restrictions in deeds from the beginning, as in the nearby Rock Ridge development, rather than ordinances to segregate after property was already sold. She blinked back tears to read the final paragraph.

> But it is not in the province of legislative bodies to say
> that the law-abiding citizens' full passion of his civil
> rights, may not live on any property to which he may
> obtain lawful title or that the right of such a citizen to
> own property may be abridged.

Naomi put the paper down with a loud sigh.

"Is this a two steps forward, one step back headline?" Maggie asked. "Or one step forward, two steps back?"

Naomi shook her head at her daughter. "For our family it is two steps forward. But for any of our people who come to Oakland from now on—I suspect it's two steps back.

"We get to keep our home, but it allows deeds preventing sales to colored people, Chinese, Japanese, foreigners—anyone they want, I suppose. Only white people will be allowed to buy homes in lovely, new neighborhoods in Oakland. We'll be forced to live in run-down areas without modern amenities."

CHAPTER 23

NAOMI

December 1917

Home after work, Naomi sat down with the *Oakland Tribune*. She took a deep breath and prayed her sons' names would not be in the newspaper. The military was supposed to notify families directly, but she knew people who learned their son had been wounded or died from the press.

The first article was devastating. Naomi held back a wall of tears and fury as she read that thirteen Negro soldiers from the Twenty-Fourth Infantry in Houston, Joseph's infantry, were hanged early in the morning on Monday. The young men sang "Amazing Grace" as they were led to the gallows. She pictured the boys, just the same ages as her sons, somehow finding the dignity and faith to sing in the face of such terror heart wrenching. Tears poured down her cheeks.

She imagined their mothers reading this account in the paper. It could have been her. In many ways it was. All colored women were being told the lives of their sons were not valued by their government.

Gramma Jordan rushed in.

"Naomi?" Gramma Jordan asked, terror in her eyes. She must have heard her wailing.

"Our boys are fine, but . . ." Naomi pointed to the article.

The two women stood side by side and read the account.

General Ruckman explained that the executions were completed without any notice or witnesses to avoid unrest from the Negroes and to prevent the president from being deluged with petitions for clemency. The news, reported without empathy or anger, conveyed none of the outrage pouring through Naomi.

"What can we do?" Gramma Jordan asked.

"There's nothing to do. It is done," Naomi hissed.

"There is always something to do. You know that," Gramma Jordan replied.

Naomi exhaled. "Today I will pray for those young men and for their mothers . . . and grandmothers. Tomorrow I might have another idea."

"Prayer is a good start." Gramma Jordan nodded and reached out.

Naomi took her mother's hands. "Dear Lord, please accept the souls of those young men. Every one of them, no matter their errors. They were young and forced into a terrible situation. Bring solace to their mothers, fathers, grandmothers . . . all who loved them. And Lord, please open the hearts and minds of those who carried out the executions. Amen."

"Amen," her mother echoed.

Prayer did help. She hugged Gramma Jordan and then said, "I feel like I cannot take any more, but then there's more, and no choice but to bear it."

"Baby, we are living through times that try men's souls," Gramma Jordan agreed.

"Did you notice the neighboring article?" Gramma Jordan asked, pointing to the column.

Naomi read the newspaper. Yesterday the House judiciary committee recommended extending the time for state ratification of the proposed women's suffrage amendment. The momentum to enfranchise women in the United States seemed unstoppable. After three-quarters of the states ratified it, this would become the eighteenth or nineteenth constitutional amendment. On any other day this would have filled her heart with joy, but today this news gave her only the smallest drop of pleasure. Women were getting the right to vote before colored citizens were given the opportunity to survive.

Wednesday night the three women sat in the sanctuary at the Fifteenth Street AME church for a memorial for those young men. Naomi was grateful for church, to be with others who shared her despair. Maggie would see the power in gathered community to give comfort and faith.

Singing, crying, hugging, listening . . . They honored each young man with the personalized eulogies printed in the *Oakland Sunshine*. The words written by their loved ones countered the lies from the newspapers. Naomi let a wall down; she shed tears and let rage pour through her body.

When they came to Joseph Smith the entire congregation gasped. They knew it wasn't their Joseph Smith, but it hit hard knowing it could have been.

It was right and good to memorialize these lives, but it didn't erase the pain. Naomi's sons were at risk. All their sons were.

The *Oakland Sunshine* wrote that there was no certainty that any of the young men were involved in any wrongdoing. Some were misidentified. Others were defending themselves or their comrades. These executions were a broadcast to all colored men: you will pay dearly if you dare defend yourself against the abuse of white men.

Nausea was Naomi's constant companion. She forced herself to eat, knowing she needed to keep up her strength, but the physical disequilibrium was nearly as exhausting as the emotional toll. She went through her days emotionally numb, and physically tired.

Just a few weeks later the *Tribune* reported more soldiers were put on trial: the article was so unsettling that Naomi vomited after reading it.

Determined to take some action beyond feeling sick, Naomi brought stamped postcards to church on Sunday. She and Maggie gathered more than fifty notes for the secretary of war and President Coolidge pleading for clemency. She mailed them with a prayer that these men would listen to the wisdom of Christian ladies. It was a minuscule comfort, but something she could do to plant seeds for love and justice. Would they sprout? She didn't know, but she was called by God to cast them. And pleased that Maggie was too.

Naomi's waning appetite was joined by a bloating belly that was disturbingly reminiscent of her grandmother's. She pushed aside any thought that she might have a tumor or a blockage, knowing as well as anyone there was little to be done for it. Rather than alarming her family for no purpose, she kept her observations private and pre-scribed herself the standard of treatment for an ulcer or a gastrobac-terial infection: sleep, plain food, clean water, and medicine.

One morning her mother eyed the box of Squibb's Sodium Bicarbonate—the same design as the one that was in their kitchen in Chicago as they cared for Grammy Mattie.

"I fear I am getting an ulcer or extra acid from all of my stress," Naomi said.

Gramma Jordan nodded without a word, but Naomi saw the concern in her eyes. They'd said the same about Grammy Mattie—and they'd both been wrong. She'd died too soon after her stomach started swelling.

CHAPTER 24

NAOMI

March 1918

The months of erratic sleep were over. Now Naomi slept hard and long at night, and well into the morning. For the third time that week Maggie roused her so she would not be late for work. She'd never been one to sleep late in the past.

Naomi made it through work, attended to her responsibilities, and left exhausted. She dozed on the trolley as she headed home, reluctantly standing when it got to her stop. In her front yard, three bright-yellow crocuses popped up along the walkway. Usually this sign of spring was a joy, but this year they felt like a cruel taunt.

They didn't speak openly about her condition, but they all knew something was very wrong.

Gramma Jordan tended to the garden alone and made supper each night. Maggie took up the laundry and washing the floors without being asked. Willie told her to rest and made her breakfast on the days he was home.

Naomi *must* work as long as she possibly could. Without her pay they would not make the mortgage. She didn't know how long she would have the strength to keep nursing. She prayed that by the time she was confined to a bed the war would be finished and their sons could contribute to the family income. She added her own health to her near-constant petitions for Cedric and Joseph.

One night as she changed into her nightgown she caught a glimpse of herself in the mirror. Her midriff noticeably bulged out. She ran her hands over her stomach. This degree of swelling could not be from the change of life. Any small hope she was not seriously ill flew away.

"Lord, my life is in your hands, but I beg of you, allow me to live until I can see my sons again."

She lay down and palpated her own stomach. On the right side there was a hard knot. Using the tips of her fingers she felt in a circular motion to distinguish the boundaries. It was larger than her fist. Her throat closed tight.

Her chin quivered. Not ready to draw Maggie's or Gramma Jordan's attention, she bit down on her lower lip to stop herself from wailing out loud. She rolled to her side and curled up, placing her hand on her tumor. Ovarian tumors killed before they were this large so it was likely in her uterus, liver, or perhaps stomach. She prayed for the uterus. Some women lived for many years with slow-growing tumors in their womb. Perhaps this was benign, even though it was growing rapidly.

Her favorite passage from the Bible, Psalm 23, ran through Naomi's mind:

> The Lord is my shepherd,
> I shall not want.
>
> He makes me lie down in green pastures;
> He leads me beside quiet waters.
>
> He restores my soul;

He guides me in the paths of righteousness
For His name's sake.

Even though I walk through the valley of the
    shadow of death,
I fear no evil, for You are with me;
Your rod and Your staff, they comfort me.

You prepare a table before me in the presence of
    my enemies;
You have anointed my head with oil;
My cup overflows.

Surely goodness and lovingkindness will follow
    me all the days of my life,
And I will dwell in the house of the Lord forever.

She needed to have faith that God would get her, and her family, through this. A too familiar twinge passed through her belly. She could hope this growth was benign, but she could not deny it was affecting her.

The lump pressed against her hand. She took in a deep breath to calm her twitchy body. It seemed to press again.

Naomi's chest exploded.

She pushed against the bulge; it pushed back. Her mind raced: nausea, exhaustion, bloating. Naomi palpated again, this time searching for a different answer, and she found it—this was not a tumor, it was a baby.

"Oh, dear Lord!"

She was forty-three years old. It seemed impossible, but she knew as well as anyone that it wasn't. Like so many women her age she'd stopped taking any precautions, believing she was no longer fertile.

She thought back to her last monthly. It was so long ago, more than a year. She'd been certain she was entirely through the change of life. She must have ovulated . . . without any signs. She felt her belly. How far along was she? By the size she would estimate five months. Surely she would have realized before the fifth month. Perhaps it was the fourth month. She thought to Willie's schedule, but it was little help. Obviously she was in the second trimester.

She wasn't dying. A chill of relief raised the hair on her flesh. She exhaled.

Her relief was quickly smothered by dismay. Willie would be fifty-six years old when this baby was born. She might be left to raise it alone. How could she bring a life into this horrid world?

Her mind was churning when her mother walked in and read her distress.

"Naomi, what is the matter?" Gramma Jordan asked, fear in her voice.

"I'm pregnant," Naomi said.

Gramma Jordan stared at her. Her brow furrowed in confusion and then her eyebrows rose in surprise. A huge grin grew on her face. She closed her eyes, her hand over her chest. "Oh, thank you, Lord. Thank you, Lord!"

"Thank you, Lord?!" Naomi exclaimed, furious. "How can I have a baby? Another child to be trampled and maybe sent off to be killed!"

With emotion in her voice Gramma Jordan spoke: "Naomi Smith, for weeks I've been scared of losing you. I have been terrified with every breath. I am not going to apologize for celebrating; I'm getting more of *you*, and a new life!"

"You do not understand!" Naomi argued. "I'm terrified to bring a baby into *this* hate-filled world."

Her mother's eyebrows arched. "You think you're the only Negro woman who was scared to have a baby because of how hard life might be for that baby." Her voice got steely. "My mama ran through a forest all by herself with me tied to her back to get me my measure of freedom.

"Your grandparents were enslaved." Gramma Jordan got that indignant look in her eyes. "I was born into slavery and look at me now. Every morning I send a gratitude to my parents for fighting for my life. And a good dose of spite to those who don't believe I have a right to this much dignity and life. We will not concede this world or this nation to those who won't give us our rightful place in it. There's nowhere else for us to go. This is the time and place where we stake our ground. We belong here as much as anyone. No more. No less."

Naomi exhaled hard. She was exhausted and longed for respite, not another soul to worry over. Would she ever be assured that her children were safe? She understood what her mother was trying to teach her, but in this moment all she believed was God was burdening her with one more soul to fear for. She wanted to have Gramma Jordan's courage and Grammy Mattie's strength, but Naomi wasn't confident she could bear this gift from God with the grace of her foremothers.

CHAPTER 25

MAY

July 1918

May walked home from work, a wool shawl that protected her from the summer fog wrapped around her shoulders. Today was her last day as a grocery clerk. Momma was taking her next shift. Nearly a year after falling ill, Sadie Wagner was one of the 50 percent to recover from tuberculosis. None of them knew with certainty which of the many treatments they used were most effective, but May would always hold that the Chinese herbalist saved her mother's life.

Thank you, Lenny, she telegraphed a message across the miles. His most recent letter to Elena and Peter was from Belgium, but he could be anywhere by now. Elena shared each note with May, and in more than one he sent his regards to her and Kay Lynn. *May you be safe.*

Coincidentally today was the two-year anniversary of her father's return. She only saw him that one time. When she was staying with Elena he returned for Momma's signature, making him a citizen, and disappeared again. It confirmed what her mother believed: Heinrich was not interested in knowing May. What seemed so important when she was a child, and compelled her to leave home for a few days, was so entirely overshadowed by Momma's illness that May rarely thought of him. Truly he meant so little to her.

She wished Heinrich Wagner was someone he was not, the same thing she wished about John, but she was not going to base her contentment on an unfulfilled desire. Her priorities had changed dramatically since Kay Lynn was born. She missed having a naïve belief in fairy-tale endings, but she would not trade her daughter for anything. Kay Lynn brought more joy and love to May's life than she ever dreamed possible.

Walking along the path through her front garden, she noted that the flowers were looking droopy. She and Kay Lynn needed to do one of the girl's favorite activities in the morning: water the garden.

An envelope addressed to her rested on the hall tree in the entryway. It was written on thin international mail paper. Curious, she took it into the living room, sat on their couch, and tore it open. She glanced at the signature.

Leo

Her heartbeat sped up. What a strange coincidence that she'd just sent him a mental message.

June 14, 1918

Dear May,
I send this note with a prayer that it arrives into your hands. The mail has been unreliable and slow, as you can imagine. My greatest hope is that you, Kay Lynn, your grandmother, and mother are surviving these challenging times as well as possible. I was so glad to hear from Elena that Dr. Chan's remedies have been

as healing for your mother as they were for my father. May she have a complete and swift recovery.

I've been spared the worst a soldier can face, but nevertheless this war has revealed to me that our lives are short, uncertain, and precious. I signed on willingly to serve my country and have no remorse for doing so; however, my time as a soldier has illuminated the greatest regret of my life.

I've been neither honest nor bold when it comes to expressing my deep devotion to and affection for you. I can hardly remember a time when that was not true. I've been a coward in sharing my feelings because I feared your rejection. My timidity, if unchanged, will cost me the very possibility of my dearest dream: to be your husband and make a family with you and Kay Lynn. So I'm boldly writing to you for your permission to court you when my time in this war is over, whenever that may be.

I assure you I will graciously accept whatever answer you have for me.

In the deepest admiration and affection,
Leo

A chill raised the flesh on May's arms. She rubbed them. *Did Elena put him up to this?* She didn't want his pity.

"Momma!" Kay Lynn shouted and charged her way onto May's lap. She grabbed her mother's cheeks and kissed her on the left and then the right, back and forth, at least ten times. May laughed and hugged her little girl. She carried her into the kitchen where her mother was cooking.

May smiled at Momma, hugged her with her free arm, and kissed her cheek. A welling of love filled her soul.

The shadow of tuberculosis still marked Momma's face, but the doctor was confident it was gone from her chest. She was healthy enough to walk, cook, and work for a full day.

"Well?" Momma asked, caution in her voice. "Who is the mysterious international letter from?"

May handed it to her mother to read. She watched her eyes dart across the page, her expression changing from concern to surprise to delight.

"What will you tell him?"

May shrugged.

"Are you at least flattered?"

"I fear Elena put him up to it," May admitted.

"You know he has found you charming for a long time," Momma chastised her. "Elena didn't travel back in time and cause that young man to admire you."

May took in the truth of her mother's words. She felt the weight of Kay Lynn on her hip.

"*You* made your way without a husband," May replied.

Momma sighed. "I was so afraid of making the wrong choice that I never allowed myself to come close to love again." She shook her head. "I don't regret that decision for myself or for you, though sometimes I think you would have been happier with a brother or a sister."

Momma fell silent. After a moment she shook her head as if to clear it and she mumbled, "That doesn't matter now; what is done is done."

Momma looked right at May and declared, "Dare to take a risk and do not let fear rule your life. Love is a precious gift, and aiming for it, even if you fail, is never a mistake." Momma continued, "Don't make the same mistakes as me. Make your own." She laughed.

May smiled at her mother. A wall around her heart collapsed. She'd been certain that everyone pitied her and her instinct was to close herself off to the possibility of love. Perhaps her own shame built the wall—not other people's judgment.

She considered her mother's words: *Take a risk and do not let fear rule your life.* Was she avoiding Leonardo out of fear?

"Thanks, Momma," May said and hugged her mother tight.

After Kay Lynn was fast asleep, May settled herself in on the end of their bed to listen to that still, small voice. Leo's letter was in her hand. She took a few deep breaths and read it again.

I want to be your husband and make a family with you and Kay Lynn.

Once again that sentence sent a chill down her spine and raised the flesh on her arms.

She closed her eyes, placed her hand over her heart, and pictured Leo's face.

May took in a breath and asked, *God, what should I do?*

Kay Lynn's breathing joined the question. She noticed her own heartbeat and her own breath.

Should we make a family with Leo?

She breathed the question deep into her lungs.

May's shoulders dropped and her heart opened. Another chill traveled down her spine. She smiled as she pictured his face, suddenly dear like never before. Leo was a good man.

I'm going to tell Leo he can court me.

Her heart beat in excitement. Her feelings were clear; she learned her answer, and could give him his. Peace and gratitude filled her soul.

May went to their small secretary and pulled out a piece of paper. She thought and thought, and finally wrote on two different pieces of stationery:

> *Dear Leo,*
> *Yes.*
>
> *With great hope and fondness—*
> *May (and Kay Lynn)*

Using the address from the letter he sent her, she addressed one envelope to the Army Post Office. He might never receive it. On another envelope she simply wrote his name. She would bring it to his family home so when he returned it would be waiting for him.

May smiled as she sealed the note. She ran her hand along the seam of the envelope; a sweet certainty in her choice hummed in her.

CHAPTER 26

NAOMI

August 1918

In the kitchen after work, Naomi opened the paper before doing anything else.

She scanned the front page of the *Oakland Tribune*, taking in a jumble of headlines. A sub-headline with the word *Nogales* jumped out at her. She skimmed for confirmation.

Negro Troops Cross Border

Cedric's unit! Her heart galloped like a racehorse. She blinked back tears, and forced herself to start at the top of the article:

SCORES OF MEXICANS, MACHINE GUN TOLL

Attempts of Southern Republic's Customs Guards to Start Trouble Results in Bloody Battle at Nogales, Sonora

MEXICAN MAYOR IS AMONG THOSE KILLED

Gov. Calles of Sonora Sends His Regrets to U.S. Army on Order of Gen. Carranza; Negro Troops Cross Border

BY ASSOCIATED PRESS

LEASED WIRE TO TRIBUNE

NOGALES, Ariz. Aug. 28—Sincere regrets for yesterday's clash between Mexicans and America [*sic*] soldiers were expressed by P. Elias Calles, military governor of Sonora, to Brigadier-general De Rosey Cabell, in a telegram received from General Calles at Magdalena, Sonora, today. General Calles stated he had been ordered to proceed to the border by President Carranza to express these regrets personally.

Reports that Negro cavalry crossed International Avenue at 5 p.m. and rode one block in Nogales, Sonora, to clear the adobe houses of snipers.

The Mexican casualties in the fighting are variously estimated at 150 to 200. Three Americans were killed and 28 wounded.

Several machine guns, which were placed on the hills on the American side, inflicted heavy casualties on the Mexicans, the machine-gun bullets ploughing through houses in all parts of the Mexican town.

THREE AMERICANS DIE

TWENTY-EIGHT WOUNDED

Naomi couldn't stop her tears any longer. They welled up, making it impossible to read the article. She rested her forehead on her palm, bent over the newspaper, and let them flow. When they ran out, she wiped her face with her skirt and returned to the horrid account.

A revised list of the casualties suffered by the Americans shows that one officer and two enlisted men were killed and 28 soldiers and civilians wounded in yesterday's fighting. Three of the wounded are reported seriously hurt.

The American officer killed was Captain Joseph D. Hungerford, who commanded a troop of Negro cavalry.

Among the Mexicans killed was Felix Penaloza, mayor of Nogales, Sonora, the Mexican town opposite here.

Among the Americans wounded is Lieutenant Colonel Frederick Herman, commander of the border patrol here. His wound is not serious. The fighting began at 4:15 yesterday afternoon when a Mexican attempted to cross to the United States. A. A. Barber, a United States custom guard twice ordered the Mexican to halt, and when the latter failed to comply with his command, Barber drew his pistol, but did not fire.

Two Mexican custom guards, according to Barber's account, resented his interference with the Mexican seeking to cross the line and opened fire.

FIRE IS RETURNED BY CUSTOMS GUARD

Their bullets missed Barber, but struck Corporal Barney Lots in charge of the American guards. Lots was shot through the arm and the lungs and ran to the Western Union Telegraph offices nearby on the American side, shouting for assistance. He fell unconscious at the door, and was removed to the base hospital, where he died. As the Mexicans' bullets struck Lots, Barber returned the fire and felled the Mexican guard who had mortally wounded the corporal.

The firing then became general, Mexicans appearing suddenly in the doorways of houses, on the roofs of buildings and in the surrounding hills and shooting across International Avenue, the principal street of the twin towns and which forms the boundary line.

There were no names of those others killed or wounded. Her Cedric might be dead. Or alone and in pain. She pictured his face, as dear to her as anything in the world.

Adrenaline poured through Naomi's veins. She had to move, so she channeled her energy into scrubbing, an activity she could manage with her huge belly. Stack by stack she pulled every single plate and bowl out of the cupboards until the shelves were empty. Gramma Jordan found her standing on a chair washing the wooden shelves with a rag.

"What's happened?" her mother asked.

Naomi pointed to the paper.

Gramma Jordan read and then prayed out loud: "Lord, watch over our Cedric." Then her mama got a rag wet and joined Naomi. She patted her daughter's back, but there were no comforting words.

They waited in painful uncertainty, holding the best and the worst outcomes at the same time, until they learned the truth.

Naomi and Gramma Jordan were working side by side in the pantry when the knock came. Filled with sudden panic that this was *the* knock every soldier's mother feared, Naomi stared at her mother, her heart in her throat.

"Oh, Mama, no!" Naomi cried.

"I'll be back," Gramma Jordan whispered in a hoarse voice, her eyes filled with moisture too.

She returned too soon with a terrifying envelope in her hand.

Naomi could not stop her tears. "Oh, Ma. Oh, Ma. It can't be. Please Lord, no!"

Gramma Jordan's hand shook as she tore open the horrid Western Union telegram. Her eyes darted right and left.

Gramma Jordan exhaled hard and declared, "He's only injured."

Naomi grabbed the paper and read it for herself.

> I REGRET TO INFORM YOU YOUR SON PRIVATE FIRST-CLASS CEDRIC SMITH WAS ON THE TWENTY SEVENTH OF AUGUST SEVERELY WOUNDED IN NOGALES, MEXICO. YOU WILL BE NOTIFIED AS REPORTS OF HIS CONDITION ARE RECEIVED.
> *HARRIS, THE ADJUTANT GENERAL*

Good news? How was it possible that severely wounded *was* good news? But a huge measure of relief swirled into her anxiety. Cedric was *still alive.*

And suddenly she knew with absolute certainty: *Someone has to go to him.*

"Willie, you *must* get to Arizona," Naomi insisted when he came home that night after ten days away.

"Naomi, that's not how it works. Wounded soldiers are taken care of by the military," her husband countered.

"Willie Smith, if you do not go I will," she declared.

He looked at her. His eyebrows rose and he pointed to her round belly.

"I don't care if I have this baby on the way. One of us needs to watch over him." She glared at her husband. She *was* being unreasonable; but it was unthinkable that her son was severely wounded and alone in a hospital one thousand miles away from home.

"Taylor won't just agree," Willie explained. "If I don't show up for my shift he may tell me to never come back."

"You can always find another job, but we can't replace our son. *Severely wounded* means his life is in danger," she argued. "You know as well as anyone that we cannot trust them to take care of him, to make sure he's treated right." She teared up. "Cedric has to know he's not forgotten."

Willie nodded. "I'll go."

"Thank you, Willie." She exhaled and hugged her husband tight. With her face pressed as close as she could get to his comforting chest, she repeated, "Thank you."

Willie was nearly in Arizona. He'd been gone for two days; his railroad brothers ensured his journey went well. Between her giant belly and the gnawing anxiety for Cedric, Naomi could hardly breathe. She was too far along to deliver other women's babies so she filled her days with house projects and getting ready for the new family member.

Eighteen years had passed since she'd given birth. After the first grueling labor with Cedric the next two came easy, but with so much time between labors and her advanced age, she feared what was to come.

Naomi was piecing a quilt from scraps of clothing when the Washingtons' youngest son arrived to say Willie was on the phone at their house.

Anxious to get news, Naomi yelled up the stairs into Mama's flat, "Willie made it. I'm going to talk to him on the telephone."

Not waiting for her mother, Naomi rushed up the block to the Washingtons'.

Naomi spoke into the hard, black mouthpiece. "Have you seen him?"

"He's . . ." Willie's voice was tight. "He's . . ."

Naomi's throat closed. She forced in a shaky breath.

"He's delirious with fever," Willie said. "He thinks he's in Oakland."

"Where are his wounds?"

"His arm and shoulder," he replied. "The doctor says he should not be this ill."

"Did you have trouble getting to him?"

"I know how to flatter white people in order to get my way."

Naomi sighed. "Thank you, Willie."

"I'm glad I'm here."

"Bullets?" she asked. "Does he have bullet wounds?"

"Yes," he replied without more details.

"Have they all been removed?" she asked.

"The doctor said they were taken from his shoulder and arm."

She stated, "But no chest wound?"

"Naomi, your Bible deflected a bullet away from his heart," Willie told her, awe in his voice.

"What?" A wave traveled down Naomi's spine.

"The nurse showed me the Bible from his pocket. It has a diagonal gouge. You saved him. There's no signs of entry to his lungs or chest."

"God is good," she praised. She thought and then asked, "What is the condition of the skin around the wounds?"

"It's covered by bandages," he explained, "so I didn't see the wounds."

"Willie, *you must* remove them," Naomi insisted. She gripped the black phone in her hand as if it would convey the urgency to her husband. "Look for puckering or dry skin. Look for black tissue. White doctors miss gangrene on colored boys. If you see those indications of dead tissue make them amputate."

"Lose his arm?" Willie protested.

"It's better, far better, than losing his life!" she insisted.

"Okay," he sighed. "I'll check when I see him."

Naomi sucked in her breath. "Tell him his Ma loves him very much. And I long for the day I see his precious face again."

"I will, Naomi. I will."

"I love you, Willie," she said. "I'm so grateful you are there. I'd . . . I'd . . . I don't know how I could cope if you weren't."

"I love you too, Naomi Smith. And I'm grateful to be here too," he replied. "How's the baby? How are you, besides worried about our Cedric?"

Naomi exhaled. She teared up again. "Willie, it feels like too much. All I can do is take the next breath."

"Oh, baby," he replied. "I wish I was there," he continued, "and here."

"Yeah," she replied. "Me too, but we were forced to pick—and I *want* you right where you are. Maggie and Gramma Jordan are taking very good care of me. You don't need to worry about us. You just take care of Cedric, you hear?"

In the silence she pictured him nodding.

Finally he said, "I'll call you tomorrow."

Her heart skipped a beat. It was hard to say goodbye, but long distance was very expensive. They'd said what they needed to. She forced herself to say goodbye and hung up.

Every moment anticipating another call was interminable. Waiting to learn if her son was alive or dead was excruciating. She imagined the worst: Willie's sobs coming through the earpiece as he told her their son was gone. Would she collapse to the floor? Be too overcome to cry at all? Scream with anguish? Naomi didn't want to know how she would react to her Cedric's death. She pushed the images and the questions out of her mind.

Gramma Jordan and Maggie stayed nearby all day, but there were no attempts to comfort each other with empty promises or casual chitchat. They lived in the pain of uncertainty, waiting to know if their lives would be changed forever for the worse.

Sewing kept her fingers busy, and she said a prayer each time her mind raced to a painful conclusion. Jostling from her belly was a welcome distraction and a painful reminder that if she weren't pregnant she would be in Arizona right now.

Naomi's mind was obsessed with the man she'd birthed twenty years before, her belly was occupied by the infant growing inside her, and her heart was torn between them.

She met each kick or elbow with a pat. *You're all right, little one,* she would reassure the baby and herself. For now this tiny person was safe and sound inside her.

And then she would pray:

Dear Lord, watch over Cedric and Joseph. Place my love directly into their hearts that they may know their mother is praying for them wherever they are and that I am waiting for their safe return. Amen.

After a long day waiting for a phone call Naomi went to bed without word from Willie. Her sleep was fitful—disturbed by painful dreams. Each time she woke she recited her prayer:

Dear Lord, watch over my sons. Place my love directly into their hearts that they may know their mother is praying for them wherever they are and that I am waiting for their safe return. Amen.

In the morning the vigil began again with no certain ending. The day passed as painfully as the one before. Finally, after supper, the Washington boy knocked on their door. Willie was calling. Gramma Jordan and Maggie huddled around Naomi as she held the phone.

Willie spoke in a rush: "Naomi, I couldn't leave his bedside to call you yesterday. I feared he'd take a turn and no one would help him. You were right to insist I be here; he wouldn't have come through without me at his side."

"He's alive?" she asked, needing to hear those words.

"Yes!" he confirmed. "Cedric is alive."

Naomi hung her head and a chill of relief traveled down her spine. Gramma Jordan squeezed her shoulder in a half hug. She felt Maggie's head push against her.

"Thank you, Lord. Thank you," Naomi said.

Willie continued the story: "I did as you said. The skin on his upper arm looked like it had been charred. I showed the doctor and he dismissed me, saying it was typical. After he left a white nurse told me I was right to be concerned. She offered to get a more sympathetic doctor, who agreed to do the amputation."

His voice broke. "Our boy's arm is gone."

"Which one?" Naomi asked, as if it mattered, but she needed to know.

"His left," Willie said in a quiet voice.

Naomi pictured his precious baby's hand, her thumb nestled in his tiny palm. He always wrapped his sweet fingers around hers while he ate.

She remembered kissing that hand when he left home to attend school. She'd told him, "My kiss will last for the whole time we are apart."

That hand held books, and shovels, and playing cards . . . and it was gone.

Cedric would never be a coal man again. His life was permanently changed; this mark from the war would go with him everywhere he went for the rest of his life. Would it be a badge of pride or shame? Maybe both. But that arm was a price she was glad to pay for his life.

"Tell him I love him!" Maggie shouted.

"His Gramma Jordan too."

"I will," Willie replied. "I'll send a telegram when we are heading home. No more calls unless I have something to report, right?"

"Yes." As much as she longed to hear Willie's voice with updates, the price was too dear.

"I promise to telephone if there's a problem, but otherwise, no news truly is good news," Willie explained.

"Thank you, Willie. I love you. Goodbye."

As soon as she hung up they hugged in a circle right there in the Washingtons' home. Maggie rested her head on Naomi's shoulder and Naomi rested hers on Gramma Jordan's. Her Cedric was still alive. Naomi took in a few deep breaths, reassuring her heart her life had not been destroyed, only changed. Gramma Jordan kissed the top of her head. She kissed Maggie's.

"Dear Lord, Thank you, thank you. You are good." Naomi couldn't form any other words of prayer, but God knew all that was in her heart. She exhaled hard.

"Let's go home, and focus on welcoming our newest family member," Naomi declared.

CHAPTER 27

NAOMI

October 1918

For the third day in a row a low backache with cramping woke Naomi before dawn. So long as she could lie in bed while they were happening it was just a warm-up, her body getting ready to force this baby out. The cramping went away with the sun as it did the two previous mornings, so she got up, anticipating yet another day of feeling tired and on edge.

Willie was still in Arizona at Naomi's insistence. Though she wanted her husband nearby when she delivered this baby, she preferred he stay with Cedric to ensure their son's survival.

Naomi checked her own cervix. It was continuing to get softer and shorter—a good sign that her body was readying to make one being into two. She reminded herself to enjoy each of these days when she only needed to care for herself. She only imagined caring for grandchildren in her forties, not a newborn of her own, but God had other plans for her life.

Naomi stood at the sink washing the dishes when she heard a pop instantly followed by a gush. On the floor, between her legs, was a pool of clear liquid. She exhaled hard. The wait was over, though she didn't like it when labor started with a high break because the risk of infection would hang over her until this baby was born.

Still at the sink, she squatted down and felt inside her birth canal. She didn't have to reach far to touch the very top of the baby's head. The position of the fontanel was favorable. Satisfied, she nodded. Maybe this would go more easily than she feared.

Naomi pulled herself up, wiped the floor, and washed her hands. *Willie, you're about to have another mouth to feed,* she telegraphed to her husband. She'd wait to tell her mother until she was cramping regularly, as it would most likely be hours and hours before this baby was born. Once labor progressed Gramma Jordan would fetch Maggie if she wasn't home from school, and they'd labor together until Naomi was almost complete. Nurse Hand agreed to attend the actual delivery.

Naomi mixed up a concoction of castor oil and brewed a black cohosh tea, something to help Mother Nature along. Within the hour intestinal cramps forced her to the toilet. A large uterine contraction compelled her to stand. It was accompanied by a flash of hormonal heat. Shiny with sweat and nauseated, she smiled even though she felt horrible. Her labor was beginning in earnest. It was time to get Gramma Jordan and Maggie.

Naomi was pacing in her room when Gramma Jordan returned with Maggie. Towels on the ground were spotted with bloody show and amniotic fluid.

Maggie's eyes grew round in concern. Naomi started attending births with her grandmother when she was only twelve. By the time she went to nursing school she'd been to dozens, but this was Maggie's first. Naomi couldn't very well bring her daughter to assist and observe in a hospital birth.

"It's all good," Naomi reassured her daughter. "Just the right amount of everything so far."

Maggie hugged her tight. Naomi breathed in the comfort of her daughter, and then her mother.

They played rummy, stopping for each contraction, until Naomi could no longer hold her cards. When she was ready to climb into bed, more eager for rest than the relief of standing, Naomi asked Maggie to call for Nurse Hand.

Naomi didn't track how long it took, but she was relieved when Nurse Hand's kind face smiled down at her.

"Ready for a check?" she asked.

Speaking was too hard, so Naomi nodded.

Her colleague examined her and declared, "Well done! Your cervix is nearly gone. Just a few more minutes. Do you feel the need to push?"

Naomi nodded. The pressure was building and building. She could hardly resist it.

"The baby is in an excellent position. I don't believe you will have any problems," Nurse Hand said.

"Even for an old lady?" Naomi joked.

Nurse Hand laughed and replied, "A well-experienced lady!"

"AHHHH," Naomi exclaimed. The next contraction overtook her and the urge to push was overwhelming.

"Follow your body," Nurse Hand directed.

Naomi took in a huge breath and bore down, going with the urgency of creation. All her energy focused as her instincts took over.

"Perfect. I can feel the head moving downward," Nurse Hand said. "Oh my . . ."

The contraction stopped and Naomi lay back, panting for breath.

"That one push moved your baby an entire inch," Nurse Hand declared. "It's going fast."

Naomi nodded. She reached between her legs. She could feel the baby nearly crowning.

"I don't want to tear," she panted.

Nurse Hand replied, "I'll stretch you as best as I can. Hold back on the next push if you are able."

Naomi nodded. The contraction built. This time she took in a smaller breath and used immense concentration to hold in her instinct to push with great force.

"That's it. Gentle, gentle," Nurse Hand said. "Yes! The ears are out."

The contraction ended. Naomi held back, her body taut in anticipation. She waited and waited until she felt the slightest tension in her belly and then she joined the energy of her body.

Naomi felt the rest of the head emerge.

"Wait!"

She froze up her muscles and started shaking, her legs quivering in and out.

"All right," Nurse Hand signaled.

Naomi again joined the force of her uterus and pushed until the rest of the baby flopped out. In an instant the fierce urgency to bear down fled. She laid her head back on the bed and caught her breath. A warm, wet weight pressed on her bare chest; her baby was on her instead of inside her.

"You're here. You made it. You made it." Naomi looked at the beautiful, gooey infant.

"Oh, Ma," Maggie cried. "You did it. You were amazing."

Gramma Jordan leaned over and kissed Naomi's head. "You are so strong."

Naomi beamed at the two women who'd supported her through this intense labor.

"Well?" Gramma Jordan asked.

Naomi peered between the baby's legs. Her heart leapt in joy.

"A girl," Naomi declared. "We have another beautiful daughter!"

She sobbed in relief. A daughter would never be sent to fight their wars.

Alone for the first time, Naomi was savoring the little one in her arms. She'd sent Maggie to telegram Willie and Cedric. Gramma Jordan was making her soup. The baby suckled well and was sleeping against her chest. The feel of the small body and the sound of her breathing were a balm to her soul.

She stroked her daughter's hand and love surged through her. Naomi remembered feeling dismay at the thought of having another child, but that emotion was entirely replaced by devotion to this baby.

Gramma Jordan walked in with a tray—her face traced with sorrow. "May sends her congratulations but didn't want to intrude. She came by to tell me Lisbeth is ill."

"What kind of ill?"

"Yesterday she started coughing and developed a fever." Gramma Jordan's face drew in.

"Not that horrid Spanish flu that's been in the paper?" Naomi asked.

"They fear it may be. She came to tell me, in case I want to . . ."

"Oh, Ma." Naomi teared up.

Gramma Jordan looked close to tears too. "Lisbeth met me the day I was born. She's the last person alive who's known me that long. It seems foolish to be an old woman who doesn't want to be the only one left."

Tears streamed out of her mother's eyes. "And she knew Mama. Lisbeth loved Grammy Mattie as much as I did, maybe even more. There's something so precious about those old, old friends. She's always been more like family."

Naomi replied, "Willie's mom was her half sister, so they *are* blood to my children."

Gramma Jordan nodded. "God twinned up our families in an interesting way."

"I'll pray for her," Naomi said. "For all of them."

"Me too," her mother replied.

Naomi rested and stroked her baby's back. New life was such a precious gift. And yet death continued to surround them. Sometimes it was too much to hold at once.

CHAPTER 28

MAY

October 1918

Auntie Jordan stood at the front door. She'd come to call on Nana Lisbeth. Momma welcomed her into the house without hesitating.

"Thank you for coming, Jordan. Lisbeth will be . . ." Momma's voice broke. Tears sprung to her eyes. "She will want to see you. Two masks . . . The doctor says we should double mask in the sickroom."

Momma handed the old woman another piece of cloth. Would they ever be rid of these horrid things? May led Auntie Jordan to Nana Lisbeth.

"Jordan, you shouldn't be here." Nana Lisbeth shook her head, her voice weak, and her eyebrows rose just enough to show her fear.

"I have two masks and I won't touch you." Auntie Jordan's eyes welled up. "But I had to come . . . in case it's"—her voice broke. She cleared her throat—"goodbye."

May wanted to protest, but the Spanish flu was killing people at an alarming rate. Modern travel was spreading it from city to city unlike any illness ever before. Some wondered if it would become a worldwide pandemic due to the war.

Last week the paper reported the daily cases and deaths from this horrid disease, and Oakland was considering a mask mandate like the one instituted last week in San Francisco.

They didn't know if Nana had that flu. By some accounts, this new disease came on so hard and so fast that people woke up ill in the morning and died by the same nightfall. Three days after she woke with a cough and a fever they were in the strange situation of being grateful Nana Lisbeth was alive. She was ill, but they were hopeful it wasn't the horrid Spanish flu.

May didn't allow herself to dwell over the news from the world or the thought that her grandmother might not get well. The knowledge that her mother overcame tuberculosis added to her conviction that her grandmother would recover from this illness.

Nana Lisbeth smiled at the thin woman; her eyes filled.

"Thank you," she whispered.

"I brought Mama's Bible," Auntie Jordan said. "Want to hear her favorites?"

Nana Lisbeth nodded and whispered, "The Parable of the Sower?"

Auntie Jordan replied, "You know Mattie's heart."

The elderly colored woman sat in the hard chair—many feet away from Nana Lisbeth. She opened the ancient book. May would not have said her grandmother particularly appreciated the Bible, but she looked grateful and at peace. Momma was right to let Auntie Jordan come in.

"First, tell me about your new granddaughter," Nana Lisbeth croaked. "I need to know her name so I can tell Mattie when I see her."

May bristled again. Nana Lisbeth was too certain she was leaving this earth.

"Dawn," Auntie Jordan replied. "She's called Dawn—for the new day we are going to have as soon as this war winds down all the way."

"Lovely. And Cedric?" Nana Lisbeth asked, and then coughed twice. She was getting tired. She hadn't talked this much since she had fallen ill.

"He's much recovered. Willie believes they will return in a matter of weeks."

Nana Lisbeth nodded.

Auntie Jordan continued, "And the news from Joseph is all we could hope for. Malcolm and his family are just fine as well. You rest now, while I read to you."

It took May a moment to remember Auntie Jordan's other child, Malcolm, who lived in Detroit.

Auntie Jordan read in an emotion-filled voice:

> Matthew 13 The same day went Jesus out of the house, and sat by the sea side.
>
> 13:2 And great multitudes were gathered together unto him, so that he went into a ship, and sat; and the whole multitude stood on the shore.
>
> 13:3 And he spake many things unto them in parables, saying,
>
> Behold, a sower went forth to sow;
>
> 13:4 And when he sowed, some seeds fell by the way side,
>
> and the fowls came and devoured them up:
>
> 13:5 Some fell upon stony places, where they had not much earth:
>
> and forthwith they sprung up, because they had no deepness of earth:
>
> 13:6 And when the sun was up, they were scorched;

and because they had no root, they withered
    away.

13:7 And some fell among thorns;
and the thorns sprung up, and choked them:

13:8 But others fell into good ground, and
    brought forth fruit,
some an hundredfold, some sixtyfold, some
    thirtyfold.

13:9 Who hath ears to hear, let him hear.

It was a lovely passage. May hadn't taken it in before even though the sanctuary in her church was dominated by a stained glass image of the sower.

"I'll make you both some tea," she told them, and went to the kitchen.

"They seem happy to be together," May said to her mother, who was washing dishes at the sink. Kay Lynn stood by her on a stool, stirring the rinse water with a spoon.

"Being with the people you've known since you were young is especially soothing," Momma replied.

May had lived only in Oakland, surrounded by people who knew her, with her entire family on her mother's side nearby, and the German side was never a part of her life.

In contrast, Nana Lisbeth was born and raised in Virginia, moved to Ohio, and then to Oakland. She'd been in California long before May was born, but before that she'd had entirely different lifestyles.

May returned to the sickroom with two cups of tea: one for Auntie Jordan and one for Nana Lisbeth, though she was unlikely to drink anything.

"Please get my jewelry box," Nana Lisbeth croaked to May.

May did as Nana Lisbeth asked. She carried the wooden box, worn, dull, and smooth from age, to the bedside. She opened it and

Nana Lisbeth pointed a bony finger to a cowrie shell strung on black twine.

"Give this to Jordan, please."

May pulled on the shell; it was cool and smooth.

Auntie Jordan's breath caught when she saw what May was delivering to her. Her hand went over her heart and tears spilled from her eyes.

"You still have yours," she stated.

"Of course," Nana Lisbeth replied. "Nothing but death would cause me to part from it."

May didn't know the significance of the object, but didn't intrude with a question.

"I miss her," Auntie Jordan said.

"Me too, always." Nana Lisbeth smiled. "I look forward to seeing her on the other side."

Nana Lisbeth continued in a weak voice, "Mattie would want the shell to go to Maggie or the new baby. It belongs with your branch of the family. It's only right."

"Thank you," Auntie Jordan said, rubbing the shell in her hand and staring at the air between them. "When you are gone, I will welcome this gift." Auntie Jordan stood. "Until then it belongs with you."

She carried the necklace across the room. Nana Lisbeth, too weak to hold up her arm, opened her bony fingers. Auntie Jordan lowered the small shell into Nana Lisbeth's palm.

A tear slid down Nana Lisbeth's cheek. "Wouldn't she be amazed to see your life? Living in a home your daughter owns. Your grandsons in United States uniforms. Naomi working as a nurse. All her dreams for you come true."

Auntie Jordan nodded with a tight smile, but there was a shadow of something besides agreement on her face—whether sorrow or doubt, May could not be certain.

———— ❧❧ ————

Three days later May stood at the sink washing up dishes from the gathered crowd. Every movement felt slow and heavy. She was glad to have the house filled with the people who loved Nana Lisbeth, and yet May only wanted to be left alone. There was nothing to say and nothing to do but wait. When it was over Nana Lisbeth would be gone—forever.

"May?" A quiet voice intruded. Dynamite exploded in her chest. She took a breath and turned around. Elena.

Tears streamed from May's eyes. Elena's too. Her cousin opened her arms, inviting May into an embrace. May buried her face against her cousin, clinging to her warm life in the midst of impending death. Their sobs mixed together, pain poured out of their bodies.

When the wave passed they broke apart.

Elena looked at May, put a hand on her cheek, and asked, "Can I help?"

May nodded, tears flowing again, but she had no words. She welcomed Elena's companionship, a slight balm for this time.

Aunt Diana found them in the kitchen. In a horrible, kind voice she said, "We think her last breath will be soon. Come or not as you wish."

Tears streamed again. May wiped at them with her handkerchief but it was so wet that it couldn't soak up any more. Aunt Diana gave her a tender smile through her own tears and held out a fresh one.

Her auntie said, "I promise it won't always be this painful. Our sorrow is sending dear Lisbeth off in love—never, never be ashamed of your tears. They honor her life—her devotion to you and yours in return."

Aunt Diana hugged her for a long time. May felt like a child. Everyone else seemed to know how to face this horror.

Elena spoke quietly. "I'm going in. We can face this together if you like."

May looked at her cousin, who seemed so mature. Elena had attended the passing of both of her maternal grandparents while May had seen death only in a casket, but never witnessed a last breath or lost someone she loved so dearly. Her doubts must have shown on her face.

"Or not," Aunt Diana reassured May. "It is a personal decision to be so close to death. Not everyone wishes to experience it, so you choose what is best for you."

May's throat closed up. She was uncertain, scared, and devastated. Nana Lisbeth alive was best for her, but God was not giving that option. Aunt Diana patted her arm and left.

Elena arched her dark eyebrow in question. May shook her head. Her feet would not move. Elena nodded.

"I'll see you in there if you change your mind."

May nodded back. Kay Lynn ran through the swinging door and threw her arms around May's legs. May lifted her daughter up. The girl hugged her tight, the left arm pressing a curled-up fist and the right patting with an open palm. Kay Lynn kissed both of May's cheeks. Then she pulled back and said in her sweet, high voice, "We walking to the market for lollipops. I pick one for you too. Your favorite—peach!"

She wiggled down to the ground and scampered out the door.

Stephanie, Elena's younger cousin, popped her head in and explained the plan to May: "We'll go to the park after the store to give you a quiet house."

"Thank you so much for watching Kay Lynn too," May said, tearing up in gratitude.

"Absolutely," the young woman replied. "She's delightful."

She *was* a delight; the biggest joy in May's life. It was hard to fathom that she nearly gave her up for adoption—or worse yet to the home for imbeciles. She remembered that moment when she fiercely knew Kay Lynn belonged with her. Every so often she thought about what might have happened to her precious daughter if she followed the doctor's prescription. It made her sick to imagine what Kay Lynn's life would be. She shook off the thought. She *had* brought Kay Lynn home, and while she walked with a limp and her left hand ended in a fist, she was in no way an undue burden. She was as bright, loving, and articulate as May could hope for.

May's thoughts veered to her family as she finished washing. She teared up again. Being in that room would be horrible, but it was more distressing to be outside of it. She needed to be with them to add her love to Nana Lisbeth's send off.

May pulled up her masks and opened the door to the sickroom. After her eyes adjusted to the darkness she made out Nana Lisbeth's figure in the bed. Damp hair stuck to her sweaty and swollen face. A mask covered her nose and mouth, her eyes more sunken than just a few hours before. Momma, also masked, still sat on the bed, holding Nana Lisbeth's hand directly.

Masked faces turned to welcome May into the space made sacred by their gathering. Even riddled with sorrow, Momma managed to convey a smile with only her eyes. She reached out her arm, inviting May to come close. May accepted the offer. Standing by her mother, she looked down at her grandmother, whose rattled breaths were shallow and far apart.

May leaned over and placed her warm hand on the laboring chest. She poured a blessing into Nana Lisbeth. *Thank you. I love you. Go in peace.*

Through her masks she kissed each of Nana Lisbeth's cheeks, mindful that it was for the last time. Perhaps she should care more about getting ill, but she could not let this final opportunity pass. Her tears left a lingering mark of love. Uncle Sam, occupying a wooden chair by the bed, patted May's arm.

She joined Elena and Auntie Diana standing vigil at the foot of the bed. Elena hooked her arm through May's, making a chain of three loving women. Aunt Diana held out an open palm and wordlessly recited a prayer.

May opened her hand and did the same:

Thank you. I love you. Go in peace. Thank you. I love you. Go in peace. Thank you. I love you. Go in peace. Thank you. I love you. Go in peace. Thank you. I love you. Go in peace. Thank you. I love you. Go in peace. Thank you. I love you. Go in peace. Thank you. I love you. Go in peace.

May's silent prayer was interrupted when Momma moved to listen close. Was it over? Momma leaned in to touch Nana Lisbeth's pulse. Then she sat upright with a sigh.

May's legs were getting tired, but she didn't want to disturb the room by moving. She wiggled her toes, swayed a bit from side to side, and returned to her personal blessing.

Thank you. I love you. Go in peace. Thank you. I love you. Go in peace. Thank you. I love you. Go in peace. Thank you. I love you. Go in peace. Thank you. I love you. Go in peace. Thank you. I love you. Go in peace. Thank you. I love you. Go in peace. Thank you. I love you. Go in peace.

The disturbing sound of Nana Lisbeth's erratic breaths filled the room. They went from a fast and shallow pant to stopping for a distressing number of seconds. May's heart beat hard in the booming silence. Nana Lisbeth gurgled, and a large gasp followed. Did she feel herself to be drowning?

Uncle Sam uncapped the brown bottle on the bedside table. He placed a few drops of laudanum into Nana Lisbeth's gaping mouth.

Nana Lisbeth's forehead relaxed almost instantly. She looked at peace again. May sighed in relief, grateful they could keep her grandmother's pain at bay.

Thank you. I love you. Go in peace. Thank you. I love you. Go in peace. Thank you. I love you. Go in peace. Thank you. I love you. Go in peace. Thank you. I love you. Go in peace. Thank you. I love you. Go in peace. Thank you. I love you. Go in peace. Thank you. I love you. Go in peace.

May lost track of the time as they kept their vigil, each in their own thoughts and actions. The loud sounds of breath coming and going. May studied her grandmother's hands. Those hands held her, fed her, and clapped for her since she was born. Kay Lynn too. It was unfathomable that they would never hold hands again.

Suddenly the room was silent; May felt a chill and a breeze.

She stared at Nana Lisbeth; her face was entirely changed. Uncle Sam touched Nana Lisbeth's pulse. Momma rested a hand on her chest. Then laid her cheek on her mother's heart, tears streaming down her face. Nana Lisbeth was gone.

Auntie Diana opened the curtains, letting in bright sunlight. The windows were already open to the late-October afternoon air.

"Lisbeth, you are free of your body now. Go. Go find your ancestors; they are waiting to welcome you," Auntie Diana commanded.

Elena turned to hug May. Their tears flowed, marking one another's shoulders with love and sorrow.

CHAPTER 29

MAY

November 1918

The space next to Grampa Matthew's grave at the Mountain View Cemetery was a gaping hole ready for Nana Lisbeth. Without this plot bought so many years ago she might not have gotten a proper burial. In four weeks this influenza had killed more than three hundred people in Oakland.

They stood around the open grave. Nana Lisbeth's casket perched next to it. Each of them held a scarlet-tinged carnation from their front garden. The minister spoke, but May didn't care to follow his words. During "My Life Flows On in Endless Song," Nana Lisbeth's favorite hymn, May's tears fell freely. The simple service ended with an invitation to place their flowers on her casket.

May walked forward with Kay Lynn in her arms. She kissed her mottled carnation, a mixture of sorrow and courage, and said, "I love you, Nana Lisbeth. Goodbye." Then she set it on the wooden casket.

"Bye, Nana Lisbeth!" Kay Lynn echoed. She leaned over from May's arm and placed her flower on top of her mother's. Her little hand patted the wooden box.

The others followed suit—each having a final private moment. Momma went last. She placed her hand on the casket; her lips moved as she offered a silent message and her tears left drops on the wood. She returned to May's side and their arms went around each other. Mother, daughter; Mother and daughter; the chain lost a link.

May and Kay Lynn stayed by Momma's side as she hugged the attendees. Cousin Naomi walked up with baby Dawn in her arms.

May whispered to Kay Lynn, "See the tiny baby."

The little girl nodded and rested her head against May.

Momma said, "Thank you for coming . . . especially with Dawn only a few days out of the womb."

Naomi replied, "I wanted to be here, and Ma shouldn't be here alone. She's going to take this hard. Lisbeth was so very dear to her. They didn't visit daily, but knew they could count on one another."

Momma smiled and nodded. "Your family has been a constant in my life."

She stared into the distance, her eyes welling up; then she said, "Remember our walk here when May was a baby?"

"The day you were hiding from Heinrich?" Cousin Naomi asked.

May's heart picked up at her father's name. She listened intently.

Momma said, "Life is strange, isn't it? Not so long ago I was on a slow journey toward death. Now I'm recovered and my mother, Lisbeth Johnson, is suddenly gone forever."

"If you could know the future, would you want to?" Naomi asked.

Momma thought. "Life would feel safer, but not so interesting. What about you?"

Naomi smiled and rubbed baby Dawn's head. "If I'd known she was coming I think I would have done everything to avoid her. And now that she's here, I can't imagine my life any other way. What felt horrible six months ago is now a great gift."

May smiled to herself. That was exactly how she felt about Kay Lynn. She kissed her daughter's head.

Auntie Jordan walked up and they opened their circle to include her.

"We have a few things for you," Momma said, her voice filled with emotion.

Momma reached into her bag, pulled out an envelope, and handed it to Auntie Jordan.

The older woman peered in and her eyes welled up. She pulled out that shell necklace. Her other hand covered her chest and she let her tears flow. Obviously it was very meaningful to Auntie Jordan. May remembered playing with the shell around Nana's neck when she was young, but didn't realize it was important.

Auntie Jordan's brown hands shook, with emotion or age, as she placed it around Dawn's neck.

"It looks right on her," Momma said.

"Let me know if you ever want it back," Naomi offered.

Momma pulled her lips in and shook her head. "It belongs to your descendants. Mattie was kind to give my mom that comfort of connection, but think about where it came from. Those ancestors, your ancestors, kept the faith for Dawn."

Naomi said, "Thank you."

Wanting to understand, May asked, "Where's it from?"

Naomi replied, "The family story is these shells came from Africa centuries ago. They were handed down from daughter to daughter for . . . well, we don't know how long, do we."

"Mattie left one behind for Lisbeth when she escaped," Momma explained. "I think it was Lisbeth's most cherished possession." Tears ran down Momma's cheeks.

May touched the shell on baby Dawn. If she'd known the story of it she would have been more reverent with it in Nana Lisbeth's death room.

"I'm going to miss her so much. She's been there my whole life. I don't know how I can manage without her," Momma said.

May understood her mother's distress. She'd had the same fear about her Momma while she was sick, and now Momma lived with that fear realized because Nana was gone.

Auntie Jordan spoke up: "There were many days when I felt unable to go on without my Mama, but I did. One day led to the next. And then the next. Slowly the joy of getting to be alive became even more precious—knowing it would end someday." Auntie Jordan shook her head and then continued, "Those were some hard years. So much death piled on one after another."

Momma explained to May, "Jordan lost a daughter, a grandchild, her husband, and her Mama in a brief span."

Auntie Jordan said, "It seems as if pain should be sprinkled throughout a life, but sometimes it's pressed in all at once, too much to bear. Like in our nation right now: a hateful president, and a war, and a flu pandemic."

"I fear these times will never end," Momma said.

Naomi replied, "They will. Only to be replaced by some other troubles, I'm sure."

Momma said, "There's something else in the envelope."

Auntie Jordan felt against the side. She pulled out a photo and gasped; the look on her face raised the flesh on May's arms and sent a chill down her spine.

Naomi asked, "What, Ma? What is it?"

Auntie Jordan turned the picture around. It was old, from before the Civil War: a white baby, maybe eight months old, sat on a colored woman's lap.

"Is that Grammy Mattie?" Naomi exclaimed.

Momma nodded.

May stared at her Nana Lisbeth as a baby—her eyes the same shape as Kay Lynn's. Great-Aunt Mattie's hand rested on Nana Lisbeth's head, as if she were protecting her. It was at once touching and disturbing.

Naomi said, "Look at those matching dresses. It's so bizarre, the twisted relationship, documented for . . ." She shook her head.

"Thank you," Auntie Jordan whispered through a tight throat. "This is a treasure."

Momma nodded, her eyes shining. "Lisbeth hid it for all those years. Her shame ran deep."

May looked at the circle of women, bound by the cruelty of slavery. And yet somehow they found love too.

"She was so young," Naomi spoke, her voice astonished. "What year was Lisbeth born?"

"1837," Momma replied.

"Grammy Mattie was about twenty in this picture—younger than you, May," Naomi announced.

"So young," Auntie Jordan agreed.

Momma asked, "Did Mattie's shell get tossed in the Pacific Ocean?"

Her confusion must have shown because Auntie Jordan explained, "On her deathbed, my mama told us to throw her shell into the Pacific to 'tell the ancestors we are free.'

"We still have Mama's shell," Auntie Jordan said. "It's never seemed right to tell the ancestors that we are all free. Maybe after the suffrage amendment passes and all women can vote."

Naomi shook her head and countered, "We won't be free until we are safe living everywhere."

The circle of women nodded.

"Freedom doesn't come all at once, does it?" May suggested.

Auntie Jordan nodded. "Wise words, May. After seeing my Mama's face in that photo, I know we have come so far. But when I read the news of our city, our nation, our world I despair."

Naomi wondered, "Will we ever say this is enough freedom for *us* and throw that shell into the Pacific?"

Aunt Jordan looked out at the view of the San Francisco Bay. She gestured and said, "The bigger view is a gift, but also a burden. In this modern age we hear about sorrows, not only in *other* states but also in other nations. There's too much to take it all in, and yet here we are: in pain at Lisbeth's passing, joyful that the war seems to be ending, and angry at the continued trampling on our freedoms after we sacrificed for the freedom of people across the ocean and borders."

Auntie Jordan shook her head. She laughed and said, "I apologize—for giving a second message today."

Momma took Auntie Jordan's hand and looked right at her. "No need to be sorry. Thank you for speaking the very complicated truth in my heart."

They hugged tight. After a time, Momma's shoulder pulsed up and down as sobs shook her body.

"Gammy crying," Kay Lynn said.

"Yes, Gammy is sad," May told her daughter.

"Mommy sad?" her little girl asked while touching the tears on May's cheeks.

May looked at her daughter and nodded. "Mommy misses Nana Lisbeth."

"Kay Lynn sad too," the little girl said, resting her head in the crook of May's neck.

May breathed in the feel of her daughter and kissed her soft head. Love and sorrow filled May's chest. She hugged Kay Lynn close, so grateful for her life. Joy and pain rushed through her.

She walked to the blank side of Nana and Poppa's headstone. May placed her hand on it, took a deep breath, and opened her heart.

Goodbye, Nana. Thank you for your love and guidance. I will miss you for all of my days on earth. I'll be calling on your spirit for advice as I make my way. And I promise I will take the time to listen to my still, small voice. I love you, now and always.

CHAPTER 30

NAOMI

November 11, 1918

Naomi trembled as they waited. The train, already twenty minutes late, could be here at any moment. Cedric and Willie were coming home. She could hardly breathe. Standing on her left, Gramma Jordan held Dawn. To her right, Maggie used Naomi's shoulder for balance as she rose on her tiptoes to peer further down the track. Four females waiting for the return of two of their men, coinciding with a celebration for the nation.

Their moods on this personal day of joy matched that of the entire city—and much of the world. Day after day for nearly a week the newspaper reported it was close, so close. Today, November 11, they signed the treaty ending the Great War.

Masked revelers had filled Broadway until the crowd became so thick the trolley they were riding could go no further. The women had walked the final half mile to the train station through the strange and beautiful sight. Naomi could still hear the jubilant sounds of a brass band and the shouts of revelers in the distance.

"I see it!" Maggie squealed.

Naomi raised herself up on her toes. There it was! The train that carried her son and her husband. She grinned, tears wetting her eyes, and looked at her mother.

Gramma Jordan patted her hand for the eternity it took for the train to stop. She scanned the windows, trying to be methodical, but Naomi didn't have the restraint. Her eyes darted from car to car, and she waved in case Cedric saw her first. She looked left and right. Passengers poured off the train and filled the platform, blocking her view. She bent side to side to look around them, her heart beating hard as she urgently searched for her son.

"Ma." His beautiful voice came from behind her.

Naomi turned. "Oh!" Tears sprang from her eyes. There was her Cedric, her beloved son. She touched his thin face, gazing into his dear brown eyes. Her throat closed. Tears welled up again. Then she hugged him tight, pressing his warm body against her. She felt his single arm wrap around her.

Maggie wrapped her arms around Cedric too. And then Gramma Jordan joined in, right there on the platform.

"You're back. You're back," Naomi murmured into his uniform. "Welcome home."

When they broke apart she turned to hug Willie, but he wasn't there. Gramma Jordan pointed. He sat on a bench, Dawn in his arms, delight shining on his face.

Cedric asked, "Joseph?"

Maggie shook her head.

"He's fine," Naomi declared. "Just not here . . . yet!"

Willie yelled across the three feet, "Cedric, come meet your sister." They all circled around.

"She's beautiful, Naomi," Willie said, his eyes sparkling. "Thank you."

She leaned over and kissed her husband, savoring the warmth of him.

"Wow. She's tiny," Cedric said, wonder in his voice. "Look at those minuscule fingernails."

"She looks like you did when you were a baby," Gramma Jordan told him.

"Really?" He was in awe.

Naomi studied her son, changed in the year and a half. He'd lost weight and gained gravity. Her eyes darted to the empty left sleeve of his uniform. Would he just wear a sleeve like this from now on, or would they cut them off for his new body?

"Do you want to hold her?" Willie asked.

Cedric looked frightened, then excited. He nodded and sat on the bench right next to his father. Willie carefully passed his two-week-old daughter to his son.

"Her neck isn't strong yet," Willie instructed, "so you have to take special care to keep her head up."

Cedric cradled her close, his face filled with delight. Tears in his eyes, he looked up at Naomi. "I didn't know you could love someone the moment you met them."

"It sure is something, isn't it? That love," Naomi agreed. "It gets me every time."

Naomi looked at Maggie. Then Gramma Jordan. And finally Willie. Joseph was still away, so a piece of her heart was too, but she would not let that prevent joy in this moment.

A little white girl walked up to them; she blatantly intruded on their family moment by staring at Cedric. Her father stood nearby without scolding or correcting her. Naomi's hackles rose at the rude child gaping at her son. Was this to be his life now—someone to be gawked at by curious children?

The child looked at her father.

"It's okay," he encouraged. "Go ahead."

The girl reached out, her pudgy fingers clenched around an unusual carnation: cream tinged with scarlet.

"For your courage and your loss," she said in her innocent voice. "Thank you."

The little girl waited with her arm outstretched.

"Oh." Her father gasped as he understood that one uniform sleeve was empty and the other arm held a tiny baby. His blue eyes, round with regret and alarm, darted to Naomi's. Tears sprang to hers, his watering up as well.

Naomi stared at the awkward scene. Willie could solve this dilemma by taking Dawn so Cedric could accept the little girl's gift, or he could take the carnation on Cedric's behalf. Before she made her suggestions, Cedric raised a single finger away from Dawn's yellow blanket. The girl rested the flower in the small space.

"Thank you," he said.

Her son nodded and beamed at the shy child. The girl smiled, waved goodbye, and returned to her father's side.

"I think he liked it," the child declared, her eyes shining with pride. Naomi and Willie's children handled the situation with grace and ease.

The man wiped his cheek and replied, "I think he did too."

In the man's hands there were more than a dozen cream carnations tinged with scarlet, ready to honor returning soldiers for their courage . . . and for all that they lost. The man smiled at Naomi.

"This is a beautiful and complicated day, isn't it?" he asked.

"It sure is," Naomi agreed, and watched the father and daughter walk away, hand in hand.

Naomi sat down so close to Cedric that their shoulders touched. She looked at her baby in his arm. The white-and-scarlet bloom rested gently against Dawn's cheek.

"You take this flower, Mama," he said. "You deserve it for all you've been through."

Naomi shook her head. "It's for you."

"You saved my life . . . ," he forced out of a tight throat.

Naomi took the carnation from his finger, curved the stem in half, and slid it into the pocket of the United States uniform; it stuck on something, refusing to go all the way in. She peered in the gap. She smiled at the Bible blocking the way. Naomi slipped the green stalk behind the holy book and patted the pocket over Cedric's heart.

"You wear it proudly for both of us," she told him, and then kissed his warm cheek.

She exhaled and allowed a measure of calm, sweet joy to wash over her soul. The worst of this ordeal was truly behind them. Cedric was home, right here next to her, his spirit changed, but not broken. Hers too.

She'd walked to the very edge of the unbearable; its painful mist altered her, but she'd passed this particular test of her character. Naomi lived the wisdom in Grammy Mattie's favorite Bible passage: the Parable of the Sower. Naomi's faith in God and her family was made stronger from this trial.

Naomi looked at her beautiful family, more precious to her than gold, her heart full of love and gratitude.

"Let's go home."

EPILOGUE

KAY LYNN

My parents were always honest about my conception. For as long as I can remember I knew Poppa chose to be my father, but I wasn't conceived by him, like my sister and brother. Poppa loved me so well that John's occasional, brief dips into my life were a sting, but not a mortal wound.

I believed I knew every truth about our family until the day my aunt let it slip: Momma intended to abandon me at birth, making me just a brief chapter in her long life. If I hadn't arrived different, with these handicaps, other parents would have raised me.

Soon after I was born a doctor deemed me too defective to be adopted. He blithely declared I would be an undue burden, not good enough to be in *any* family, and had to be sent to Napa, to the home for imbeciles and epileptics. But my Momma's heart told her another truth, so she kept me even though she was unwed, giving me the dual whispered labels of *illegitimate* and *defective*.

I must have been a reminder of my mother's shame, but she and Poppa—my father who wasn't my "real" father but was really my father—treasured me so much that I didn't understand I was different from other people until long after I should have noticed.

I was twenty when the truth shook apart my reality. Like the survivors of the 1906 earthquake, I had to remove the rubble before I could build a trustworthy foundation again.

When I was born the doctor—our society—considered me disposable, but we proved him wrong. *I* proved him wrong. Like all humans, I'm flawed, but the value of a life isn't measured by its perfection. It's measured in love. I'm measured in love.

AUTHOR'S NOTE

Thanks for reading this book—and my note. I've been asked many times if I should be writing novels that aren't about my own family history. I have great respect for that question and I wrestled with it before I wrote my first novel, which became *Yellow Crocus*. I wrestle with it still.

I've been consciously aware of race, gender, and "social location" for as long as I can remember. I didn't realize this was unique until I was in upper elementary school in Whittier, California. Between the ages of two and four, most humans categorize the people around them by the caste system they were born into. As the daughter of a North African college professor father and a white, Midwestern teacher mother I didn't fit neatly into the American caste system as seen on television or in the community where I lived. I didn't fit into the categories, so I believe they became more apparent to me than to people who easily fit into the system.

My goal for my stories is to shine a light on those categories and show some of the mechanisms that have been put in place to sustain the caste system baked into our nation as well as some of the ways they have been resisted or overturned. It is my honor and my calling to tell these stories as honestly and as respectfully as I can. I do diligent research. I practice empathy. I ask readers who are closer to the cultures I write about to give me honest feedback.

Should I write novels that aren't about my own family history? I hope that question is answered by my stories, graded one book at a time. I pray I'm humbly receptive when I learn that I missed the mark.

I'm deeply grateful for the activists who worked for decades in order for me to have the rights that I do. They didn't "know" me, I wasn't even born, but their work is an enormous gift.

I write stories about faith and persistence in the face of personal and systemic obstacles because of my fervent belief that total, mutual human liberation is possible. Each morning in school I pledged myself to "liberty and justice for all." I understood then, as I do now, that we have yet to realize that aspiration, but I'm called to do what I can to hold onto that dream.

When I started researching this novel I knew I wanted to bring these families about twenty years into the future and that May and Naomi would most likely be my point-of-view characters. I knew their histories, but I didn't know their "present."

I had two historical nuggets in my mind: in 1915 there was a huge presence of eugenicists at the Pan-Pacific Exhibition in San Francisco and some home deeds in Oakland still say they have racial restrictions, because they were not automatically revised after the Fair Housing Act of 1968. With those two tidbits as the start of my research trail, I started reading the front pages of the *Oakland Tribune* between 1910 and 1915. I wanted to read the *Oakland Sunshine* as well, but there are very few editions preserved from that era. The few that are provided greater depth and accuracy to this novel.

When I read about Ishi, I imagined he would be a major character, but he ended up in the edges. A few people suggested that his thread be dropped, but I valued his place in this story, which seemed similar to George Floyd's presence in my life in 2020. George Floyd's killing is an example of an enormous social tragedy embodied in one human's story that happened at the edge of my life. It is at once heartbreaking, infuriating, and a source of despair, but also holds hope that his tragic death can make us a better society.

I was fascinated by many things I discovered in my research, but one that stood out was the image of revelers wearing white face masks on Market Street in San Francisco in November 1918 as they celebrated the end of the war. In the fall of 2019 I knew I had to include something about that in this novel. By March of 2020, it felt strangely prescient.

In *Scarlet Carnation* the disease comes up suddenly, without a lot of introduction, because that is true to reality. I included only information from the *Oakland Tribune*—the news May had access to. With the lens of time we have more complete knowledge of the devastation of the 1918 flu than these characters did while they were in the midst of it, especially since censors around the world were keeping information about the disease out of the newspapers.

A theme in all my novels is the movement for human liberation and human rights. In *Scarlet Carnation* I added disability. Our oldest daughter, Kalin, was diagnosed with cerebral palsy in 1993, when she was four months old. As she grew, I was acutely aware that the services and opportunities she had came directly from the work of the disability activists who fought for the civil rights of differently abled (diff-abled as Kalin says) US citizens, which culminated in the Americans with Disabilities Act in 1990.

Kay Lynn in this novel is named after my daughter, with her permission, and has about the same level of disability as my Kalin. I am deeply indebted to those people who fought for my daughter's right to develop and grow her capabilities in order to have a rich and full life.

And finally, a bit of information about the title. Mother's Day was started by peace advocate Julia Ward Howe after the Civil War and the Prussian wars. She imagined a day on which mothers from around the world would unite to demand peaceful forms of conflict resolution rather than sending their sons to be killed in wars. Anna Jarvis continued advocating for a Mother's Day of Peace after Julia Ward Howe died. In 1914, Woodrow Wilson signed a proclamation making the second Sunday in May a day to celebrate Mother's Day.

The holiday quickly evolved into a celebration of motherhood rather than a day for mothers to demand peace. In some parts of the United States a red carnation was worn to honor a living mother while a white carnation became a sign of mourning for a deceased mother.

During World War 1 many mothers wore red carnations to show they had a son who was a soldier.

I mixed the two colors of carnations, scarlet and white, as a symbol of complicated times that call for love, courage, and mourning. We chose *Scarlet Carnation* as the title to honor May's new motherhood, to honor Naomi's role as the mother of a deployed soldier, and in respect to *The Scarlet Letter* and Hawthorne's exploration of the cultural shaming of women.

In faith and gratitude,
Laila

ACKNOWLEDGMENTS

My gratitude is overflowing for all that has conspired to allow me to bring the stories of my heart and soul into being.

I'm deeply indebted to the readers who have reviewed, purchased, and spread the word about my novels.

Thanks to

- the readers and editors who made this a better story and gave me the encouragement I needed to keep going: Jacqueline Duhart, Rinda Bartley, Kayla Haun, René Delane, Ida Harper, Jane Cavolina, Shaundale Rena, Stephanie Thames, Jessica Aaron, Darlanne Mulmat, Margie Biblin, Kelly Kist, Charles Masten, Heather McCleod, Akberet Hagos, Katrinca Ford, and Kalin Brooke.

- all the wonderful people at Amazon Publishing, Lake Union, and Amazon Crossing that bless me with their hard work and devotion to bring these stories to readers around the world: Jodi Warshaw, Gabriella Dumpit, Tiffany Yates Martin, Danielle Marshall, Alex Levenberg, Michelle Li, Michael Schuler, Shasti O'Leary Soudant, Nicole Burns-Ascue, Carrie O., and all of you whose names I don't know (extra shout-out to marketing whose emails bring great joy to my day every single time I get one).

- Terry Goodman—always!
- my agent—Annelise Robey of Jane Rotrosen Agency.
- my family in its many forms.

RESOURCES

These sources were invaluable in making the historical details more accurate:

African American Women and the Vote, 1837–1965, by Cynthia Neverdon-Morton (Author), Evelyn Brooks Higginbotham (Author), Martha Prescod Norman (Author), Bettina Aptheker (Author), Ann D. Gordon (Editor), and Bettye Collier-Thomas (Editor)

African American Women in the Struggle for the Vote, 1850–1920, by Rosalyn Terborg-Penn

American Babylon: Race and the Struggle for Postwar Oakland, by Robert O. Self

"'Black is Beautiful': From Porters to Panthers in West Oakland," by Mary Praetzellis and Adrian Praetzellis in *Putting the "There" There: Historical Archaeologies of West Oakland I-880 Cypress Freeway Replacement Project*, edited by Mary Praetzellis and Adrian Praetzellis

A *Black Women's History of the United States*, by Daina Ramey Berry and Kali Nicole Gross

"Camp Logan 1917: Beyond the Veil of Memory," by Matthew Crow (https://houstonhistorymagazine.org/wp-content/uploads/2017/05/Camp-Logan.pdf)

"A Comparative Study of White and Black American Soldiers during the First World War," by Jennifer D. Keene

Crip Camp: A Disability Revolution (film), directed by James Lebrecht and Nicole Newnham

The Crisis, Vol. 9, No. 6 (April 1915)

Family limitation, by Margaret Sanger

Imbeciles: The Supreme Court, American Eugenics, and the Sterilization of Carrie Buck, by Adam Cohen

Ishi in Two Worlds, 50th Anniversary Edition: A Biography of the Last Wild Indian in North America, by Theodora Kroeber

The Negro Trail Blazers of California, by Delilah Beasley

No There There: Race, Class, and Political Community in Oakland, by Chris Rhomberg

Oakland: The Story of a City, by Beth Bagwell

Oakland Tribune, accessed at Newspapers.com

The Pullman Porters and West Oakland, by Thomas Tramble and Wilma Tramble

"The Site of Origin of the 1918 Influenza Pandemic and Its Public Health Implications," by John M. Barry (https://www.ncbi.nlm.nih.gov/pmc/articles/PMC340389/)

Stamped from the Beginning: The Definitive History of Racist Ideas in America, by Ibram X. Kendi

"'This Is Our Fair and Our State': African Americans and the Panama-Pacific International Exposition," by Lynn M. Hudson, in *California History*, Vol. 87, No. 3 (2010)

War Against the Weak: Eugenics and America's Campaign to Create a Master Race, Expanded Edition, by Edwin Black

BOOK DISCUSSION

1. Who was your favorite character and why?
2. What character do you wish you knew more about?
3. If you've read the companion novels, was this a satisfying part of these characters' journeys?
4. If you haven't read the companion novels, were there any parts you found confusing?
5. Did any scenes raise strong feelings in you?
6. What do you think Laila Ibrahim's purpose was in writing this book? What ideas was she trying to get across?
7. Did May's desire to end her pregnancy change your understanding of her character?
8. Why do you think Laila Ibrahim chose to have Ishi, a historical figure, in this novel? What does he represent to the other characters? Is there any person that plays that role in your life?
9. What do you think about the book's title? Would you choose something different?
10. Laila Ibrahim writes about characters struggling to overcome personal and systemic hardships. She does not share the characters' cultural background. Is it problematic for an author to write about cultures that are not their own?

11. Did the book's pace seem too fast, too slow, or just right?
12. Were you surprised at Kay Lynn's development?
13. Did the book have the right balance between history and story?
14. Did any historical details surprise you?

ABOUT THE AUTHOR

Laila Ibrahim is the bestselling author of *Golden Poppies, Paper Wife, Mustard Seed,* and *Yellow Crocus.* She spent much of her career as a preschool director, a birth doula, and a religious educator. That work, coupled with her education in developmental psychology and attachment theory, provides ample fodder for her novels.

She's a devout Unitarian Universalist, determined to do her part to add a little more love and justice to our beautiful and painful world. She lives with her wonderful wife, Rinda, and two other families in a small cohousing community in Berkeley, California. Her young adult children are her pride and joy.

Laila is blessed to be working full-time as a novelist. When she isn't writing, she likes to take walks with friends, do jigsaw puzzles, play games, work in the garden, travel, cook, and eat all kinds of delicious food. Visit the author at www.lailaibrahim.com.